D0854133

COVENTRY LIBRARIES

3 8002 02274 209 4

TERROR
by GASLIGHT

By the same author

The Shadow of Treason

TERROR
by GASLIGHT

EDWARD
TAYLOR

ROBERT HALE · LONDON

© Edward Taylor 2015
First published in Great Britain 2015

ISBN 978-0-7198-1661-1

Robert Hale Limited
Clerkenwell House
Clerkenwell Green
London EC1R 0HT

www.halebooks.com

The right of Edward Taylor to be identified as author of this
work has been asserted by him in accordance
with the Copyright, Designs and Patents Act 1988

2 4 6 8 10 9 7 5 3 1

Coventry City Council	
WIL	
3 8002 02274 209 4	
Askews & Holts	Mar-2016
CRI	£19.99

Typeset in New Century Schoolbook
Printed in Great Britain by Berforts Information Press Ltd

1

THE BANGING ON the garden door started just after ten
o'clock. Irregular, sometimes frantic, sometimes feeble, it
resonated through the house, somehow amplified by the dark
and the absence of any other sound, save the hoot of a distant
owl somewhere out on the Heath.

After two minutes the drawing-room door opened and two
women entered nervously, both in night attire and dressing
gowns. They carried hastily lit oil lamps, for the gaslights on
the drawing-room walls had been put out half an hour ago,
when the Austin sisters retired to their rooms for the night.

As Harriet and Mrs Butters came in, the banging on
the door was beginning to weaken and now they could hear
moaning.

'Lord help us!' cried the terrified housekeeper. 'It sounds
like the devil himself!'

Harriet pulled back the curtain on one of the windows and
tried to see who or what was outside the door but it was pitch
dark and the angle was wrong.

Now Clare entered the room, wearing her day clothes and
displaying annoyance rather than terror. She had a strength
about her that comforted Mrs Butters.

'Oh, Miss Clare!' she pleaded. 'What are we to do?'

'Make sure the doors and windows are bolted as well as

locked,' said Clare briskly. 'Then we must wait and watch until this nuisance goes away.'

The banging seemed to increase again, and the moaning became louder and more piteous.

'No, Clare, we must help,' insisted Harriet. 'Someone is in dreadful pain.'

'Father told us never to open the door at night. Especially when he's not here.'

'But we cannot ignore those cries! There must have been an awful accident!'

'It might be a trick,' said Clare. 'Some drunken rogue bent on mischief. It could even be the Heath Maniac!'

This thought doubled the housekeeper's fears. 'Don't open the door, Miss Harriet!' she wailed. 'He's likely out for blood!'

'But there are three of us! We can defend each other! Come, Clare, a fellow human being is in distress!'

Clare was persuaded. 'Very well, sister, if you are so determined. But let us at least find weapons, in case it is a trick.'

'No, no, Miss Harriet,' the older woman begged again.

'Don't worry, Mrs Butters,' Harriet said. 'The chain is on the door, it will open only a few inches. If I see danger, I shall slam it shut! And my sister is right, we must arm ourselves.'

Harriet took a heavy statuette from the mantelpiece and then went to the garden door. As she slid two bolts back and turned the key in the lock, Clare picked up the poker from the fireplace.

The banging and the moaning petered out as Harriet opened the door the short distance the chain allowed. She peered through the gap and then reacted with alarm and amazement.

'Great heavens!' she cried. 'It's Robert! Robert! What's happened to you? Come in! Come in!'

She unhooked the chain and pulled the door open, and the women saw a man standing unsteadily on the threshold, his eyes glazed, his face contorted with pain and his clothing soaked in blood.

The man took one small shambling step inside, then fell forward face down on the carpet. Harriet knelt down beside him and tried to turn him, so that she could cradle his head in her lap.

But as she did so, Robert Kemp let out one final, awful, choking groan and lay still.

Tears flowed down Harriet's cheeks as she looked up at the other women. 'I think he must be badly hurt,' she sobbed.

Clare's voice was calm as she looked down and said, 'I think he's dead.'

2

HILLSIDE WAS ONE of a row of houses on the Highgate Road and though basically a modest middle-class dwelling it had one priceless asset. The front of the house was mundane, separated from the street only by a thin strip of grass and paving stones. But at the back was something special.

The rear of Hillside faced south and had a magnificent view across Hampstead Heath, with the ground sloping gently down towards the City and the Thames. In the latter years of Queen Victoria's reign, the skyline was not yet cluttered with high buildings, and St Paul's Cathedral stood out as a thing of immense beauty, solitary and imposing. On a clear day, one could see across the river to the Crystal Palace and sometimes even to the North Downs far beyond.

The architect had made the most of all this, creating a long drawing room with wide windows. Between the windows a door opened on to the well-kept garden, and then the acres of grassland, woods and ponds that made up the Heath.

It was through this garden door that the mortally wounded Robert Kemp had stumbled last night. Then the scene had been all darkness and horror. This morning everything was bathed in glorious sunshine.

It would have dazzled Mrs Butters, as she went about her work, had she not drawn a curtain across one of the windows. She did not want to be dazzled this morning. She had scarcely slept and was polishing the furniture without much vigour.

On the other hand, when Meredith Austin came in, he was showing all his usual pent-up energy. A dapper man in his early fifties, he wore a sober city suit and an expression of disapproval. His shoes were highly polished, and his neat black hair seemed to be glued in place. He was not pleased to see his housekeeper's sluggish behaviour, and he spoke brusquely.

'Have the police gone?'

'Yes, sir. The inspector said they'd be back tomorrow. They want to speak to Miss Harriet.'

Austin's disapproval mounted. 'Do they indeed? We'll see about that.'

'What a terrible thing, sir! I don't know whether I'm coming or going this morning.'

'Well, kindly ascertain your precise direction quickly, Mrs Butters. We should all have grown used to horrors after the events of the last few months.'

'The murders on the Heath were bad enough, sir. But on our own doorstep! And all that blood! I've had the mat soaking in the kitchen copper all morning. I doubt if the stain will ever come out. We may need to have a new one.'

'Certainly not! I do not intend to waste money on new mats. You must dye the old one to match the stain.'

'Very well, sir, I'll do the best I can,' sighed Mrs Butters.

'Never mind your best, Mrs Butters, just get it done,' was Austin's harsh response.

A childhood of genteel poverty had left its mark on Meredith Austin. The sole companion of an ailing mother, living on a widow's pension, he had learned the value of money. It had been a small pension, earned by his father's lifelong barren years as a junior bank employee, and Austin had seen too much of it spent on keeping up appearances, rather than more practical needs. It was a mistake he didn't intend to make. He wanted respectability, of course, but respectability with economy.

He went to his desk and sat down. He kept his desk in the drawing room, to get the benefit of the view. But he was in no mood to appreciate that this morning. He quickly noticed shortcomings.

'Mrs Butters, you have not tidied my desk this morning,' he said sharply. 'Nor have you adjusted my calendar.'

Mrs Butters hurried to remedy the omissions. 'I'm sorry, sir. All these shocking goings-on, it's enough to drive a body out of her wits!'

Prominent on Austin's desk was a small wooden frame, in which cards displayed the date. Mrs Butters moved the top two cards to the back, to show Monday, 26 November. Then she busied herself lining up pens and pencils, and removing the used sheet from the blotting pad, chattering as she worked.

'I hope they won't pester Miss Harriet, sir. She's taken it very badly – as you'd expect, the young man being her fiancé.'

Austin reacted angrily. 'The young man was not her fiancé! I had given no consent for an engagement!'

'No, sir. Sorry, sir.'

'Ask Miss Harriet to come here at once!'

'She's resting in her room, sir. She was crying all night.'

Austin glowered at the woman. 'Tell Miss Harriet to attend me immediately, Mrs Butters!'

'Yes, sir.' The housekeeper put a final pen in place and scuttled off to obey his order.

Left alone, Austin thought intently for a moment, and then began writing on a blank sheet of paper. After completing several lines, he stopped to think again. Then he screwed up the paper and threw it into his wastepaper basket.

After further thought, he retrieved it from the basket and tore it into small pieces, which he put in his coat pocket. This barren activity completed, Austin began pacing back and forth between his desk and the door. His eyes lit on two ornamental Indian daggers fixed horizontally on the wall, one above the other. They seemed to have got out of alignment. He went over and took down the upper dagger, which he studied thoughtfully, before replacing it more neatly on the wall.

As he finished this task, the drawing-room door opened and in came Harriet, pale but composed, as if she had no more tears to shed. She was carrying a small brown cat in one hand, and stroking it gently with the other. Her voice was quiet. 'You wished to see me, Father?'

'Yes. You have hidden away long enough. And please do not bring that beast in here. I require your undivided attention.'

'Oh. Very well,' said Harriet. 'Ella, you must go back to our room.' She opened the door, put the cat carefully down outside, and closed it again. Then she turned to face her father.

Austin addressed his daughter sternly. 'Harriet, there are matters we have to discuss. Something I have to ask you.'

'But Dr Frankel said I was not to answer questions today.'

'Dr Frankel said that to deter the police. It is essential that you and I confer before you talk to them. Sit down. Will you take a glass of Madeira?'

'Yes, please. I am still feeling a little weak.'

As Harriet sat down, Austin filled two small glasses from a decanter and handed one of them to his daughter. Then he confronted her.

'Harriet, why was Robert Kemp visiting this house at ten o'clock last night?'

'We do not know that he intended to visit us. He was attacked on the Heath outside. Naturally, he would come to our door for help.'

'Do not be devious, child. Kemp's home is ... was ... in Gospel Oak. He would not be in this area without a purpose. And I believe he has crossed the Heath to impose himself on you several times before.'

'He came first to see you, Father.'

'He presented himself to me once in a proper manner and asked permission to speak to you. After I refused, he made clandestine visits, did he not?'

Harriet took a sip of her wine and looked down at her lap.

'Answer me, miss!' Austin thundered. 'Did Kemp call here on several occasions? Answer me! At once!'

'He called three times.'

'On Sunday nights, when I am known to be at my club!'

'Sunday night is the only one possible for him. He has classes on other evenings.'

'He *had* classes. Master Kemp's attempts at counter-jumping are now at an end.'

Austin's brutality had found another reservoir of tears and ruptured it. They flowed down Harriet's cheeks in great translucent drops. Her father's attitude softened; he went to her side and put his hand on her shoulder.

'I am sorry to speak harshly, my dear,' he said. 'I much regret the grief that has been caused to you. Though I suspect that Robert Kemp was always destined to bring you grief in one way or another.'

'But why, Father? Why? He was kind and courteous. He shared my love of reading. He came here to lend me books, or borrow mine.'

Austin scowled. 'Romantic novellas! Trash!'

Harriet became more spirited. 'No, important books! Robert was interested in so many things – in travel, in art, in ideas! He was gentle and caring. Yet the first time you met him, you made it plain you disliked him.'

'I was perfectly civil. If I was somewhat cold, it was

because I am well able to recognize a fortune-hunter when I see one.'

'Fortune? What fortune? He cannot have supposed that I am rich!'

'You are not rich at present. Though your station in life would always exceed Robert Kemp's. But you are aware that you may inherit wealth in due course. You may have been unwise enough to mention that.'

'I did no such thing! You know I do not understand these matters.'

'Indeed. But I am sure that Master Kemp did.'

'We never discussed such things. And our circumstances here would not suggest that we are rich.' Austin's frugality was evident throughout his home. All was neat and adequate, but there was no luxury.

'Not to others of our class, perhaps. But to a clerk, living in diggings, you would seem a pretty catch. Hillside is not a mansion but it is very far from poverty.'

'This house is yours, not mine.'

'One day it may pass to you or Clare. And Kemp must have known of my prosperous business. He was a fortune-hunter, my child. However, he is gone, and I would not have wished such a fate on him.'

Harriet dried her cheeks with a small pink handkerchief, and drank a little more of her wine. There was no point in arguing further. Instead, she sighed and said, 'I still cannot believe it. He was so alive. So strong.'

'Stronger men than he have fallen prey to the Heath Maniac. What we must now discuss is what you will tell the police.'

Harriet was surprised. 'Why, surely I tell them the truth.'

'The truth, yes. But not the whole truth.'

'You would have me withhold information?'

'Certainly. You will tell them how he banged on our door in

the night, and how he fell dead when you let him in. You will tell them that he was merely a family acquaintance, whom you met in my company. They must infer that Robert Kemp came to us only because he was wounded, and this was the nearest refuge. You will not tell them of his previous visits, when I was out. There must be no hint of a liaison between you.'

'But why should I conceal our friendship?'

'Because of the family's reputation. The newspapers get their stories from the police. And a man in my position cannot afford any sort of scandal.'

'There is no scandal. Robert was a dear friend. His visits here were innocent.'

'Indeed? I have extracted from your sister the admission that you were in here alone with him. Clare was scribbling in her room, as usual. And Mrs Butters was in bed.'

'We were alone with our books. Robert would never ...'

'Silence!' Austin was now exasperated. 'I don't wish to discuss this further. You will tell the police what I have instructed you to tell them, and no more. Now, that's the end of it. Go to your room and rest. Mrs Butters will bring your luncheon to you there.'

Harriet seemed about to protest. 'Father ...'

Austin was having none of it. 'Go!' he bellowed, and then added more quietly, 'We shall talk again this evening.'

Harriet hesitated briefly. Then she rose and left the room, closing the door behind her.

Her father picked up a small hand-bell from his desk, opened the door again, shook the bell vigorously, and called for his housekeeper.

He had scarcely time to replace the bell on his desk before Mrs Butters appeared, quietly awaiting orders. Perhaps she had not strayed far from the door during her employer's confrontation with his daughter.

'Mrs Butters,' said Austin. 'I now find I have to make some notes before I finally get away to the City. This infernal business has totally disrupted my timetable.'

'I'm sorry, sir,' said the housekeeper humbly.

'Don't talk nonsense, woman! This is one fiasco that cannot be blamed on your incompetence. The point is, when I eventually get there I shall have no time to go for lunch at the chop-house. Prepare a packet of sandwiches I can take with me and eat at my office.'

'Very good, sir. I'm afraid the ham was finished on Saturday. Will cheese do?'

'It seems it will have to.'

'There's a good piece of Cheddar, sir, and a nice ripe Stilt—'

Her employer cut her short. 'Yes, yes, anything. I'm a busy man. I can't waste time discussing catering trivia!' And then, after a moment, he added, 'Just make sure there's a good pickle. The strong, not the sweet. Put in some slices of cucumber. And a small bottle of pale ale. And some sweetmeats for the digestion.'

Clare Austin closed the front gate behind her, turned right, and walked briskly eastward along the Highgate Road.

Five years older than her sister, Clare did not share Harriet's good looks, partly due to a two-inch horizontal scar on her left cheek. She was used to this being the first thing people registered when they met her. She had seen so many eyes drawn to that side of her face, and then instantly flick away, pretending the scar hadn't been noticed. There'd been a time when the reaction had hurt her. But that was long gone. Now, as a keen observer of human nature, she found it mildly amusing, a prime example of compulsive behaviour.

But she would never forget the day the wound was inflicted. Nor would she ever forgive the perpetrator. It was one of the factors that made her more determined, stronger, and more self-possessed than her sibling.

Like all the residents of Hillside, she had lost most of her night's sleep, and she had then been subjected to an hour of questions from a detective inspector, with a portly police sergeant taking notes. (The ordeal which Harriet had so far been spared on medical grounds.) Clare had remained calm and articulate throughout and, when the inquisition was finished, had felt no inclination to retire to her room and lie down. Her remedy for stress and weariness was not rest, but fresh air and exercise. Besides, she had a mission to complete.

Clutching the precious envelope in her gloved hand, she approached the pillar box on the corner. At this moment a little girl was being lifted up by her mother to put a letter in the slot, an adventure she was clearly enjoying.

The woman looked up at the approaching Clare, and there was the usual tiny flicker of the eyes before she smiled and apologized for keeping her waiting. Then mother and child moved off, the little girl skipping with pleasure.

Clare checked again that her envelope was correctly addressed and stamped and securely sealed, and then she thrust it into the pillar box. She paused briefly to think what consequences might arise from what she had just done. Then she turned on her heels and walked back the way she had come.

She was not returning to Hillside immediately, however. It was a bright day, her father was in a foul temper, and the atmosphere in the house would be even more oppressive than usual. There would be many hours spent indoors today as she took refuge in her room, writing at the small table. No need to start too soon.

Beside her, the heathland stretched for miles, wild and exciting in the morning sunshine. And she had her nature notes to compile. There should be no danger on the Heath at this time of day. There was no reason why she shouldn't take a good walk.

She turned left and entered the Heath by the broad path that led due south towards Gospel Oak. But she quickly left this, branching off onto a narrow footpath that took her downhill and westward into a clump of trees. Passing quickly through this, she emerged into open country.

Away to her right, she could see Hillside and, on the grassy plain in front of it, half a dozen policemen pacing the area, and sometimes going down on hands and knees to examine the ground. They were looking for traces of blood, or anything else that might tell them exactly where Kemp had received his fatal wound last night. And they hoped they might find evidence of a struggle.

Clare gratefully turned her back on that scene; she had swallowed her fill of crime and police work in the last twelve hours. Now it was time to relax.

At first she thought of heading for the tumulus, over towards Parliament Hill, the ancient burial mound, where she had often sat musing on life, mortality and the frailty of human existence; thoughts that might eventually be useful when she settled down to the melancholy Gothic novel she would one day write.

But she changed her mind, reflecting again that there had already been enough horror and misery today. She would instead make her way to a more cheerful spot, and concentrate on the practical matter of assembling her December nature notes.

She had already decided that these might include some observations on the waterways of the Heath, and the wildlife that flourished in and around them. It would be a good idea to go and sit a while by one of the ponds. She would avoid the larger ones that were frequented by fishermen and, even at this time of year, the occasional swimmer. She would go to Heron Pool, one of the lesser-known stretches of water on the Heath, and probably the most secluded.

She took a path in that direction, walking purposefully and enjoying the gentle breeze on her face, but she was also looking diligently around her, mentally recording the natural charms and curiosities the Heath had to offer at this time of year.

She noted that although the wild rose bushes had lost their blooms they still retained a great array of sturdy rose hips, their pretty pink skins contrasting with the bright red of the nearby holly berries, which were abundant. The holly leaves were a shining vivid green. It would be a cold winter this year. She even saw mistletoe clinging to a gnarled old apple tree. There was no point in taking any home: no kissing took place at Hillside.

All these things Clare observed. But, strangely, she did not notice the man who had been following in her footsteps ever since she left the Highgate Road. He was a pale, unsmiling man, almost gaunt, and he wore a dark broad-brimmed hat and a grey greatcoat. He moved silently.

It was easy to miss him. By accident or design, he remained a constant fifty or sixty yards behind Clare, and while the young woman walked out in the middle of the fairway the man stayed close to the trees.

There was still much colour in this sprawling wilderness, even as November drew to its close. Southern England had enjoyed a mild autumn, and large areas of gorse still had their yellow hue. There were still a few leaves on many of the trees, and these by now had changed colour to an assortment of brown and golden tints. And, of course, masses of evergreens stood out boldly alongside their threadbare neighbours.

There were also pleasing sounds to enjoy. Most of the songbirds had gone by now, or become silent, but the faithful robins still trilled their pleasant song. And the bleating of sheep, grazing over by the Vale of Health, carried for a mile in the clear atmosphere.

Here and there flocks of starlings chattered as they busied themselves on the grassland, picking up any seeds or insects that remained from summer, and when the starlings suddenly and inexplicably took off and went wheeling skywards in close formation, cheeky London sparrows moved in to glean the remnants.

After fifteen minutes, Clare approached Heron Pool, which owed its seclusion to being situated in the middle of a small wood: chiefly fir trees with foliage reaching almost to the ground.

As Clare entered the wood, the silence was broken by the cawing of rooks, who had just arrived in the treetops. The other arrival was the man in the greatcoat, who had quickened his pace once Clare was in among the trees. He avoided the path which the young woman had taken. Instead, he slipped in among the adjoining bushes and firs.

Two or three minutes later, Clare emerged from the gloom of the wood into the light of the open space that was mainly occupied by Heron Pool. Obligingly, a statuesque heron was standing in the shallows, motionless, as it watched for fish.

Clare's heart sank momentarily as she saw that the heron had competition. On the opposite side of the pool two fishermen had rods projecting over the water. However, they were sitting quite still in their folding stools, eyes fixed on their floats, which were undisturbed out on the water. The men seemed not to notice her, as she made her way along the narrow beach that fringed the pond.

Separating the beach from the trees there was a modest margin of turf and, halfway along this, Clare came upon a fallen tree; she found a patch of the trunk where the bark had been broken off to reveal the smooth wood underneath.

19

This would be a comfortable enough perch for forty or fifty minutes.

She sat down, took a notepad and pencil from her pocket, and began to jot down the things she had seen and heard on her walk: the trees and bushes, the animals and birds, the vistas and views, the latter more extensive now many trees were almost bare. She had seen two hares, not boxing as they would do in the spring, but lolloping around together on the greensward before disappearing into the undergrowth. She had also seen an owl, apparently asleep up a tree, resting before nightfall, when he would begin his relentless hunt for prey.

When she felt she had captured all the treasures she had met with on the way, Clare began to survey the scene in front of her.

The lake, protected from the breeze by the surrounding wood, was placid, its calm ruffled only occasionally when the tip of a pike briefly broke the surface. Pike were too big to interest the heron, and the fishermen could only wait and hope that one of them would take one of their lines. So neither heron nor humans reacted.

All around the pool's perimeter coots and moorhens were bustling about, forever engaged in some urgent but obscure activity; a total contrast to the elegant heron, which hadn't moved a feather since Clare arrived.

As she studied the scene, Clare herself was being observed by the watcher in the wood. The man was leaning against a tree a little way back from the clearing, where he could see and not be seen.

For a while Clare sat absorbed by the beauty around her. And then last night's sleepless hours began to take their toll. She had chosen a spot where a gap between two tree-tops allowed a ray of sunshine to caress her face. She felt her eyelids beginning to close.

For half an hour she slept, and then was awoken by a fierce burst of quacking from four ducks at the far end of the water. For some reason, few ducks ventured to Heron Pool. But those that did were especially jealous of their territory.

The altercation ended when one duck went scuttling away into the trees, briefly pursued by the other three, still flapping and squawking.

Once the intruder had been seen off, silence was restored. The water and the woodland glade resumed dozing in the winter sunshine.

Then came more excitement.

Clare was suddenly aware of movement on the pond's tranquil surface, and saw two small blobs swimming towards her. She watched as they reached the shore in front of her and came out to shake the water off their little bodies. They were water voles. Then, to her delight, they began to sport on the beach, almost as if they were playing catch.

For more than a minute the game went on, and then a bad thing happened. There was a flutter of wings, followed by squeals of panic from the voles, and then a bird of prey was airborne with one of the little creatures in its beak. The other vole raced for cover under a bush.

Clare sighed. Then she picked up her notepad again and wrote a few more words: 'Peregrine active on Heron Pool, 27 November.'

It was the most dramatic event she had witnessed this morning, as well as the saddest. But there had been many other happenings of a more pleasing nature. Now she must go home and log them all in her Heath file, and then select the items for her December article.

She stood up, stretched, and put away her notepad and pencil. Across the pool, the two fishermen had also decided it was time to leave. They were starting to secure their rods and lines. One of them had just transferred the few fish they had caught from the water-net into a fish-basket. It all seemed a lengthy business.

Clare began to stroll back along the waterside, pausing briefly to examine a plant in the grass at her feet. It was yarrow, a long way past its due season, which had survived because of the gentle weather and its sheltered situation. She decided that a mental note should be enough to preserve this phenomenon for her file.

She reached the path by which she had come and turned into the wood. The sun, low in the late autumn sky, scarcely penetrated the dense fir trees, and the way ahead of her was dark. The air was chilly here, and she fastened an extra button on her coat.

Once Clare was out of sight of the pool, the watcher moved swiftly through the trees to a point by the path that she must soon reach. He remained concealed three yards from the track.

In the poor light Clare was no longer studying her surroundings; her mind was on her nature notes, and she was toying with phrases she might use to bring them to life.

The man took something from his pocket. The young woman was getting closer now.

Then there came a shout from twenty yards behind her. It was one of the fishermen, who were catching up with her on the same path.

'Oi, miss!'

Clare stopped and turned towards them.

'Can you tell us the way to the 'ighgate Road? We come up from Kentish Town. Don't know this bit of the 'eath.'

Clare responded courteously. 'The Highgate Road? Well ...' She tried to marshal complicated directions in her head, and then decided on a simpler solution. These were elderly men and seemed like decent fellows. 'That's where I'm going,' she said. 'If you'd like to walk with me, I'll show you the way.'

'Ta,' said the fisherman, and his friend said, 'Not sure if we can keep up with your young legs, miss, but we'll try.'

The watcher turned and retreated into the trees.

The hand-bell in the drawing room rang again.

Mrs Butters had completed Meredith Austin's luncheon order and had managed to squeeze it into a package that wasn't too thick to fit into his copious briefcase.

She took it with her to the drawing-room door and knocked. Austin called for her to enter and she went in, brandishing his lunch-pack.

Her employer was standing up, transferring documents from his desk to that same briefcase, which had once been shiny and stiff but now was rough and saggy. It was well used to accommodating too many items.

'I've got your lunch here, sir,' said Mrs Butters.

'Good,' said Austin tersely, taking it unceremoniously from her hands. Without another word he forced it in among the papers, and was just able to make the case close and lock. Then he addressed his housekeeper sternly. 'Mrs Butters, I am at last going to my office, to get on with the job that feeds every member of this household.'

'I'm sure we're all very grateful, sir,' said Mrs Butters meekly.

'I certainly hope so. I have lost half a day through this intolerable disturbance, so I shall undoubtedly be late home this evening. Have dinner available at eight o'clock and keep it hot till I arrive. You know I cannot abide food that is luke-warm or dried up.'

'Very good, sir,' said Mrs Butters, wondering how that might be achieved.

'Take lunch to my daughters in their rooms. They are both still in a state of shock, and need to rest.'

'Yes, sir. I'll see they're looked after.'

She thought of telling him that she had seen Clare leave the house an hour ago, looking fit and untroubled, but she decided against it.

She was aware that there was something more important she ought to say to him, something that was sure to cause displeasure, and she was wondering if she could face it. Yesterday Austin had told her she must be sure to give him this reminder, but things were different today.

She asked herself whether her employer would be angrier now if she spoke up, or later if she hadn't done so. Finally she concluded that the wrath would be greater if delayed. She cleared her throat and forced the words out.

'Excuse me, sir. You haven't forgotten the inquiry agents?'

'Inquiry agents?' said Austin blankly. Then he remembered. The Heath Dwellers' Association had voted to employ private investigators to speed the solution of the Heath Murders. 'Dammit! I had forgotten!' He thought for a moment. 'Well, that appointment was made last week. They cannot hold me to it after what's occurred.'

'They were due at twelve o'clock, sir.'

'Indeed. I had intended to come back early today, deal with them, and then work at home this afternoon. Instead, I find myself going out abominably late.' He grunted irritably. 'You will have to send them away. Tell them today is not convenient.'

'Oh. Yes, sir.' Mrs Butters was clearly nervous. The visitors might be stern, important men. 'What reason shall I give?'

'None. Dammit, woman, I don't have to explain myself to people. Just tell them to go!'

Meredith Austin was an impatient man, indifferent to the feelings and problems of others. He had been fond of his mother, and had cared for her dutifully through her long final illness. That had seemed to exhaust his supply of human kindness. No one had helped him then; he had seen no reason to help anyone else since. He had emerged from those difficult years with a determination to achieve prosperity and status. His office was the centrepiece of his life and he bitterly resented any enforced absence from it.

His housekeeper stood for a moment, looking uncertain.

'That will be all, Mrs Butters,' snapped Austin. 'You've heard my orders.'

And then came a brisk emphatic knock at the front door.

'That'll be them now,' said Mrs Butters. 'They'll be on the doorstep when you go out.'

Austin pondered. All Heath Dwellers were expected to grant these men an interview. If he didn't see them now, they'd come back. He changed his decision with a sigh.

'Very well, Mrs Butters. As they are here, I'd better see them. Then they won't need to return and spoil another day.'

As Mrs Butters departed, Austin sat at his desk, frowning. He noticed one of his scarves on the seat of an armchair, and it seemed to cause him some alarm. He hurried across, picked up the scarf in a disorderly tangle, and thrust it into one of his desk drawers. He had resumed putting things into his briefcase when Mrs Butters ushered the visitors in.

She did her best to manage a formal voice as she struggled to read from the card she had been given.

'Major Henry Steele,' she announced. 'Private Invigorator and Inquiry Agent.'

'Investigator, actually,' said the taller of the two men, advancing with outstretched hand. 'I'm Henry Steele, and this is my colleague, Mr John Mason.'

When Steele retired early from British Military Intelligence, he had kept his service rank, but his sergeant, whose simultaneous release he had paid for, had warmly embraced civilian status.

Austin's glance took in the new arrivals as he shook their hands. Steele, in light green Donegal tweed, was lean and very upright, with greying hair and sharp features. Mason was a little shorter but a lot broader, built like a prizefighter. He wore a plain brown suit that had probably served him well for several years.

Austin spoke briskly. 'You'd better sit down. I can spare you twenty minutes. This house has been in turmoil, and I am already four hours late for work. I'm sure you're aware of the tragedy that took place on our doorstep last night.'

'We are, sir,' Steele confirmed. 'We wondered if we should still impose on you. But then, as this latest outrage seems related to matters we are due to discuss, we thought perhaps you would bear with us.'

'Very well,' said Austin. He took a round silver watch from his waistcoat pocket and propped it upright on his desk. 'I am at your disposal for a further nineteen minutes. But I should start by telling you that when the Heath Association discussed employing your services, I spoke against it.'

'So we heard.' Steele spoke dispassionately. 'I gather it went to a show of hands, and you and Dr Frankel were the only dissenters.'

Austin was not pleased that Steele should know this, but decided not to make an issue of it. 'There was nothing personal in the matter. Frankel and I both feel that, as we pay extortionate rates and taxes, we are entitled to full protection from the constabulary without paying additional fees.'

'I sympathize, sir,' said Steele genially. 'And I have to say that, for our part, we were not keen to get involved. It appeared to be a routine job for dogged police work. But then we noticed that there were strange aspects that intrigued us.'

'Strange? It seems to me a straightforward instance of a homicidal maniac who must, sooner or later, be caught and hanged.'

Steele demurred. 'Not quite straightforward, I think.

Mason, you have a list of the victims to date. Would you kindly read it out for us?'

'Shall be done,' said Mason, taking a folded sheet of paper from his pocket. He straightened it out, cleared his throat, and began his recital.

'Ambrose Rennie, a clerk, stabbed to death on 7th October in Parliament Hill Fields.'

'Near the Stone of Free Speech, I think,' said Steele.

'On 28th October, James Tate, a professional boxer, was similarly killed, after leaving a public house in the Vale of Health.'

Steele interrupted again. 'Note, however, it was established that the man was not drunk, and should have been well able to defend himself.'

'November 11th,' Mason continued, 'Philip Agnew, a trader, was murdered on the Heath, and then pushed into one of the ponds.

'Last night, Robert Kemp was fatally stabbed outside this house. In the first three atrocities, death was due to a single stab wound, but no weapon was found near the scene of the crime. We believe the same is true of last night's murder. Is that the case, sir?'

Austin shrugged. 'I understand the man was stabbed. I have not concerned myself with any other details.'

'Note,' said Steele, 'that all these crimes took place on Sunday nights, between the hours of 9 and 11 p.m.'

'The killer is a lunatic, as I said,' observed Austin testily. 'No doubt he is obsessive.'

'He is also audacious. The third and fourth murders took place in spite of police patrols, brought in after the second death, and doubled after the third. Truly, a man now needs a strong reason to venture on the Heath at night.'

'British citizens will not let a thug deter them from going about their normal purposes.'

'Ah, yes, one has to have a purpose. Which brings us to Robert Kemp. I believe he was a friend of your daughter's.'

Austin bridled instantly. 'You have been misinformed, sir. Kemp was merely a family acquaintance. He was not a friend. And he had no particular association with any one of us.'

'Oh. I had supposed that Kemp was on his way to visit the young lady.'

'Good God, man! My daughter does not receive young men in the absence of her father!'

Steele remained cool. 'You were not at home last night, then?'

'I was not!' snapped Austin. After a brief pause, he decided to add, 'Your man can add to his jottings that I was at my club.' Austin was annoyed to see that Mason was making notes.

'But your daughter would not have been alone, surely. I believe you have two daughters residing here, as well as that pleasant housekeeper who let us in.'

'Major, I thought you were here to ask about the Heath Maniac. I was not expecting questions about my family, or my household. The point is, the man Kemp was not expecting to call at this house. Clearly, he was passing this way on some other business. When he was attacked he came to the nearest door for help.'

Steele was non-committal. 'Let us assume so. Mr Austin, was Kemp a fit and vigorous young man?'

'He seemed so to me. I met him on only two or three occasions.'

'Then we come to the most surprising aspect of this case. You note that all the victims have been healthy young men in the prime of life.'

'It had not occurred to me, but now I see that it is so.'

'Is it not curious that none of them was able to put up any sort of resistance?'

'I assume each attack took the victim by surprise.'

'Well, I'm sure they were not expecting it. But one might anticipate that, in at least one of the first three crimes, the initial blow would be less than fatal. One of the victims might have survived long enough to grapple with his assailant: the boxer, perhaps.'

'Possibly they did, but were overcome,' Austin suggested.

'Not so, Mr Austin. In no case were there any signs of a struggle. Is that correct, Mason?'

Mason looked up from his notes. 'Yes, sir. Perfectly correct, sir. No cut hands, no bruised knuckles. Just one deep stab wound to the heart every time.'

'This man is obviously a skilled assassin,' said Austin.

'Also a lucky one,' said Steele. 'And devilish clever. To get close enough to deliver the deadly blow without the victim seeing or hearing him.'

Encouraged by Steele cueing him in, Mason now ventured an observation. 'Almost as if he arrives on wings, like the Angel of Death.'

Steele bestowed a little smile on his companion. 'My colleague enjoys a touch of fantasy, Mr Austin. But I assure you our inquiries will be totally down to earth. We shall not be seeking any sort of winged creature. We shall be tracking down a wicked human being. And we shall find him.'

'Then the local community will be very grateful to you, sir.' Austin shifted in his seat, his movement suggesting an early end to the interview. 'I hope our brief discussion has helped you clarify your thoughts.'

'I think it has,' said Steele. 'But I hope we may detain you a little longer. There are certain facts we need to ascertain.'

'The police were here for many hours this morning,' Austin responded. 'They obtained enough facts to fill an encyclopaedia. I suggest you liaise with them.'

'We shall do so, of course,' said Steele. 'But our approach

doesn't always coincide with that of the constabulary. I think first of the psychological aspect. I ask myself what sort of man would have the motive for these vile crimes.'

Austin seemed astonished. 'Motive? You seek a coherent motive? We are dealing with a madman!'

'Are we? Then what drove him mad? Would his family and friends not notice that he was mad?'

'Why should he have a family? He's probably a lonely wretch, living in lodgings in Kentish Town. Or a perverted vagrant from the stews of Cleveland Street.'

'Of course, we shall search those areas. But first I intend to visit the wealthy and prosperous, who often attract envy and resentment, and therefore enemies.'

'Your last point is true enough. But how is it relevant? No one wealthy or prosperous has been attacked.'

'Not directly. But the Heath Association tell me that the climate of fear is affecting all its members. Traders are losing revenue because people are avoiding the area. Already property values are falling. Thus the Maniac is effectively damaging local society.'

'That, of course, is why the Association sought your help.'

'Quite. It is also the reason why we need your further assistance.'

Austin sighed, sat back in his chair, and thought for a moment. Then he grudgingly conceded. 'Very well, Major. I must submit to your questions a little longer.' He opened a silver box on his desk, took a pinch of snuff, and inhaled it vigorously.

'Thank you,' said Steele. 'Mr Austin, it's just possible that one of these big houses on the Highgate Road could unwittingly provide sanctuary for this monster. I need to know who is resident in each household. Also whether there are any rooms, attics or outbuildings which are not normally in use.'

'You seem to know already, sir, that my household consists

of myself, my daughters, and a housekeeper. There is a garden shed, if that is of any interest to you.'

'It might be,' said Steele, glancing to check that Mason had noted the fact. Then he turned back to Austin. 'Do you have a gardener?'

'I no longer keep a permanent gardener. A man comes in twice a week.'

'I see. From the description of your family, I assume you have the misfortune to be a widower.'

Austin's response was chilly. 'You assume wrong, sir.'

Steele waited briefly, hoping the other man would expand on the subject, but he showed no signs of doing so. Steele took the plunge.

'As I said, Mr Austin, I need to know the circumstances of all local residents. May I ask where Mrs Austin is?'

'You may ask, sir, but I may not tell you.'

'I understood I was to have your full co-operation.'

'I cannot tell you where she is, Major, because I do not know. She chose to leave me ten years ago. I do not know her whereabouts. We do not speak of her.'

Steele inclined his head a little. 'I am sorry I had to raise the matter. You have my sympathy.'

'Save your sympathy, sir, for the rogue with whom she ran away.'

'Ah. There was a man involved.'

Austin's temper was rising. 'If you choose to call him a man! A young whipper-snapper, full of airs and graces, enough to steal an honest man's wife, but not man enough to face him!' While speaking, Austin had picked up a heavy ebony ruler from his desk and was now squeezing it with both hands.

'Steady, sir, you are distressing yourself,' said Steele. And then he noticed a thin line of blood, trickling back towards Austin's right wrist. 'Good Lord! You are bleeding!'

31

Austin controlled himself with difficulty. He took his bleeding hand off the ruler and peered at the palm, which was covered with blood. 'I cut my hand yesterday. A small flesh wound, which seems to have reopened. It is nothing.'

'It will not remain nothing if you continue to reopen it,' Steele cautioned. 'I urge you to wash and dress the wound.'

'I shall attend to it in due course. Now I have to go to my office. Monday is a busy day, and I have lost five hours already. Must there be more questions?'

'Just a few, if you please. I take it you are in business, Mr Austin?'

Austin had put down the ruler and taken a crisp white handkerchief from his pocket. He was winding it round his hand as he replied, 'I am senior partner in a firm of insurance brokers.'

'Ah. How came you to cut your hand yesterday?'

'I cut it with my razor. I foolishly left it open on the rim of the basin. When I reached for the soap, I accidentally grasped the blade.'

'Alas, the kind of mistake we all make.'

'I think that's enough about my mishap. I cannot think it has any bearing on the problem you are here to investigate.'

Steele was not deflected. 'Interesting that you did it with a razor. I had supposed you might have hurt yourself with one of those daggers.' He rose, and walked to the wall which displayed the weapons Austin had recently adjusted.

Austin was too taken aback to protest, and his response was surprisingly defensive. 'The daggers? Why should you think that? They are simply for decoration. I never handle them.'

'Indeed?' Steele was scrutinizing the objects closely. 'Yet someone has handled the upper one quite recently. With all due respect to your good housekeeper, I see a little dust on the lower one. But there is none on this one.'

'I daresay Mrs Butters dusted the higher one, but was distracted before she could complete her work.' Austin rose, to indicate that he had no more to say.

'Distracted,' said Steele. 'Yes, that's possible. These are distracting times.' He sighed. 'Well, I shall distract you no longer on this occasion, Mr Austin. The world of insurance must not be kept waiting any longer.'

'I am glad to hear that,' said Austin, as Steele moved towards the door, but then John Mason intervened.

'Excuse me, sir, but you usually ask about enemies.'

'Ah yes,' said Steele. 'Thank you. As Mr Austin was not the direct victim, I had almost forgotten. But, as we observed, the Maniac's activities are a blow at everyone living in this area. It would be useful to know, sir, if you're aware of anyone who might wish to harm you or your family. Or, by extension, your daughter's ... er ... your acquaintance.'

'No,' said Austin tersely. 'I do not know of any enemies, though no doubt we all have them.'

'Have there been any business disputes that might have led to bitterness?'

'Clients often make unreasonable demands on their insurers and are angry when they have to settle for less.'

'Ah, indeed. It is surprising how many people still expect to be paid in full. But you cannot recall any particular instances that gave rise to threats?'

'No,' said Austin. 'I can't.'

'Have any employees or tradesmen been dismissed in acrimonious circumstances?'

'No,' was Austin's first response. But then he thought again. 'Except ... ah ... you mentioned gardeners. For a short time last year I did employ a man on a permanent basis, to work in the garden and do odd jobs. Then I found he was stealing vegetables, and I told him to leave.'

Mason had put his notebook away, so Steele sat on the arm

of a chair, and took a pad and silver pencil from his pocket.

'This may be important,' he said. 'What was this man's name? Where did he come from? What became of him?'

'I cannot recall his name. Mrs Butters may remember. I believe he came from Camden Town.'

'How was he recruited?'

'He knocked on the door, looking for work. He had references, which I now believe were falsified.'

'And you had to discharge him. How did he react?'

'When I accused him of stealing, he was insolent. When I dismissed him, he was abusive. However, I cannot recall any threats. I have no idea what became of him. But I now recall his name was Scully.'

'First name?'

'I don't think he had one.'

'Thank you, Mr Austin. We shall endeavour to trace the man. Of course, there may be several Scullys in Camden Town.'

'More than enough, I imagine.' Austin consulted his watch again. 'And now, sir, I can spare you no more time. I have to go.'

'Of course,' said Steele. 'We shall detain you no longer.' Austin returned the watch to his pocket, visibly relieved. And then Steele added, 'However, I should like to speak to your daughters, if you please.'

Austin's response was a mixture of anger and astonishment. 'My daughters? That is quite out of the question! They are both distressed and must not be disturbed.'

'Nevertheless, it is important that we talk to them. Perhaps if we returned tomorrow ...'

'Not today, not tomorrow, not any other day! I have given you all the information you could possibly need!'

'Different people see things in different ways—'

Austin cut him short. 'Do not persist, Major! You are

bordering on impertinence! I must ask you both to leave at once! My woman will show you out.'

Austin picked up the little desk bell again and shook it furiously. While he was doing this, Steele deftly slid his silver pencil down inside the armchair, beside the cushion. Then he sighed and stood up, restoring the pad to his pocket.

'Very well, sir,' he said. 'If you insist. May we leave by this garden door? I should like to see where Mr Kemp came in from the Heath.'

Austin was by now thoroughly exasperated. 'You may go by any door you wish, sir, as long as you go!' He spoke sharply to Mrs Butters, who had appeared in response to his summons. 'These gentlemen are leaving by the garden door. Fetch their coats at once!'

As Mrs Butters went to comply, Austin had more fierce words for the visitors. 'Pray do not pry or probe in my garden. The police have done enough damage there already.'

'I cannot give any undertaking, sir,' said Steele. 'I must tell you that, as well as our commission from the Heath Association, our friends at Scotland Yard have asked us to give them our views on this matter.'

'Tchah! Clearly a case of too many cooks! My lawyer will demand recompense for any nuisance!'

Mrs Butters gave the men their hats and coats and, as they put them on, she opened the garden door.

'Good day to you, Mr Austin,' said Steele, as he and Mason stepped outside. 'And thank you for your assistance.'

Austin could not bring himself to reply. And then, as the housekeeper closed the door on the men, he turned his fury on her.

'Mrs Butters!' he thundered. 'You have disgraced my house!'

'I beg your pardon, sir?' The woman's voice mingled fear and bewilderment.

'You may well ask my pardon! Those meddling busybod- ies discovered dust on this ornament!' Austin took the top dagger from the wall and waved it under his housekeeper's nose. 'How the devil did you let that happen?'

'I'm sorry, sir. I must have missed it. All these goings-on.'

Her master plunged the dagger into a pile of newspapers on a table. 'I am surrounded by disloyalty and incompetence!' He was shouting now. 'I am hounded by spies and enemies! You are not to allow those men in the house again, d'you understand?'

'Yes, sir.'

'Where is Miss Harriet? She is the cause of all this turmoil, with her foolish flirtations and silly ideas. Where is she?'

'She is not in her room, sir. I think she is having a bath.'

'Had she not defied me, we should not have been involved in this infamy!'

'I'm sure she meant no harm, sir.'

'Silence, woman! She disobeyed my orders about that rascal Kemp! And all this disruption is the result! She should be taught a lesson!' Austin seemed to make a decision. 'By God, she shall be taught a lesson! She shall pay a penalty she will not forget!'

The angry man picked up his briefcase and strode to the hall door. There he paused, turned, and glared at his housekeeper.

'I've already told you, Mrs Butters, that I shall certainly be late home tonight, due to all these appalling events. Now it seems I shall be even later, thanks to your persuading me to receive those presumptuous pests!'

'I'm sorry, sir,' said Mrs Butters, yet again. These were words that were often used in this house, though never by Meredith Austin.

'You had better delay the evening meal till nine o'clock on

this occasion. I suggest you use the extra hour to do some proper cleaning. If I find a speck of dust anywhere in this house tomorrow, you will lose a week's wages!'

And with that Austin stormed out of the room, slamming the door behind him.

Left alone, Mrs Butters stood for a moment, shaking her head unhappily. Then, nervously, she prised the dagger out of the newspapers and wiped it on her sleeve, before replacing it on the wall.

She noticed the end of Austin's scarf protruding from a desk drawer. Puzzled, she opened the drawer, extracted the scarf, and folded it neatly before replacing it and closing the drawer again. Austin had never been an easy man to work for but this last month his temper had become worse. She wondered why.

She was straightening the curtains when the hall door opened and Harriet's sister came in. Clare's cheeks were still a healthy pink from her outing. She had deposited her notes in her room and given her face a refreshing wash, but she still retained much of the impetus from her walk. She spoke briskly. 'My father came upstairs looking very angry, Mrs Butters.'

'He is angry, Miss Clare. Angrier than a rabid stoat. When he's in this mood, I dread what he'll do next.'

'He likes people dreading what he'll do next. It's better if you don't let him frighten you.'

'But he does frighten me, and that's a fact. And he frightens Miss Harriet too.'

Clare smiled a neat little smile. 'Well, please remember that he doesn't frighten me.'

Mrs Butters took a cloth from her apron pocket and began dusting the windowsills. 'It strikes me nothing frightens you, Miss Clare.'

'Not true, I'm afraid. Smallpox frightens me. The Heath

Maniac frightens me. The Liberal Party frightens me. But I am not frightened by a blustering bully.' Clare went to the stack of bookshelves which lined the wall opposite the window. 'I hope I'm not holding up your work, Mrs Butters. I need to consult some reference books for a piece I am writing.'

'Bless you, no,' said the housekeeper. 'There's not much more to do in here. But how you're managing to write today, I do not know. All this fuss, and bobbies everywhere.'

'Writing is actually a great escape from the stresses and strains of life.'

Mrs Butters was carefully dusting a small china cat. 'But it must be hard work, finding the right words and so on. It takes me ten minutes to write a note for the milkman.'

Both women were startled by the noise of the front door being violently slammed shut. Although there was a door and a long hallway between her and the noise, it was loud enough to make Mrs Butters drop the china cat. It landed on its feet on the carpet, as cats do, and no damage was done.

'Ah,' said Clare. 'My father's gone, as gracefully as usual. You will be able to breathe more easily now.'

'For a few hours at least, thank the Lord. His temper's no better, from the way he slammed that door.'

Clare sighed. 'His temper's a fact of life, I'm afraid. He simmers like a latent volcano. It's something we all have to live with.'

'It wasn't always as bad as this, was it?'

Clare changed the subject. 'Oh, Mrs Butters, perhaps when you've finished working in here, you could kindly put the carpet sweeper away. I think it's rather dangerous at the top of the stairs.'

Mrs Butters was puzzled. 'Top of the stairs? I don't remember leaving it there, miss. I don't know what's happening in the house this morning.'

3

FROM THE HILL Top Cafe opposite, Steele and Mason watched Meredith Austin close his front gate and walk briskly off down the Highgate Road.

'Shall we go, guv'nor?' asked Mason.

Steele demurred; his cup was not quite empty. 'No hurry, Jack,' he said. 'There's time to finish my coffee.' Now there were just the two of them, the formal use of 'sir' and surname was jettisoned. In front of clients it enhanced the impression of military efficiency. But in private the two men's relationship was much more relaxed.

They had been a good team throughout twenty years in British Military Intelligence. In particular, their undercover work in Mesopotamia had forged a unique mutual respect. It had also done much to protect British interests and the welfare of the local population in that troubled region, where European powers were conniving to extend their influence. The methods employed by the two men, however, had tended to be unofficial and unorthodox, and had often raised eyebrows in senior circles.

Then came the mishap that eliminated a ruthless and dangerous German agent. It had undoubtedly saved hundreds of lives, and possibly averted war in the Middle East. The man's fatal fall from a hotel balcony had, of course, been a drunken accident. But a *Times* journalist, seeking a story, had hinted at British involvement, and military authorities had hurried to distance themselves from the incident. Major Steele had been encouraged to resign and return to England and civilian life. It had been his idea that his sergeant should do the same, and join him in starting a detective agency.

In this new enterprise, their instinctive teamwork continued to serve them well. Each normally read the other's thoughts without effort. But at the moment Mason was puzzled. 'Excuse me asking,' he ventured, 'but why are we so interested in that lot over the road? I mean, our job is chasing the Heath Maniac. That's not going to be Mr Austin, is it?'

Steele took a sugar lump from the bowl and sucked it. 'We don't rule out anything at the start, do we? And the reason we're probing a little deeper into the Austin household is because it's aroused my interest.'

'I can see that, guv'nor, but why?'

'You know that I am always intrigued when I perceive that someone is lying, or concealing something. There's a mystery at Hillside House. It may have to do with the Heath Maniac, or it may not. Either way, I think we should find out what's going on.'

As Mason considered this proposition, he peered out through the cafe window and watched a man walking along the other side of the road. The man wore a grey greatcoat, and had a broad-brimmed hat pulled down low over his forehead. Curiously, although it was still a mild day, the muffler round the man's neck had been dragged up to cover most of his mouth. Mason thought perhaps he had a toothache. There was certainly nothing jaunty in his walk.

Mason turned back to look at Steele again.

'Well, you give the orders, guv. And you're usually right.' He sniffed. 'I must say, I don't much care for Mr Austin. I reckon if he ever smiled his face would break up. And I could never trust a man with shoes as shiny as that.'

Clare was still making notes by the bookshelves when Mrs Butters returned.

'I've put the sweeper away in the cupboard.' She'd had second thoughts. 'I wonder if it was me that left it on the landing. Tell the truth, I'm in such a tizzy today.'

'After being shouted at by my father, it's not surprising,' Clare consoled her. She closed a large volume and returned it to its place. 'What time is luncheon today?' she enquired.

'Any time you like,' said the housekeeper. 'There's some nice cold steak and kidney pie from yesterday. The master said to serve you and Miss Harriet in your rooms.'

'Ah, not for me, thank you. There are papers all over my room. I'll have mine as a snack downstairs. Lay it out on the kitchen table.'

'Very good, miss.' Mrs Butters was glad to be spared an extra trip up the stairs.

'With a little English mustard, please.'

'Yes, of course, miss.' The housekeeper was eager to please: she always saw Clare as an ally. 'And perhaps you'd like some potato salad.'

'Yes, that would go well. Thank you.' Clare was about to leave when there came a knock at the garden door.

'Hello, who can that be?' Clare turned back into the room. 'Can you see, Mrs Butters?'

Mrs Butters peered through one of the windows. In the sunshine she could see Steele and Mason, standing back from the door.

'Mercy me!' she said. 'It's the two gentlemen who were here just now. The detectives. They made your father very angry.'

'That sounds interesting. Open the door and let them in.'

'Oh no, Miss Clare!' cried the housekeeper. 'Mr Austin

said I was never to let them in this house again! And he said I was to tell you not to speak to them!'

'That sounds even more interesting. Open the door, please.'

'But Mr Austin said—'

Clare cut her short. 'Mr Austin is not here. Open the door at once, Mrs Butters.'

Reluctantly, the housekeeper opened the door.

Henry Steele stepped forward with a smile. 'Ah, Mrs Butters, I'm sorry to trouble you again. I seem to have left my silver pencil in here. May we come in and retrieve it?'

Clare took charge. 'Yes, come in, by all means, gentlemen. I'm Clare Austin. My father just left, I'm afraid.'

'Ah, indeed. Thank you,' said the major, as the two men stepped into the room. 'How do you do, Miss Austin. I'm Henry Steele, and this is my colleague, John Mason.'

'How do you do,' said Clare. 'I've heard that the Heath Association have engaged your services. You have mislaid a silver pencil?'

'Your father was giving me useful information, and I was making notes. I think the pencil may be on Mr Austin's desk.'

Steele crossed to the desk and surveyed everything on it. He looked at a pad on which there was writing, then he raised it and looked beneath. 'It may have got pushed underneath here. No. Then it must be somewhere else.'

For a moment Mason feared his colleague might suggest that the pencil had somehow rolled into one of the closed drawers. But Steele knew when to temper audacity with discretion. 'Perhaps it's on one of the windowsills,' he said, and set off in that direction.

Then Clare intervened. 'Where were you sitting?'

The suggestion seemed to come as a surprise to the major. 'Ah. A good idea,' he said. 'I was in that armchair.'

Clare reached down inside the chair, felt around, and swiftly produced the missing item. 'Is this it?' she enquired.

'Yes, it is,' said Steele gratefully. 'Good gracious! In the chair! My word! Thank you, Miss Austin.'

Clare handed him the pencil and he put it in his pocket. Then he smiled and said, 'As we've met, madam, I wonder if I might ask you a few questions?'

'Certainly, Major. I should be pleased to help, if I can. I believe the Heath Association would wish all of us to assist you in any way we can.'

Mrs Butters was appalled. 'Miss Clare, your father said you weren't to talk to these gentlemen!'

'I'm sure that must be a misunderstanding. I will take full responsibility.'

'But, Miss Clare—'

'Thank you, Mrs Butters. That will be all for now. Please go and deal with the lunch.'

Once again shaking her head disapprovingly, the housekeeper left the room and closed the door behind her.

'Now, gentlemen,' said Clare. 'Please be seated. And tell me how I can help you.'

The men sat down. Steele cleared his throat and voiced the cautionary words his conscience demanded. 'Miss Austin, it's only fair to warn you that Mrs Butters is right. Mr Austin has forbidden us to talk to his daughters. There could be unpleasantness for you if he found out.'

'There will be no unpleasantness in this house whatever happens,' said Clare. 'In the meantime, my father has gone to the City. I am twenty-five, and will talk to whomever I please.'

Steele's admiration was genuine. 'You are a woman of spirit, Miss Austin. I hope to speak to your sister also. May I ask if she shares the same attitude?'

'My half-sister,' Clare corrected. 'And no, she is only eighteen and entirely under our father's thumb. I doubt she will be willing to talk to you.'

'A pity,' said Steele. 'We were especially keen to hear from her, as I believe she had an association with last night's victim. Am I right?'

'Yes,' said Clare firmly.

'Although your father vehemently denies it, for some reason.'

'Snobbery is the reason. He felt Robert Kemp was beneath our station in life.'

'I see.' Steele glanced across to check that the faithful Mason was taking notes again. He was. Steele continued. 'Will you tell us a little about your sister, please.'

'Harriet has always been young for her age. Her main concern in life was always her pets. That is, until she met Robert. Under his influence, she began to take an interest in books, and show a little independence. Alas, I fear all that will now be snuffed out.'

Steele smiled gently. 'We must hope not, Miss Austin. Independence is a powerful beast, once it is unleashed. You knew Mr Kemp yourself, I take it?'

'I was the first to meet him. Last year, through an old school friend. After I introduced them, Harriet saw him more frequently. Often at the Hampstead Arts Club, which I no longer attend.'

'You are not a lover of the arts, then?'

'On the contrary, I am. But I am a doer rather than a critic. I do not care for the chatter at the Arts Club.'

'Ah. Loud talk and floppy bow ties, perhaps?'

Mason chuckled dutifully. Clare merely said, 'I think that might be fair comment.'

Steele pressed on.

'So a friendship developed between your sister and Robert Kemp?'

'Yes. He called on her several times here. To exchange books, or simply to talk about them. He and I spoke only briefly. I thought it right to leave them alone together.'

'Quite. Was there a feeling that this friendship might blossom into something stronger?'

Clare paused fractionally and then said, 'Yes, there was.'

'And your father reacted unfavourably?'

'To say the least. He was determined to destroy the relationship. The first time Robert called, Father was rude to him. Then he forbade Harriet to see him. So Robert had to come on Sunday nights, when Father is always out.'

'And you feel his hostility was due to snobbery?'

Clare hesitated briefly. Then she took the plunge. 'Well, snobbery was the obvious reason. But, in truth, I think there was something else. Something stronger. Father called Robert a fortune-hunter.'

'Oh. A fortune-hunter.' Steele thought for a moment. Then he leaned forward and said, 'Miss Austin, will you allow me an indiscreet question?'

Mason looked up, a little apprehensively. But Clare Austin was unperturbed.

'You may ask me anything you wish,' she said.

Steele chose his words carefully. 'Is there a fortune for Robert Kemp to have hunted?'

The young woman looked around, and then there was something in her tone that might have been a rebuke. 'You have observed that we live somewhat modestly, no doubt.'

Mason rushed to the aid of his leader. 'The major was not suggesting that anything was shabby, miss.'

Clare gave a little humourless laugh. 'Of course not. But there is no sign of conspicuous wealth, is there? My father is not an extravagant man. However, Harriet's mother seemed to have money. I imagine Harriet will eventually inherit some.'

'One would assume so,' said Steele. 'Can you tell us anything of Harriet's mother?'

Clare's reply was brisk. 'A very sensible woman. She left my father.'

'So I understand,' said Steele, and waited for more. After a few seconds it came.

'She ran away with another man. Mention of her name is forbidden in this house. Like so many other things.'

Again there was quiet for a moment. Then Steele risked another indiscreet question. 'It's clear you are not happy here, Miss Austin. May I ask why you stay?'

Clare was not offended; indeed, she seemed relieved at a chance to air her problems. 'I am the daughter of his first wife. There is no fortune for me. My father gives me a very small allowance while I am under his roof. A legal obligation, I'm sure.'

'A legal obligation?'

'A condition of my mother's will, I think. He would not do it out of kindness. At all events, it is a mere pittance, which I try to augment by writing articles for publication. At present, that income is tiny. So, until it improves, I would rather endure my father than go and starve in a garret.'

'Ah. I understand,' said Steele sympathetically. And then, more brightly, 'Well, well. So you are a writer, Miss Austin?'

'I aspire to be. So far I have succeeded only with nature notes. I observe the wildlife of Hampstead Heath, and write a monthly piece for the *Hampstead and Highgate Express*. They pay me a token fee: very small, I'm afraid.'

'Indeed?' Steele smiled admiringly. 'I'd say that makes you a professional writer. In my experience, for anyone to get anything published anywhere is a considerable achievement.'

'Thank you. But it does nothing to alleviate my financial plight.'

'Have you tried submitting material to other publications?'

'Oh yes. I have sent articles to various natural history journals, but none has so far been accepted.'

'Keep trying, Miss Austin. It is the only way.'

'I know that, Major, and I do. I recently completed a short story, and I have offered it to *The Strand Magazine*.'

Steele and Mason were both visibly impressed.

'*The Strand Magazine*!' said the major. 'You are aiming high! When do you think you may have their response?'

'Not for a while, I think. I posted it only this morning. I am already asking myself if I have simply wasted precious pennies on postage. One has to send a stamped addressed envelope, you know.'

'So I understand. Well, let us hope and pray that it will prove a good investment.'

Mason nodded his head cheerfully. 'We both wish you luck, miss.'

'We certainly do,' Steele echoed. And then he reverted to business. 'Now, may I ask you about your own mother? What are her circumstances?'

Clare paused, sad to leave the brief literary diversion. Then, for the first time, she showed signs of emotion. There was a slight tremor in her voice as she answered.

'My mother lies in Highgate Cemetery. She drowned when I was five years old.'

This reply was so unexpected that the men reacted with surprise rather than sympathy. 'Drowned?' said Steele.

'An accident. While boating with my father on the Thames.'

Clare was wiping moist eyes with a tiny handkerchief, and now Steele's voice was full of compassion. 'I am very sorry, Miss Austin. I regret arousing unhappy memories.' He took a large, spotless white handkerchief from his breast pocket and handed it to her. 'Perhaps you would do better with this,' he said. Clare took it with a murmur of thanks.

Mason went and put a fatherly hand on the young woman's shoulder. 'The major didn't mean to upset you, miss,' he said.

Then he turned a critical eye on Steele. 'Excuse me, sir, but do these questions help us find the Heath Maniac?'

'I think they might do,' said Steele. 'I think they might do.'

Silence was hanging heavy in the air as the door opened and Harriet came in, speaking as she did so.

'Clare, have you seen – oh, I'm sorry. I didn't know you had company.'

Her sister had regained her composure. 'It's all right, Harriet. These gentlemen were hoping to speak to you. They are engaged by the Heath Dwellers' Association.'

The two men rose. 'How do you do, Miss Harriet. I am Henry Steele and this is John Mason. We are hoping to shed some light on the recent outrages on the Heath. May I offer you our condolences? I understand that last night's crime was a personal tragedy for you.'

Harriet did not advance her hand, and stood looking perplexed. Then she managed a nervous, 'Oh. Thank you.'

'The Association has asked everyone to give these gentlemen all possible assistance,' said Clare.

Steele spoke gently. 'Our first task is to learn all we can about local residents, in case some vendetta or grudge is involved. We would welcome your observations.'

Harriet seemed unsure how to reply. So Clare put it more directly.

'They need to ask us some questions, Harriet. It is our duty to give them answers.'

Now Harriet found her voice. 'I don't think our father would approve of that,' she said firmly.

'I'm quite sure he wouldn't,' Clare responded. 'But he's gone to his office, hasn't he, to make himself more filthy lucre. So he won't know.'

'I am not willing to deceive him.' Harriet turned to the visitors. 'I'm sorry, but recent events have been too painful to discuss. I must ask you to spare me.' And with that she changed the subject. 'Clare, I came in to ask if you had seen Ella.'

Clare sighed. 'She was sleeping on the landing an hour ago.' She turned to Steele. 'Ella is my sister's cat.'

'She was in my room when I went for my bath. Now she's nowhere to be seen. I get so worried when she strays, after Freddie going.'

'Freddie was Harriet's guinea pig,' said Clare patiently. 'He disappeared from his hutch last month.'

'If I lost Ella as well, I don't know what I'd do.'

'You would still have your rabbit to console you.' Clare's manner was friendly but firm. 'Now calm yourself, Harriet. Ella may have gone to find her basket. I think Mrs Butters was going to clean it. She may have put it in the scullery. Or the cellar.'

'Oh. Yes. I'll go and see.' Harriet turned to leave, but not without a nervous warning to her sister. 'Do be careful, Clare. We mustn't do anything to upset Father.' And then she was gone.

'Please forgive Harriet,' said Clare. 'She has had a terrible shock. And her nerves are not good at the best of times.'

'Of course, Miss Austin. I was foolish to think of questioning her today.'

Then John Mason spoke up. 'Your sister doesn't look well, miss. I think she may have a temperature.'

'Mr Mason has some experience in these matters,' said Steele. 'During his army career, he was at one stage a medical orderly.'

'Perhaps she should see a doctor,' Mason added.

'Harriet is in the care of our family physician, Dr Frankel,' said Clare.

'Dr Frankel?' Steele mused for a moment. 'Another member of the Heath Association, I think.'

'Yes, he's one of our neighbours. A rather disagreeable

person, as you might expect, since he's our father's best friend. In fact, probably his only friend. Dr Frankel is always giving Harriet tablets and telling her to rest.'

There was a small pause; Steele was hoping Clare might say more on the subject. But she didn't. It was Mason who broke the silence.

'Your sister is very fond of her cat.'

'Yes. Ella is her special companion.'

'Really?' said Steele. 'More so than you, Miss Austin?'

'I'm afraid so. Over the years I've tried to establish a bond between us. But I cannot say we are really close.'

'I'm sorry to hear that.' Steele had now decided on his next line of inquiry. 'Miss Austin, another personal question if I may. You've told us frankly of your lack of funds. Did your unfortunate mother not leave any money?'

'Whatever she left went to my father. I believe he used it to start his insurance business.'

'I see. Now, as to the boating accident. You would have been too young to take in details at the time. But did you later find out any information?'

'As far as I could, Major. Father would never speak of it. But there were two newspaper accounts, plus a report of the inquest. A lady at our church had cut them out, and she gave them to me when I was older.'

'Ah. Good.'

'I also have my mother's diary, which records events in preceding days.'

'Excellent. I wonder if I might borrow those items and study them at leisure.'

'By all means. But I'm afraid it will take me some time to find them. I have not seen those things for years. All my shelves and drawers are taken up with my scribblings: notes, pieces abandoned halfway, rejected manuscripts and so on. I find it hard to keep track of personal documents.'

'We plan to call here again, if we can come to terms with your father. Or even if we can't. Our next visit will be soon enough. Now another matter, Miss Austin. Do you recall a man called Scully, who worked here briefly as a gardener?'

For a moment, something seemed to startle the young woman. Was it just the abrupt change of topic? Steele wondered. Then she quickly regained her composure.

'Scully? Yes. Yes, I do. Luke Scully. A rather wild-looking man, with a mass of red hair. And very piercing eyes, I remember.'

Mason looked up thoughtfully. He recalled a mention in the Heath Maniac file of a man with long red hair, seen at the pub on the night James Tate died.

Steele continued. 'I believe he left here on bad terms?'

'Yes,' said Clare. 'Father never liked him. Finally, he dismissed him for stealing vegetables, which he probably didn't do.'

As Steele digested her words, there came from somewhere upstairs a piercing scream, a single, shrill shriek of terror. All three reacted with shock. 'What was that?' said Mason.

Clare rose swiftly. 'It sounded like Harriet. I must go to her.' She hurried to the door.

'Can we assist?' said Steele.

'No. No. She sometimes has hysterics, and does not welcome witnesses. I'll call if your help is needed.' And with that she was gone.

Steele went to the open door. 'That didn't sound like hysterics. It was too sharp and sudden. Something bad has happened.'

'It won't be the Heath Manic,' said Mason. 'He's never struck in daylight.'

'And never indoors,' said Steele, 'as far as we know. But there's always a first time. Anyway, the young woman's obviously in distress. You have the smelling salts?'

Carrying the phial of reviving chemical was one of Mason's tasks, a throwback to his medical orderly days. The salts had often proved valuable to witnesses at crime scenes. He patted his waistcoat pocket. 'Yes, guv'nor. They're here.'

From the hall came the sound of female voices, one sobbing, the other attempting to give comfort. 'Have them ready,' said Steele. 'I think they will be needed.'

Then, through the door came the two sisters. Clare had her arm round Harriet's shoulders. Harriet, with tears flooding down her cheeks, was carrying a pet's basket, from which protruded pieces of bloody fur and mangled flesh.

'Ella!' she cried. 'Somebody's butchered my Ella!'

4

THE NEXT HOUSE along the Highgate Road, fifty yards to the west of the Austin home, was Dunblane. A grey building, slightly more austere and sombre than its neighbour, it had been built eighty years earlier for a wealthy Scottish entrepreneur, and reflected a lingering puritan streak which he had never quite managed to shed. By the same token, though he kept a succession of mistresses, he always insisted they go to church regularly. Not with him, of course.

Dunblane was a little larger than Hillside. In fact, it seemed a little too large for its four permanent occupants: Dr Otto Frankel, his secretary, and two servants.

But the doctor had made good use of at least one of the extra rooms, turning the one at the rear of the first floor into a laboratory. Here he had installed enough equipment and resources to carry out the research which appeared to be his main preoccupation.

He was in there now; a tall, powerful man, with a face like a medieval gargoyle, he was pounding at some hard matter with pestle and mortar. The substance was reluctant to crumble and he paused, from time to time, to relax and look out of the window. This, like the Austins' south-facing windows, enjoyed a panoramic vista of Hampstead Heath. Dr Frankel's window also offered a good view of his neighbour's house and garden. Standing on a footstool, he could even see into Clare Austin's bedroom, if she forgot to draw her curtains.

He had just resumed his work when there was a knock at the laboratory door. 'Come in!' barked Frankel, and his secretary entered. Charles Stone was a thin man of medium height, forty-five years of age. But he was made to look older by his grey complexion and thinning hair. His lean body was held stiff and upright and his thin lips were clearly not much accustomed to smiling. His words came quickly but precisely.

'I'm sorry to interrupt you, Doctor. But I wonder if you know where the boy is. Prosser needs his help in the kitchen.'

'I sent the boy on an errand to the City,' said Frankel. 'Prosser will have to manage on his own for once.'

'Very good, sir,' said Stone. 'I'll tell him.'

'You can also tell him that if he serves up any more meat as tough as last night's, I'll rub it in his face.'

'I will inform him, sir.' Stone turned to go, but Frankel stopped him.

'Another thing, Stone.'

'Yes, sir?'

'The incident that took place next door last night. You'll have noticed that police have been at Hillside all morning.'

'Yes, sir. They seem to have left now. But there are several still busy just out on the Heath.'

'They will undoubtedly be back at Hillside shortly. And, in due course, they will be here, pestering us.'

'No one's called yet, sir.'

'But they soon will, you may be sure. And, when they do, remember this. And tell Prosser and the boy. No one is to talk to those interfering busybodies without my prior permission. And I must be present at any interview with any officers of the law. I shall tell you in advance what to say. Is that understood?'

'Yes, sir.'

'In that case, you can go. Tell Prosser I wish to eat at two o'clock sharp.'

As Stone left, Frankel gave the stuff in the bowl an extra strong blow with his pestle, and the lump finally shattered into fragments.

Dark clouds had now obscured London's morning sunshine, and the light that had flooded into the Hillside windows was beginning to turn somewhat grey.

Left alone in the big room, Steele was taking the opportunity to examine the items in and on top of Austin's desk. He was thwarted by the drawers on the left-hand side, which were locked, but the drawers on the right opened easily, and some of the contents were interesting. He had just extracted a small green notebook, and was turning the pages as Mason returned.

'How is the girl?' asked Steele.

'She was very emotional, obviously. But Clare's given her a strong sedative, and she's sleeping now.'

'A strong sedative? Where did she acquire that?'

'Harriet has a substantial supply, prescribed by Dr Frankel.'

'Good heavens! A ready supply of strong sedatives? At the disposal of a girl of eighteen?'

'Frankel's ordered small regular doses, apparently, with a reserve of tablets for bigger doses in emergency. According to Clare, the doctor thinks her sister's on the verge of a nervous collapse.'

'Considering the tension in this house, it's hardly surprising.'

'She seems to be living in a state of suppressed hysteria. Incredible that she should mistake a butcher's hare for her pet cat!'

'Not that incredible, surely, since the hare had been put in her cat's basket and was mangled beyond recognition. Same colour fur, I imagine. It was a fiendish trick.'

'Was it a trick, guv'nor? The housekeeper thinks it may have been an accident. She told me she was busy when the hare was delivered and she left it on the kitchen table. The cat could have dragged it to her basket and tried to eat it.'

'Unlikely. You saw for yourself, the head had been removed, and the carcase violently mutilated. All to blur the picture.'

'The cat could have done that.'

There was no doubt in Steele's mind. 'I think not. I'm sure someone intended Miss Harriet to assume her cat had been murdered, in order to drive her further out of her wits.'

Mason blew out air through pursed lips. 'Well, that would certainly be a vile trick,' he conceded. He watched Steele turn the pages of the green notebook. The point he'd made in the cafe continued to nag at him. 'Still, it's not a criminal offence, is it? Not like stabbing four men to death.'

Steele raised his eyebrows. 'What are you saying, Jack?'

'I don't see why we're spending so much time on the Austins. We're supposed to be catching the Heath Maniac, aren't we? There are a lot of other people we have to visit.'

'I understand your concern.' Steele closed the notebook and returned it to the drawer. 'You'll have to trust my intuition, old chap. There's something wrong in this house. It may have a bearing on the Heath Maniac, or it may not. But I sense evil here. Bad things could be about to happen, and I think we should try to stop them.'

Mason sighed; nothing was going to change the major's mind. But there were still practical matters to raise. 'You haven't forgotten we're due at the Gilberts' house at 3.30?'

'We have plenty of time. While we're in this house I must find out all I can. I have more questions for Clare Austin. And she might provide me with a key to these locked drawers.'

'What about lunch?' Mason had a big frame to nourish.

'I noticed a fine side of cold beef at the Hill Top Cafe, which I would guess they use for their sandwiches. It is on the way to the Gilberts.' Having explored all the unlocked drawers, Steele was now sifting through Austin's wastepaper basket. The search quickly produced an exclamation of triumph. 'Ah!'

'You've found something, guv'nor?'

'A lawyer's change-of-address card!'

'Is that important?'

'Yes it is, because it tells us who Austin's solicitor is. Would you like to guess?'

'No, thanks. I'll save my brain for finding the meat in the sandwiches.'

'Austin's business affairs are in the hands of none other than Cedric Jamieson!'

'That rogue! Is he still in business?'

'Not only in business, but apparently prospering. He's gone up in the world, moved into Chancery Lane.'

Steele put the card in his pocket. 'Well, Mr Austin has thrown this away so we are entitled to keep it. We shall call on Master Jamieson at his new premises.'

'Not before lunch, I hope.'

Steele smiled. 'No, not before lunch, Jack. Not even today. But soon. These matters need thinking about.' Steele rooted about in the wastepaper basket for a few moments more, inspecting papers and discarding them. Then he straightened up.

'I think I have garnered all the information that's freely available,' he said. 'We must wait and see if Miss Austin can supply keys to these other drawers. And that bureau over there.' With that, he sat down in an armchair and stroked his chin thoughtfully.

Mason was not letting go of the main issue. 'If you're

laying off Austin for a minute,' he said, 'can we talk about the Heath murders?'

'By all means. I haven't lost sight of our basic purpose.'

'I mean, they make no sense to me. Four random killings. Four fit young men, unable to defend themselves. No connection between them.'

Steele corrected him. 'No apparent connection.'

'All right, no apparent connection. Have you got any ideas yet?'

'I have a few,' said Steele. 'For one thing, I find myself recalling the case of Arthur Nesbitt.'

'Nesbitt.' Mason thought for a moment and then remembered. 'Nesbitt! The Bristol Monster!'

'Precisely. The young man who slaughtered five strangers before killing the man he needed to be rid of.'

'A rich uncle, wasn't it?'

'A very rich uncle.'

They were recollecting an investigation they'd worked on four years ago. Arthur Nesbitt, a dissolute young gambler, was sole heir to Alexander Nesbitt, the cotton millionaire. Had Alexander been a single murder victim, Arthur's lifestyle and his prospects of inheritance would have made him the obvious, probably the only, suspect. By bludgeoning to death five other men, by night in the streets of Bristol, Arthur hoped to obscure his motive. He might have succeeded had Alexander's friends not called in Steele and Mason.

'A very nasty young man,' said Mason. 'But clever. He'd have got away with that but for you.'

'You flatter me, Jack,' said Steele, not displeased. 'It was the police who found the hair on Nesbitt's golf club.'

'Only because you told them where to look.' Having softened up the senior man, Mason ventured further. 'You think this may be the same thing? Someone's doing random murders before he kills his real target?'

'It's possible.'

'So there may be more deaths?'

After brief consideration, Steele's reply was measured. 'Perhaps not. I hope not. My instinct suggests that Robert Kemp may have been the assassin's ultimate target.'

'Any reason, apart from intuition?'

'Consider the difference between the previous crimes and this last one. The first three were casual killings, in remote parts of the Heath. Pitch darkness, deserted areas, no police patrols, at least in the first two cases. Easy crimes for a ruthless killer who knows how to use a knife and has the advantage of surprise. Am I correct?'

'Yes, guv'nor. You're always correct.' Mason allowed himself a slight smile. 'But how was last night different?'

'Kemp's murder was scarcely on the Heath at all. It was behind a house, facing the main road. Street lamps. The possibility of passers-by, even at night. If this was another random killing, the villain could have found an easier victim in a quiet place. But he was determined to kill Kemp, and did so at some risk to himself.'

'You mean, risk of retaliation?'

'Risk of being observed. Someone looking through the window of one of the houses. Someone taking a short cut. Such was the risk that he dared not stay to finish the job. He left his victim dying, instead of already dead, as on all previous occasions.'

'Right.' It all seemed obvious, now that Steele had pointed it out. 'So we're looking for someone who wanted Robert Kemp dead.'

'That is my present feeling. Of course, we mustn't close our minds to other possibilities. Kemp's killer may have wanted to strike a blow at the Austin household.' Steele paused. 'I am interested in this man Scully.'

'The gardener who was sacked.'

59

'Precisely. A man with long red hair and piercing eyes.'

'You may recall a man with long red hair was near the scene of the Tate murder?'

'Indeed. I also recall that Clare Austin seemed a little startled when Scully was mentioned. What was his first name, Jack?'

Mason consulted his notes. 'Luke. Luke Scully.'

'We must find Luke Scully as soon as possible.'

'I'll ask around the Hampstead pubs.'

'That shouldn't be too onerous for you. We'll talk to friend Willoughby, and enlist the help of the constabulary.'

When the two had made their discreet exit from the army, there had been some quiet liaison between Military Intelligence and senior figures in the Metropolitan Police. Officially, of course, the latter had to disapprove of the duo's unorthodox methods as strongly as the army had done. But Scotland Yard recognized the value of two astute investigators who were not bound by the same rules as the police were, and a senior policeman, Chief Inspector George Willoughby, had been appointed to maintain an unofficial link with Steele and Mason, with a view to mutual assistance.

The alliance had already borne fruit, when Steele and Mason had helped Scotland Yard solve the murder of a Russian diplomat. The police would never have been able to penetrate the ambassador's study and examine his papers, something which, of course, never happened. So Anglo-Russian relations remained unruffled.

The hall door opened, and Clare Austin came in. The men rose to their feet.

'Please be seated, gentlemen,' said Clare. 'Forgive me for leaving you. You'll understand my concern for Harriet.'

'Of course,' said Steele. 'How is she now?'

'She's still sleeping. It took a while to convince her that what she saw in the basket was a hare from the butcher's.

But I succeeded in the end.'

'Poor girl,' said Mason.

'Poor girl indeed,' echoed Clare. 'Ella is still missing, and Harriet fears she'll come to harm, if she hasn't already.'

'Small wonder,' Steele observed. 'The evil mind behind that trick may have other unpleasant plans.'

'Let us not beat about the bush, Major. The evil mind we are talking about is that of my father.'

Steele sighed. 'Yes. It does appear so.'

'There can be no doubt of it. He told Mrs Butters that Harriet was to be punished. And he had time to do it before he left the house.'

Mason shook his head sadly. 'Extraordinary! For a man to do that to his child.'

'I do believe he hates her,' said Clare. 'I fear for her safety.'

Steele stared at the young woman. 'For her safety? You put it as strongly as that?'

'I do. I think my father is bent on driving her mad.'

As the detectives digested these remarkable words, Clare seemed to make a decision. There was new frankness and urgency in her voice. 'Major, I thank heaven that you gentlemen have come into our lives. I beg your help in saving her. Please protect us both from our father!'

Steele spoke calmly. 'Our help you shall certainly have when needed, Miss Austin. But it's hard to see how we can act against your father at present. Putting a dead hare in a cat's basket is wicked but it is not an illegal act. Unless he breaks the law there is little we can do. Is there anything more you can tell us?'

'Yes. I was too restrained in answering your questions earlier. This latest atrocity has convinced me I must speak out.'

'Please do. What you say will be treated as confidential.'

'I believe our father's cruelty to Harriet has some financial motive. I do not understand business but my instinct tells me so. I think he may be planning to steal her inheritance. Or there may already have been some improper use of funds. Such things would be against the law, surely. Is it possible you could look into that aspect? As an act of kindness. I cannot pay any fees.'

'You need not worry about fees, we have our own reasons for probing your father's affairs. We can assist each other, Miss Austin. It's difficult to pursue our inquiries when we are barred from this house. Will you continue to admit us at times when your father is absent?'

'I can do better than that.' As she spoke, Clare went to the mantelpiece, removed the lid from a small pewter pot, and took out a key. 'This is a spare key to that garden door. Please take it. But have a copy made and put this back in place before it's missed.'

'Thank you. I can return it at once, if you have water and a bar of soap available.'

'Soap and water? Well, there is a washbasin in the conservatory there.' She was pointing to a door at the end of the room. 'But I don't understand.'

Steele took the key and went to the door. 'Mr Mason will explain while I do the job,' he said. He opened the door and disappeared into the conservatory.

Mason welcomed the chance of some cheerful chat. 'A little trick we have learned from the criminal fraternity, Miss Austin. You soften the soap with water, and then press the key into it. If you take the key out gently, it will leave an exact impression. We know one or two craftsmen who can use that to produce a perfect replica.'

'Oh. Is that legal?'

'Er ... not entirely. But if it's done in a good cause ...' Mason smiled. 'Say no more.' He now broached a new subject. As the medical half of the team, he felt it was his province.

'We were surprised that your sister is prescribed strong seda-tives. Is Dr Frankel an experienced physician?'

'I doubt it. He doesn't seem to do general practice. His interest is in research, we're told.'

'Yet he's your family doctor!'

'That's because he's my father's crony, as I told you. Since Dr Frankel moved in last year, they've been as thick as thieves. They go together to their club every Sunday night. To play whist, I think.'

Steele returned from the conservatory, using a small towel to dry his hands, the key, and the bar of soap. 'Thank you, Miss Austin.' He handed Clare the key, then wrapped the soap in a piece of paper from the wastepaper basket and put it in his pocket. 'I hope this soap won't be missed.'

'I shall replace it with a new bar. I know where Mrs Butters keeps them.'

'I think that would be wise,' said Steele. 'We'll have a duplicate key by tomorrow. And, speaking of keys, it might help us uncover your father's activities if I could unlock these desk drawers. Also that bureau over there.'

'I can assist you with the desk,' said Clare. She replaced the door key and extracted a small key from the same pot. 'But I cannot help you with the bureau. I've never seen it opened, and I've no idea where the key is kept.' She held out the desk key for Steele, but he declined.

'I won't take that now, Miss Austin. I have a lot more ques-tions to ask while I'm with you. If you'll kindly replace it in the pot, I'll know where to find it when I need it.'

Clare returned the little key to the pot, and turned to face the detectives. 'What more can I tell you, gentlemen?'

At that moment the hall door flew open and in rushed Mrs Butters, in a state of great alarm.

'Miss Austin, Miss Austin!' she cried. 'The master's back!'

Clare was visibly shaken. 'What? He's come home?'

'And he told me not to let these gentlemen in! What are we to do?'

Mason glanced at the garden door. 'Should we make a dash for it?'

'No,' said Steele. He shut the hall door as they heard the front door open and close beyond. 'We could scarcely get away unseen. And if Austin glimpsed us fleeing, our friends here would be in worse trouble.'

Mrs Butters was gibbering. 'What can we say? What can we do?'

'Calm yourselves, ladies,' said Steele. 'I shall deal with this situation.'

'But he has such a temper, sir! You haven't seen him in one of his rages!'

'No,' said Steele. 'It should be an interesting sight.'

From the hall came the sound of a cupboard door opening and closing.

'Oh dear.' Clare spoke evenly, her self-control now restored. 'He has gone to the hall cupboard. That's where he keeps his gun.'

'A gun?' said Steele. 'Even more interesting.'

Then the hall door was flung open, and Meredith Austin entered, incandescent with rage, and carrying a shotgun.

'You blackguards!' he roared. 'You have invaded my house again! You have flouted my orders!'

Steele remained cool. 'You cannot be surprised to see us, sir.' He indicated the shotgun. 'You have come prepared.'

Now Austin's voice was steely. 'I received a message from my neighbour, Dr Frankel. He saw you both skulking back here. And you treacherous women let them in! Against my instructions!'

'These good ladies had no option, sir. I had left a valuable silver pencil here.'

'Ha!' said Austin. 'And it has taken you over an hour to

find it! Do not waste time dissembling! You two scoundrels came back to pry, and I will not have it!' He pointed the gun at Steele. 'Leave my house at once, both of you! Or you will be sorry!'

Mason intervened. 'Have you got a licence for that gun?'

'Yes, I have. Though it is none of your business, I am licensed to shoot game on the Heath. Also vermin, in which category I include unwelcome intruders!'

'I don't think a court would share that view,' said Steele.

'A householder is entitled to defend his property.'

'He is not entitled to harm visitors calling on lawful business. However, we shall not stay to bandy words; we have work to do.'

'Then go and do it, by God, and cease to pester me!'

Steele moved towards the garden door. 'Time to leave, I think, Mason. Next time we call, perhaps we should bring our friend from Scotland Yard with us.'

Austin was not intimidated. 'Then make sure he brings a warrant with him, or he will fare no better.'

'Do not trouble to show us out, Mrs Butters. We can leave by this door.' Steele inclined his head to the women. 'Good day to you, ladies. We apologize for barging in. Mr Austin must understand that you could not prevent us.'

The two men went to the garden door and Steele opened it. As Mason passed Austin, he grasped the barrel of the gun and swung it up to point at the ceiling. 'If you're going to wave that thing about, you should put on the safety catch,' he advised. 'Otherwise you might shoot yourself in the foot.'

'Get out!' thundered Austin. 'Go now! Get out!'

Steele and Mason did so. Austin slammed the door behind them, and turned to face the trembling housekeeper and the stoical Clare. He was shaking with anger, and almost at a loss for words.

Clare spoke first. 'I'm sorry you seem distressed, Father.

Please calm yourself. Dr Frankel has warned you against excessive tension.'

'He'd have done better to warn me against meddling troublemakers and disobedient women! I strictly forbade you to admit those men, Mrs Butters, and you have chosen to defy me!'

'I'm sorry, sir,' pleaded Mrs Butters. 'It was the silver pencil.'

'Silence!' Austin shouted. 'Do not insult me with that absurd pretext! I told you not to let them in, and within an hour you had done so!'

Clare's voice was firm. 'You must blame me. I told Mrs Butters to open the door to them.'

Austin stared at his daughter. 'Oh, you did, did you? By thunder, I shall deal with you presently, madam!' He turned back to Mrs Butters. 'Does this young person pay your wages, woman?'

'No, sir,' mumbled the housekeeper.

'"No, sir" indeed! I provide your wages and your home! So you will take your orders only from me, and not from junior members of my household. Do you understand?'

Mrs Butters affirmed that she did.

'Very well,' Austin continued. 'That's for the future. As to the past, you have disobeyed my direct orders. You will forfeit two weeks' wages.'

'Oh no, sir!' begged the woman. 'Not two weeks, please!'

'Very well,' said Austin, enjoying the moment. 'Three weeks. Now leave the room and go about your work, before you lose your job altogether.'

'Yes, sir,' sobbed Mrs Butters. 'As you say, sir.'

The dejected servant left, and Austin spent a moment closing the door behind her. Then he moved quietly, almost imperceptibly, to the other two doors, before rounding on his daughter.

'So, you wretched girl! You admit to instigating this outrage!'

'Yes, if that is how you describe an act of common courtesy.'

'Courtesy? Courtesy?! Your first duty of courtesy, my girl, is to obey your father! That is your duty, and that is what you have wilfully failed to do!'

'I merely helped a visitor retrieve his lost property.'

'Poppycock! You brought enemies into my house, to spy on me. You have betrayed and dishonoured me, and you must be punished. You will learn that I do not tolerate disloyalty!'

Clare was quietly defiant. 'You are welcome to fine me. The pittance you allow me is so small its absence will scarcely be noticed.'

'For your shameful behaviour, madam, a fine will not suffice. A more severe penalty is appropriate.'

Austin went to the bureau and took a key from his waistcoat pocket. 'It is fortunate that I never got rid of the horsewhip!'

Now Clare was very afraid, and her hand went automatically to the scar on her face. 'No!' she cried. 'No!' But she still disdained to use the word 'please'.

It would have made no difference. Austin took the whip from the drawer and watched his daughter rush to the three doors and try each in turn. But her father had locked them all.

A moment later, Clare's screams were heard throughout the house. Indeed, they reached the house next door.

Dr Frankel looked up from his work and smiled.

5

CEDRIC JAMIESON WAS indeed moving up in the world, as Steele had observed. Abandoning the one-room office in Stepney, he had installed himself in Chancery Lane, the heartland of London's legal profession. But the advance had been limited: his new premises were not palatial nor were they at the better end of the road.

As Steele and Mason approached the street number on Jamieson's change-of-address card, they found themselves looking at Dolly's Dairy, from which customers were emerging with jugs of fresh milk. Several churns stood outside on the pavement and through the shop window a young woman in a white hat and striped apron could be seen patting slabs of butter into shape with two small wooden bats.

Next to the long window, at the other end from the shop entrance, was a street door beside which cards in a small frame identified the occupants of the upper areas. The first floor was ascribed to 'C.R. Jamieson, Solicitor', the second to 'Jas. Hoskins, Fruit Importer' and the third to 'Miss Lamour, Personal Services'.

The street door was unlocked. The two men entered and climbed a steep flight of narrow wooden stairs. At the first landing the staircase twisted round on its way to the higher regions. But the detectives had reached their destination, being in no need of imported fruit or wild oats at that time.

The door ahead of them amplified the information displayed downstairs. Here the lawyer was described as 'Cedric R. Jamieson. Solicitor and Commissioner for Oaths'. This door also was unlocked. Steele opened it and the pair went in.

They were impressed to find that Jamieson now had an outer office, with a couple of chairs and framed certificates on the walls. There was also a desk, at which sat a spotty youth perusing a comic paper, his lips moving as he wrestled with occasional clusters of words.

He looked up at the new arrivals and said, 'Yeah?'

'We've called to see Mr Jamieson,' said Steele, pleasantly.

'You got an appointment?'

'No. We thought we'd give him a nice surprise.'

'Mr Jamieson never sees no one without an appointment,' said the youth.

'I think you'll find he's about to make an exception,' said Steele, handing the youth his card. 'Tell him Major Steele and Mr Mason would like a word with him. Say some new facts have emerged about the Slattery case.'

Steele's manner made the youth disinclined to argue. He took the card and went into an inner room, closing the door behind him. For a short while, indistinct male voices could be heard, one raised in anger. The detectives passed the time studying Jamieson's certificates. These all bore spectacular red seals, but came from American universities of which neither man had heard.

Jamieson had first come to the detectives' attention as an East End lawyer, defending local villains on routine charges. He was known for exploiting legal loopholes to the limit and sometimes, they felt, rather beyond.

After he'd progressed to more salubrious areas of the law, Jamieson had crossed their paths again in the notorious case of Edwin Slattery. Slattery had tried to execute a series of elaborate share-dealing frauds, using a network of false proxies and non-existent companies. Steele and Mason, working for a firm of stockbrokers, had been the first to uncover wrongdoing, before the police took over the investigation. Slattery and an assistant had gone to jail.

They had employed a number of lawyers in weaving the dense web of legal complexities which were intended to hide their criminal activities. One solicitor, Silas Crutchley, had been struck off by the Law Society. And suspicions remained that others had been involved in misconduct.

Jamieson had been a minor player, with no firm evidence against him. Steele had always believed that a deep and thorough probe would reveal some misdeeds but justice had been done, investors had been reimbursed, and the detectives had more urgent work on their hands, protecting a prominent politician from assassination.

So the matter lay dormant. But Steele and Mason and Jamieson all knew there were dark secrets to be unearthed if anyone had the incentive to dig.

Just as the certificates on the wall were starting to lose their entertainment value, the spotty youth returned and said, 'Mr Jamieson will see you in five minutes. He has an important job to finish.'

'Ah. Perhaps we could go in and help him,' said Steele, already moving briskly towards the inner door. 'Many hands make light work.'

The youth seemed about to protest but before he could find the words Steele and Mason were through the door and into the lawyer's inner sanctum.

Cedric Jamieson, somewhat agitated, was trying to secrete a whisky bottle in a desk drawer into which he'd just crammed a bulky file that he must have thought rather sensitive. The drawer wouldn't close, and the neck of the bottle protruded. The Commissioner for Oaths was uttering several very coarse ones.

Steele was reassuring. 'Don't bother to get drinks out, Cedric. We're here on business.'

Jamieson regained his composure, laid the bottle on the floor beneath his desk, closed the drawer and managed a smile that was rancid enough to curdle the milk downstairs. 'Major Steele!' he cried. 'And Mr Mason! Good to see you!' He rose and extended a hand.

Mason did the job of shaking it so his senior didn't have to. Steele just grinned affably at the lawyer and said, 'We'd like a little co-operation from you, Cedric.'

Jamieson enthused. 'Of course, Major, I'm always ready to help, you know that.' He cleared his throat, and then spoke a little nervously. 'Arthur said it was something to do with the Slattery case.'

'That was just to get your attention, old chap.' Steele was still sounding genial. 'You'll be pleased to hear that at present we have no plans to delve deeper into the Slattery affair. Unless new circumstances arise, of course.'

The solicitor concealed his relief effectively and instead registered mild puzzlement. 'I'm not sure why you feel the Slattery case is of special concern to me, Major. However, if you tell me the actual purpose of your visit, I'll do my best to assist you.'

'We're interested in the affairs of one of your clients. Mr Meredith Austin of Highgate Road, Hampstead. We need to know about various transactions.'

'Major Steele,' said Jamieson sternly. 'You know I can't discuss a client's business with a third party. Unless I have the client's express permission, of course. Has Mr Austin given his consent to this approach?'

'We've had several meaningful discussions with Mr Austin,' said Steele. 'He's aware of our interest.'

'But has he given you written authority to make these inquiries?'

'Now I come to think of it,' Steele conceded, 'I'm not sure that he has. In fact, I think it might be best if none of us mentioned them to him.'

Jamieson was shocked. 'This is most irregular. In the circumstances, I don't see how I can help you.'

'Well, let me make a suggestion,' said Steele. 'That cabinet must contain clients' files, surely? Mr Austin's will be in the top drawer, marked "A to C", I daresay.' He turned to Mason. 'Jack, perhaps you could find it for Mr Jamieson.'

'Shall be done,' said his burly assistant, moving swiftly into action.

Jamieson objected vociferously. 'This is outrageous! Come away from there! I shall have to call the police!' But he thought it wise not to intervene physically, and Mason quickly took out Austin's file and laid it on the desk.

'Here we are, sir,' he said. 'Right at the front. Very orderly system Mr Jamieson has. I didn't have to disturb anything.'

'Very good,' said Steele. 'Now you have the file in front of you, Cedric, it should be easy for you to help us. We'll ask questions and you can look up the answers.'

'That's out of the question,' the lawyer protested. 'Completely unethical.'

Steele smiled. 'And of course you would never do anything unethical, would you? Not like poor old Silas Crutchley in the Slattery case. He got struck off by the Law Society, didn't he?'

Jamieson ran his tongue over dry lips, and said nothing.

'Of course,' Steele continued, 'if our way is blocked on this Austin inquiry, we'll have time on our hands. We could take another look at the Slattery business after all.' He turned to Mason. 'What d'you think, Jack?'

'Certainly, sir. I've felt all along we should go into that more thoroughly.'

The lawyer sighed. 'Be reasonable, Major. The fact is, I cannot supply you with information about clients. I dare not.'

Steele considered the situation and then offered his solution. 'All right, Cedric, I see your problem. You can't answer our questions. We'll have to acquire the information we need without your knowledge.'

'What does that mean?'

'If you leave this office for half an hour, you won't be responsible for what goes on here, will you? Why don't you go and help Arthur with his reading? He seems to have difficulty with the longer words. Or perhaps Miss Lamour would welcome a visit. Does she offer special rates for neighbours?'

Jamieson looked at Steele and then at Mason. Both faces were smiling but quite relentless. Mason tilted his head briefly towards the office door.

Without another word, Jamieson gave a resigned shrug and left the office, closing the door behind him.

Steele sat down at the desk and opened the Austin file. Mason took out his pocket notebook.

It had turned colder overnight, and now the afternoon was as bleak as a judge's smile.

Some thin November sunshine was totally outgunned by a freezing east wind, not spectacularly fierce but very cold. This wind was apparently blowing all the way from Siberia, crossing the North Sea and the flat plains of East Anglia, and arriving undiminished on Hampstead Heath, eager to chill new victims.

Harriet Austin still looked pale but was largely recovered from the crisis of four days ago. She was glad of her overcoat, with the scarf and the hood brought up over her head. She was grateful, too, for the leather gloves, lined with warm fleece, and much more comforting than any gloves she had worn in the past. She'd found this expensive pair in the attic. They'd been tucked away in a chest of drawers, which contained some of her mother's belongings Meredith Austin had failed to burn or throw away. These items had survived because his hatred had been surpassed by his reluctance to part with anything that might be worth money.

The gloves were of good quality, soft and supple, and Harriet had hoped she could carry out her mission without removing them. But then she found she couldn't. Although the bark of the trees was firm and fairly soft, the drawing pins were too small and fiddly for gloved fingers, and two pins had fallen to the ground. As she took off a glove to grope for them in the grass, she relaxed her grip on the leaflets and one of them detached itself from the rest, to go skittling away in an eddy of wind.

Harriet had spent hours composing the text of her leaflet, and many more making a dozen copies by hand. She had felt that twelve was the minimum required, and she still thought so. Besides, she hated litter. So she stuffed the rest of the bunch into her overcoat pocket and set off in pursuit of the miscreant.

Harriet was slim and light but not much accustomed to physical exercise, and the leaflet was well airborne. It seemed an unequal chase.

But then the leaflet was blown against the side of a prickly bush, becoming briefly trapped. And before it could free itself and resume its flight, a figure emerged from a clump of trees and intervened.

It was a boy who had been using a knife to whittle a stick into a sharp spike. Now he thrust the knife and the spike into the belt of his trousers and moved swiftly to retrieve the paper.

The rescuer was a lad of about fourteen years, with tousled fair hair and a grubby face. His face and body were thin and his frame was wiry. He wore long scruffy trousers, with a tear at the right knee and, above them, a coarse jerkin over some sort of woollen garment.

He grabbed the paper and studied it keenly for a few moments. Then he looked at Harriet.

'This yours, miss?' he asked. His voice was hoarse and had already broken.

'Yes,' she said nervously, uncertain whether or not to advance and take the leaflet from him. It was broad daylight and there were other people in sight, including a distant police constable on patrol. But the boy looked wild, almost feral, and he had that knife in his belt.

So she stayed where she was and simply said, 'Thank you for catching it for me.'

The boy showed no sign of wanting to part with the leaflet. He continued to peer at it closely, and eventually managed to master one of the words near the top.

'Woss this about a cat?' His delivery was slightly aggressive. But there was a naive pride in his words that was somehow touching. 'I can read, you know. My mate taught me,' he went on. 'Before he had to go away.'

'My cat's disappeared,' Harriet explained. 'I think she may be lost on the Heath. I'm offering a reward to anyone who finds her.'

The boy's interest was aroused. 'Woss this cat look like?'

'She's small and brown, not much more than a kitten. She's called Ella, her name's on her collar. There's more about her in the leaflet.'

The boy sniffed. 'Yeah. Well, I don't read no more than I have to. My mate said too much reading's bad for your eyes.' He got quickly to the main point. 'Woss the reward?'

'I'll give a guinea to anyone who brings Ella safely back to me.'

'A guinea? 'ow much is that?'

'A guinea is one pound plus one shilling.'

The boy whistled in amazement. 'Gor! More than a quid! When I bring home a cat to my gaffer, he just give me tuppence!'

Harriet was pleasantly surprised. 'Your father runs a refuge for lost cats?'

The boy gave a brief, mirthless laugh. 'Nah! He ain't my father. And the cats don't have to be lost. Just any old cat I can lay my hands on. Or a rabbit. Or a squirrel, if I can ever catch one. See, he just likes something he can cut up.'

The smile froze on the young woman's face.

'He cuts them up?'

'Yeah. Research, he calls it. I think he just enjoys it.'

Harriet winced. 'That's awful!'

'Well, he won't get no more moggies from me. Not when he pays tuppence and you'll pay a quid. I'll bring 'em all to you in future!'

Shock waves began to course through Harriet's brain, triggered by the dreadful thought that this boy might start bringing a succession of kidnapped cats to her home, creating huge problems; not least, the fury of Meredith Austin.

On the other hand, if she declined the offer, any cat unlucky enough to be caught by this ruffian was doomed to be butchered.

Briefly, she struggled for words. Then she gave in. The other cats would have to take their chance. The alternative was impossible.

'No, you must bring me only Ella, if you find her. As I said, her description's in the leaflet. I cannot pay for any other cats. I have little money.'

'Gor!' said the boy again, this time in disappointment. He summed up. 'Right. So I just look out for this small brown cat, then. And if I fetch her to you, you give me a quid and a shilling?'

'Yes,' said Harriet. At least if she sent this boy roaming

the Heath with a financial incentive, it might be her best chance of recovering her pet. Then a hideous thought struck her.

'Pray God you haven't already found Ella and delivered her to your master! She's been missing for more than a week.'

The boy thought, then shook his head. 'Nah,' he said. 'I ain't seen a brown cat lately. Fact is, I ain't caught any cats these last ten days.' His voice took on a darker tone. 'I had other things to do.'

As Harriet wondered what those other things might be, and how she could bring this encounter to an end, the youth changed the subject.

'You live in that 'ouse over there, don't you?'

The young woman was shaken. She hadn't expected, or wanted, this rough lad to know where she lived. But then she remembered her address was on the leaflet anyway. It had to be, for her to get the cat back.

'Yes,' she said. 'I live at Hillside. I'm Mr Austin's daughter.'

'I thought so. I seen you in the garden there. I was watching you the other day, walking up and down.'

Harriet shivered, and realized it was not just the cold. But there was worse to come.

'I live next door, see? Dunblane. I can watch you from our window.'

Harriet was dismayed. She had supposed that this unkempt creature came from one of the dingier corners of the Heath, from Gospel Oak, perhaps, or Archway. She had even imagined him living rough in the woods. But no, in fact it seemed he was her neighbour! Dear God! Did that mean that the person who slaughtered animals in the name of research was actually the man her father had chosen to be her doctor? Fearing she knew the answer, she still had to put the question.

'Do you work for Dr Frankel?'

The boy was becoming animated. 'Work for 'im? Not arf! Morning, noon and night I work for 'im. I'm only out here now cos I'm supposed to be gathering firewood! I'm 'is bloody slave, that's what I am!'

The swear word jarred on Harriet. She'd heard it before, when Luke Scully worked at Hillside. In fact, it had rent the air several times. But it always bruised her ears. Then she reflected that this lad probably had no idea that the word was offensive.

'But I won't always be,' he declaimed, a new passion in his voice. 'I'm going to get away, I am! When the right time comes. I'm going to make a lot of money, I am! Cos I know secrets! I seen things other people don't know about! One day I'll be rich. And then I'll do what I like and have lots to eat.'

'Well, I hope all those things happen for you,' was all Harriet could find to say.

The boy calmed down, as the thought of money prompted a more practical question.

'''Ow much you gonna give me for this paper, then?' He waved the leaflet teasingly in the air.

Harriet was taken aback. 'You have to keep that,' she said. 'You need it for my address and the description of my cat.'

'No, I don't,' the boy announced. 'I know where you live, don't I? And I know about the moggie. Small and brown, ain't she?'

'With a white patch on her tail,' Harriet added.

'Right. So now I know it all. You can have this paper back, and give me a tanner for catching it for you.'

'Well, I suppose the more leaflets I can pin up the better. But I have no money with me at all at present.'

Then she saw the solution. 'Give me the leaflet now,' she suggested. 'And when you bring my cat back I'll give you an extra sixpence.'

The boy considered this proposition for a moment, and

then concluded it was the best bargain he could get.

'All right, you can have it,' he announced. 'Cos I like you.'

He moved forward and gave the leaflet to Harriet, and having done so, he put his hand on her wrist.

'You're quite pretty,' he said. 'You and I could be friends. And when I'm rich I'll buy you lots of nice things.'

Had she been told in advance that such a thing might happen, the young woman would have expected to recoil and scream for help.

But now that it had occurred, she astonished herself by doing neither. The proposition was absurd, of course. But she found that she didn't want to hurt this vulnerable fellow human.

His voice had become quieter, and his touch was tentative and reasonably discreet, not the brutal groping she'd heard of other young ladies enduring on rare encounters with males of a lower class. And she was looking at a pale, sad face that seemed as if it had never known any affection.

So she produced a nervous smile and responded courteously, gently removing his hand from her arm. 'Thank you,' she said, 'but I don't think that would be possible. My father would not approve.'

The boy hesitated, looking uncertain for the first time. A frown seemed to be gathering on his face. Anger? Or merely regret?

It was with relief that Harriet observed the patrolling constable was now quite close and heading in their direction.

'Now please excuse me,' she said. 'I want to have a word with that policeman. I can tell him about Ella.'

The moment he became aware of the law approaching, an inbuilt alarm galvanized the boy.

'Bloody rozzers!' he said, and marched off swiftly.

As he went, he took the knife from his belt and hurled it at an oak tree that stood ahead of him, throwing it skilfully so that the point thudded into the trunk at head height and stayed there. When his retreat took him past the oak, the boy wrenched the knife from the bark and restored it to his belt. Then he disappeared into the trees.

Harriet watched him go and then stood there, bewildered, shaken by this confrontation, and wondering if she could carry on with the job she had come here to do.

Nervousness was mingling in her mind with a curious excitement. Then, as she havered, the constable arrived and greeted her respectfully, touching the side of his helmet in salute.

'Good afternoon, miss.' His voice was strong and reassuring, with a Berkshire accent. He was one of those hefty, stalwart country bobbies the authorities were always glad to recruit, to keep the peace in London.

'Good afternoon, Officer.' She gave him a small smile.

'Was that boy annoying you?' the policeman enquired.

'Oh no.' Harriet was surprised to find herself oddly protective about the ragamuffin who had so recently alarmed her. 'No, not at all. He's going to try and help me find my cat. I think she's lost on the Heath.'

'Hmm,' said the constable. 'Well, I strongly advise you not to trust him. He's no good, miss. We think he's been thieving food down Camden Market.'

'He looks as if he needs it,' said Harriet. 'He seems half starved.'

'That's as may be,' said the officer. 'But thieving's not the way to go about it. If we catch him at it, he's going to cop it and no mistake.' He noticed the leaflets in the young woman's hand. 'You're putting up notices about your cat, are you?'

'That's right. It's not illegal, is it?'

The policeman pondered. 'Well, strictly speaking I suppose you might need permission. But I don't think anyone will bother. Specially not in these times. If you like, I'll take a couple and show them round at the station.'

'Oh yes, please do.' Harriet handed him two leaflets and he studied the top one with raised eyebrows.

'A guinea reward! That's very handsome. I'll be keeping a lookout myself, I can tell you.'

He turned to resume his patrol and then paused. 'I'm sure I don't need to warn you, miss, to be very careful out here. Make sure you're home before dark. There's some rum customers about on the Heath these days. It's not just the Maniac you have to worry about. Take care.'

'Thank you, Officer,' Harriet called, as the policeman strode away.

Buoyed up by the thought that she now had help from both sides of the law, she decided that she would complete her mission. There was just time to pin up the remaining leaflets before dusk.

The polishing fluid had dried on the cutlery, and Mrs Butters was now busy wiping off the powdery residue with a soft cloth. In a gentle way, she was quite enjoying herself. It pleased her to see the metal start to shine like silver.

Also, although it was a task that should properly be done in the scullery, Mr Austin was out, and Mrs Butters knew that neither of his daughters minded her bringing it to the more congenial surroundings of the drawing room. Here she worked at a small table, which she'd covered with a green baize cloth.

The scullery managed to be damp and dark at all times of the day but here in the drawing room she'd been cheered by the huge sky that filled the windows, and by the view across the Heath. This was a pleasant place to work. Earlier on, there had even been some weak sunshine. That was now fading into dusk but the view remained, and there was even a little lingering warmth on this side of the windows.

Mrs Butters had learned to get satisfaction from simple domestic tasks: not the strenuous, back-straining heavy work, of course, nor the less salubrious jobs. But sedentary ones that showed a good result always gave her modest pleasure.

There were not many joyful activities in Mrs Butters' daily round. The exciting and romantic penny novels, on which she spent part of her hard-earned wages, brightened the last half-hour of her long day, though she sometimes found it hard to read the bigger words.

In the summer she enjoyed taking the sun for a few stolen minutes in the kitchen garden alongside the house. And, of course, she shared with Harriet the delight of stroking and fussing over household pets. It was a limited existence but at least a relatively secure one. At least, that was what she'd always thought.

There had rarely been much frivolity in Grace Butters' life. Daughter of a parlourmaid and a footman, she herself had begun in domestic service at the age of fourteen, as part of a big household in Sloane Square. Here she had toiled her way from kitchen skivvy to assistant cook in eight years, before marriage changed everything.

Michael Butters was a handsome, lively fellow, a soldier by profession and an athlete from choice. He had boxed for his regiment with some success. The two years during which he was stationed at Chelsea Barracks had been the happiest time of the young woman's life, and it was then that their daughter Ann was born.

But all too soon things changed. Michael's regiment was posted to India. Here he was involved in a skirmish on the Kashmir border, which left him with a head wound, a minor medal and a medical discharge from the army. On his return to England, he was a changed man: moody, violent and unpredictable, often berating, and sometimes beating his wife. She put up with his behaviour, telling herself it was not his fault. She would never have left him. But then he left her.

Their love and their marriage had both ended twenty-five years ago, in dramatic fashion. Embittered by years of unpleasant menial jobs, frequent sackings, often for violent conduct, mixed with long periods of unemployment, Michael Butters launched a fierce attack on his wife and child, hitting them with his fists and then threatening them with a knife. Grace had saved their limbs, and probably their lives, by locking herself and her daughter in a room with a stout door.

When they nervously emerged hours later, Michael Butters was gone. And neither of them had seen or heard of him since. Grace had reported his disappearance to the police, but there had been no outcome. For years Grace and Ann had lived in fear, before at last accepting that his exit from their lives was final.

Mrs Butters had gone back into service to support herself and her daughter. Then, at eighteen, Ann had married a decent young man, a carpenter, who had heard of great opportunities for skilled tradesmen in the New World. And Ann and her husband had sailed steerage to America, with her mother's blessing.

Mrs Butters' occasional exchange of letters with her daughter was the highlight of her year. One day Ann and John would return to England with her grandchildren. That was something to look forward to. For now, Mrs Butters must get on with her daily routine and make the most of its lighter moments.

It was getting colder. Mrs Butters went to the fire and brought it to life by means of a few ferocious prods with the poker. Then she returned to her chair and contemplated the results of her labour.

But the temperature took a sharp tumble as Harriet

opened the garden door and came in. She shut it quickly behind her but there'd been time for the icy wind to sweep across the room.

The housekeeper shivered. 'Brrr! You must be frozen, Miss Harriet. I'll wager it's colder than a dead frog out there!'

In fact, Harriet was now glowing from her achievement in pinning up ten leaflets, every one of which had been affixed by a drawing pin at each corner, to prevent the wind getting underneath it.

She was also warmed by the effort involved, and by the excitement of her encounter with the boy. Looking back she had mixed feelings about this but it had certainly been an adventure. So there was more than a touch of cheerfulness in her reply.

'It's chilly, yes. But it was pleasant while the sun was out.' She made for the fireside and announced triumphantly, 'I've put up all the notices!'

'Well done, miss. But I'm glad to see you safely home and that's a fact. I wouldn't want to be walking on the Heath these days. It's too dangerous for me.'

'Oh, I'm sure there's no danger in the afternoon, Mrs Butters. The Maniac has never struck in daylight.'

Mrs Butters sighed. 'There's always a first time, that's what I say.'

'Besides, the police are everywhere. There's a bobby behind every bush. I had a nice talk with one.'

'Talk's all very well but they didn't stop those poor young men being murdered, did they? With respect, miss, I say you were taking a risk.'

'A risk worth taking, if it brings my Ella back.'

'Well, I pray it does. With all my heart.' Then the housekeeper remembered her duties. 'Shall I put your things away, Miss Harriet?'

'Don't get up now. They can wait till you've finished that

job.' Harriet took off her coat and gloves and put them on the back of a sofa. Then she sat down in an armchair and picked up a piece of embroidery. Now she was ready to impart the big news of the day.

'I met a young man on the Heath this afternoon.'

The older woman's interest was swiftly aroused, together with considerable alarm.

'What sort of young man, if you don't mind my asking?'

'A very young young man. More of a boy, really. Fourteen or fifteen, perhaps.'

'A boy of fourteen? Out there alone?' Mrs Butters was shocked. 'What can his mother be thinking of?'

'Alas, I fear he may not have a mother,' said Harriet. 'But he appeared well able to look after himself, and he seemed quite at home in those surroundings. He said he was gathering firewood.'

'Well, there's plenty of that about. But what was he going to do with it?'

'That's the surprise. He seemed so at home out there, I thought perhaps he lived on the Heath. Some people do, I'm told. But no, he lives in the house next door! Dunblane! He was gathering firewood for Dr Frankel!'

'Oh. The boy from Dunblane,' said Mrs Butters, a little disappointed at having the mystery peter out so tamely. 'Yes, they always keep a boy at Dunblane. Mrs Piper at the grocer's says they use him very badly. They feed him scraps, and he has to do all the rough work. It seems he's just a slave.'

'That's what he told me. He wants to get away.'

'I wish him luck, poor little devil. To tell you the truth, Miss Harriet, although it's not my place to say so, I don't like that Dr Frankel. I wish the master didn't have him treating you. I don't think he's a nice man.'

'Oh,' said Harriet, without much conviction, 'I'm sure my father knows best. Dr Frankel has an unfortunate manner but I believe he's very clever. He does a lot of research, you know.'

'So they say,' said the housekeeper, darkly. 'Goodness knows what that means. Mrs Piper says there's a lot of funny things go on in that house. I hope that poor boy gets away soon.'

Harriet attempted to drive from her mind the picture of her medical adviser cutting up animals, and strove to regain her former cheerfulness.

'Anyway,' she said brightly, 'he's going to try and find Ella for me. And the policeman said he'll keep an eye open too.'

'Well, the more the merrier, I say.' Mrs Butters held up a fork, to inspect it in the fading light. There'd been a blemish which had required extra polishing. But now it seemed to have gone. She gave the fork a final rub, replaced it with the others, and asked, 'D'you think those notices will help, Miss Harriet?'

'One can only hope, Mrs Butters. But I believe the guinea reward should create some interest.'

The housekeeper was impressed. 'Goodness me! If a guinea doesn't do the trick, I don't know what will!'

'I only wish I could afford to offer more,' said Harriet.

'It's my belief your Ella just wandered off. Cats like a change, you know. She may come back of her own accord.'

'Pray God she comes back alive,' said Harriet. 'I miss her terribly.' She snipped the silk thread she was using, and changed the subject. 'I suppose my sister's writing in her room?'

'That's right, miss. These days she seems to spend all her time there.'

Harriet sighed. 'She loses herself in her work, lucky girl. And she'll do anything to avoid speaking to our father.'

'Such a shame, that is. It's not natural.'

Suddenly, Harriet was alert. 'What was that? It sounded like our garden gate.'

'I didn't hear anything, Miss Harriet.'

Harriet put down her embroidery and hurried to the window. 'I'm sure I heard the gate open. Or close.'

'Well, your ears are younger than mine, and that's a fact.'

Harriet peered through the window and instantly cried out in alarm.

'What is it, miss?'

'There's a strange man by our gate! A horrid-looking man, all wild and dishevelled! He's staring in!'

Mrs Butters rose. 'Let me come and have a look.'

'Come quick! Oh heavens, he's seen me!'

The housekeeper dropped a spoon, picked it up, and advanced across the room, mumbling, 'These legs aren't as fast as they used to be.'

'Yes, he's seen me!' cried Harriet. 'He's running away!'

The housekeeper arrived at the window and surveyed the scene outside. 'Well, I can't see anyone, miss.'

'Too late. He's disappeared into that clump of trees.'

'Sounds like he's more frightened of you than you are of him. So you needn't worry, miss.'

'But I do, Mrs Butters. I saw him yesterday. Some sort of tramp, with dirty clothes and hair down to his shoulders. He comes up to the gate and stares at our windows.'

Mrs Butters plodded back to her chair. 'You'd better tell your father, miss.'

'I don't think he'd believe me.' Harriet sat down again in her armchair and picked up her embroidery, without enthusiasm. 'He'd say I was imagining things. Like he did when I told him about the whistling I sometimes hear at night. He got angry when I mentioned that.'

'He's not an easy man to talk to, that I will say. Makes things awkward, that does. I've got something I'd like to tell someone about. Something very odd. But I don't fancy speaking to the master.'

Harriet looked up with interest. 'Something odd? What do you mean by that?'

'Well … a sort of … a contraption.'

'A contraption? Where?'

'It was when I moved some logs in the garden shed. There was this funny-looking thing behind there, like it might be some sort of weapon. And it had some sticky stuff on it. I thought it might be … well … dried blood.'

'Blood?' The younger woman was amazed. 'Surely not. It must be paint. Or something for the garden.'

'Well, it might be. But I wondered if I should tell the police.'

Harriet was very alarmed at the suggestion. 'Oh no! You mustn't tell the police, Mrs Butters! Father would be furious! He says the police always create scandal! He doesn't want them coming here any more.'

The housekeeper pondered as she shone up the last of the dessert spoons. Satisfied, she laid it in the large-spoon section of the velvet-lined case in front of her. Then she yielded the point. 'I daresay you're right, miss. But I do feel I should tell someone who might know about these things.'

'In that case,' said Harriet, 'perhaps you should tell that Major Steele. He may be more discreet than the police.'

It was the older woman's turn to be shocked. 'The detective? But he's not allowed to come here! I shan't be seeing him!'

'I'm afraid you will, Mrs Butters. Quite soon. My sister is determined to collaborate with him, and she's advised him to call when Father is out. I think she's arranged for him to come this afternoon.'

'Oh no!' cried the housekeeper. 'Not again! That Miss Clare, she'll never learn! She'll bring disaster on all of us!'

'I cannot dissuade her, she is older than I am. I can only try to avoid being involved myself.'

'Heaven help us! Those men are coming here today?'

'Apparently. And as they're to be with us anyway, you might as well tell them of your discovery.'

As the housekeeper struggled to digest this advice, the hall door opened and Clare came in, with a bright greeting.

'Good afternoon, Harriet.'

The response was muted. 'Hello, Clare.' Harriet bent over her embroidery without looking up.

'Mrs Butters,' said Clare, 'I'm expecting two visitors.' She glanced at the clock. 'Twenty minutes to five. Not too late for tea, I think. Will you bring some, please?'

'If you say so, Miss Clare. But ... would it be that major and his friend?'

'Yes, Mrs Butters, it would. So please serve the best tea. I expect they're quite discriminating.'

'Forgive me, miss, but is that wise? You remember what the master said.'

'I do,' said Clare. 'And I remember what he did. But tyrants must not prevail. You may rest assured that all precautions have been taken. I have ascertained that Mr Austin has an important meeting in his office at half past five, which he will not want to miss. And our visitors will use the front door.'

'The front door, miss?'

'When they used the garden door, Dr Frankel saw them and warned Mr Austin. He's less likely to observe them approaching by the road. Also, I believe Major Steele has some other plan to avoid detection.'

'Well, I tell you, Miss Clare, I'm frightened.'

Clare sought to reassure her. 'You need not be. Should this visit ever come to light, which is very unlikely, I shall make it known that you were out shopping and knew nothing of it. Now the tea, please, Mrs Butters.'

'Very well, miss. I pray you don't have cause to regret this.'

Shaking her head, the housekeeper left the room and closed the door behind her.

Now Harriet looked up. 'Clare, why are you so keen to help these detectives?'

'You have it the wrong way round, sister. It is not a question of us helping them, but of them helping us.'

'Helping us? By catching the Maniac, you mean, and making the Heath safe again?'

'That, of course. But we have a more personal need. I truly believe that our father has wicked plans affecting our future. Especially yours, Harriet. I think he may already be embezzling money which should come to you.'

Her younger sister was appalled. 'Oh, Clare, surely not!'

'We shall see. We've been given the heaven-sent opportunity to have two professional detectives look into the matter. We must make the most of it.'

'You are wrong about our father, Clare. He is strict and bad-tempered but I believe he has our welfare at heart.'

'If you believe that, dear sister, you must also believe that the earth is flat.' Clare went to the door, opened it, and paused. 'I've found some items relating to my mother that Major Steele wishes to see. I must fetch them from my room. If the gentlemen arrive before I return, please receive them well. They are our friends.' And with that she left, closing the door behind her.

Harriet tried to resume her needlework but her mind was too troubled. She put down the silk and went to the window, half excited, half fearful, at the thought of what might meet her eyes. But this time there was nothing to see in the gloom, except a tall man walking an Alsatian dog. The man carried a heavy stick, as walkers did on the Heath these days.

As she surveyed the darkening scene, Harriet heard a knock at the front door, and then male voices mingled with that of Mrs Butters.

Moments later, the drawing-room door opened, and the housekeeper ushered in the two expected guests, unexpectedly dressed in expansive blue overalls and large boots. John Mason carried a toolbag. This unwelcome duty completed, Mrs Butters withdrew, still shaking her head.

Somewhat startled, Harriet nevertheless recalled Clare's words and greeted the newcomers pleasantly, if a little uncertainly. 'Good afternoon, gentlemen. It is Major Steele and ... er ... your colleague, isn't it?'

'It is, Miss Austin. Please forgive this attire. I thought our arrival might attract less attention if we looked like workmen, here to do a job. Mind where you put that bag down, Jack. We don't want the ladies tripping over it.'

'You look very convincing, I must say,' ventured Harriet.

'Thank you, miss,' said Mason. 'I think you're right. A lady in the street asked us to come and repair her pipes.'

'Alas,' said Steele, who seemed to be in good humour, 'we had to say we were too busy. It would have made a pleasant change from poring over documents.'

'No doubt,' said Harriet brightly. 'My sister will be here shortly, gentlemen.' And then she added what she felt she needed to say. 'Major Steele, I must make it clear that your business here is with Miss Clare. I fear I cannot be of any assistance in your inquiries.'

'That is understood, Miss Austin. However, you could do us, and yourself, one small service without becoming involved.'

Harriet could not help being intrigued. 'A service? Of what kind?'

'I should like you to ask your father one small innocent question, which cannot give offence. Your sister could convey the answer to us.'

'Then could not she be the one to ask Father the question?'

'They are not on good terms, I think. I doubt if he would give her the courtesy of a reply.'

Harriet acknowledged her error. 'You are right, of course. It is a very sad situation.' She took a deep breath. 'Well, Major, what is this question? Will my father suspect it comes from you?'

'Not at all. It is a very natural question between father and daughter. You can ask it as if it had just come into your head.'

'Please tell me what the question is.'

'You know that many local people bathe in Highgate Ponds in the summer?'

'Yes. Dr Frankel recommends it as good exercise.'

'Excellent. That will make it easier for you. I want you to tell your father you'd like to take up swimming. Ask him if he will escort you to the ponds. Ask if he could help if you got into trouble. In short, Miss Austin, I want to know if your father can swim.'

'How strange.' For a rare moment, Harriet was almost amused. 'Well, that seems harmless enough. I will ask him when I have the opportunity, and give the answer to Clare.'

'Thank you,' said Steele, and then the door was pushed open and Mrs Butters brought in a tray bearing tea things and a plate of biscuits.

'Miss Clare asked me to make tea for the guests,' she said, putting the tray down on a table. 'I'm sorry, there's no cake.'

'Thank you, Mrs Butters,' said Harriet. 'I'm sure biscuits will be fine. Will you serve the tea, please? My sister is fetching some things from her room.'

'Very good, miss,' said the housekeeper. She addressed the major with a mixture of respect and nervousness. 'How do you take your tea, sir?'

'Strong, please. No milk or sugar.'

As the woman served him, Steele glanced at the ornamental daggers on the wall. Both were now spotlessly clean and shining, and perfectly aligned.

Mrs Butters turned to Mason. 'What about you, sir?'

'Milk and sugar for me, please,' said Mason. And then, assessing the size of the cups, he added, 'Two lumps, please.'

'Help yourselves to biscuits, gentlemen,' said Harriet, rising to her feet. 'And now I'll ask you to excuse me. I have been out on the Heath this afternoon. I feel in need of a rest.'

'Very wise,' said Steele. 'Thank you for your co-operation.'

The young woman's response was polite but firm; she was conscious of the housekeeper's presence. 'I have not co-operated, Major. Please remember that, officially, I have no knowledge of your visit. You have come to see my sister.'

Steele made a slight bow. 'Of course, Miss Austin. We thank you nevertheless.'

Harriet moved to the door and Mason opened it for her. 'Thank you,' she said, and was gone. Mason closed the door behind her and then returned to his teacup. He took a Bourbon biscuit.

Major Steele turned a warm smile on the hesitant housekeeper. 'An excellent cup of tea,' he remarked.

'Thank you, sir.'

'Clearly you always warm the pot.'

'That I do, sir,' said the housekeeper, with some pride. 'And I take the pot to the kettle, not the kettle to the pot.'

'Ah. A commendable policy,' purred the major, before turning to more serious matters. 'Mrs Butters, I have heard from Miss Clare that your master punished you for letting us in the other day.'

'He did, sir, and no mistake. Three weeks' wages he docked me! And me saving for a winter coat. Now I'll be too late for the sales.'

Steele produced some coins from his waistcoat pocket. 'I should not wish to be the cause of that disaster, Mrs Butters. Perhaps you would be good enough to accept some compensation.' He held out the coins, and Mrs Butters took them with a gasp.

'Oh! Sir! Three sovereigns! That's far more than I lost, sir!'

'But I've no doubt you also suffered some unpleasantness. And, furthermore, I hope you may be able to give us some slight assistance from time to time in the future.'

This aroused considerable alarm. 'Oh! I don't know about that, sir. I don't know if I dare.'

'You will not be put in peril again, never fear. I merely ask that if you notice anything unusual in this house, or indeed in the neighbourhood, you will tell us on one of our visits.' Steele took further coins from his pocket, inspected them, and put them back again. 'There are more sovereigns where those came from.'

Mrs Butters lost some of her hesitancy. 'Well, sir ... if I could be sure the master would never hear of it ...'

'You have my word on that.'

'Well ... as it happens, I did come across something odd the other day. I was already wondering if I should tell you about it.'

'Yes, Mrs Butters, you should. It will be kept entirely confidential.'

'Well, sir ... of course, it may not be of any importance ...'

'Let me be the judge of that. Please tell us what you came across.'

'Well, sir ...'

As Mrs Butters sought the right words, the door opened and Clare came in, carrying a large envelope and a small book.

'Ah, Major Steele,' she said, in a businesslike manner. 'And Mr Mason. I'm sorry I wasn't here to receive you.'

'Don't worry, Miss Austin. We have been well looked after.'

'I've found the souvenirs you wanted.' She handed the items to Steele. 'The newspaper reports are in this envelope. And here is my mother's diary for the last year of her life.'

'Thank you, Miss Austin. We shall guard these most

carefully, and return them as soon as possible.'

Clare turned to the housekeeper. 'Thank you, Mrs Butters. I'll take charge of the tea now.'

'Very good, miss,' said the housekeeper, turning to go.

Steele held up a hand. 'One moment, please. Mrs Butters has something to tell us.'

'Oh, never mind that now, sir. That can wait for another time. I must go and start on the vegetables for dinner.' She was on the move before Steele could protest further. Clare took up the conversation as the door closed behind her.

'The diary is mainly full of trivia, I'm afraid, and there are several gaps. But there may be something of interest.'

'Anything that sheds light on events of that time will be useful,' said Steele. 'The boating accident is one of our main lines of inquiry.'

'Have you any news for me, Major?'

'Yes, I think we have. We asked our contact at Scotland Yard to look at police records relating to the incident. His report is sad but interesting.'

Mason was concerned. 'Maybe you should sit down, Miss Austin.'

'Yes … yes. Perhaps we should all be seated. What have you learned, Major?'

'The police were extremely concerned about your mother's death. But the boat was in a secluded reach of the Thames, and there seemed to be no witnesses.'

'That much I learned from the inquest report.'

'Your father testified that your mother insisted on attempting to punt. He said she unbalanced and fell overboard when she took the pole from him. Strangely, she didn't try to save herself by clinging to the side of the punt. Mr Austin claimed that was because the current took the boat away from her. He couldn't steer it back because the pole had fallen in and drifted away.'

Clare spoke contemptuously. 'An extraordinary chain of circumstances.'

Steele continued his account. 'Your father said he didn't dive in after her because he couldn't swim. The police were unable to disprove that.'

'Alas, neither can I,' said Clare. 'The question has never arisen.'

'We hope your sister may elicit that information. If so, she will pass it on to you to give to us.'

Clare raised her eyebrows. 'Harriet is willing to help?'

'In that one small way only. We must not ask for more.' Steele concluded his narrative. 'Your father said he thought it better to stay on the punt and shout for help. Unfortunately, by the time that arrived it was too late.'

There was a pause, while Clare sadly considered what she'd just been told. Then she observed, 'It doesn't seem to have been a very thorough investigation.'

'Our contact, Chief Inspector Willoughby, was not involved at the time, of course. He has been consulting an older colleague. It appears that the police considered bringing a charge of culpable homicide against your father. But it was felt at the time that there was insufficient evidence to pursue it.'

Clare sighed. 'A pity. And was that the end of the matter, as far as the police were concerned?'

'It was, Miss Austin. But no longer. Inspector Willoughby is having the case reopened at our request. And it now appears there may have been a witness after all.'

Clare was animated. 'A witness? Why did that person not come forward at the time?'

'For the understandable reason that he might have been prosecuted himself. My colleague has the details.'

Mason consulted his notebook. 'It seems that a local character named Dan Croucher habitually fished on that stretch of river without a licence. Poaching, in fact. He was seen there early on the day in question. After the accident he made himself scarce for a while. But it's thought he's still alive and the police will now try to trace him.' He closed his notebook. 'And that is how things stand at present.'

Clare sighed. 'Well ... it seems my thoughts may be confirmed. Have you been able to discover anything about my father's business affairs?'

'We have,' Steele responded. 'And, there again, it seems your suspicions may be justified. We were fortunate in finding that your father's solicitor is one Cedric Jamieson, who is well known to us. A man of very few scruples.'

'About the most devious rogue in the legal profession,' said Mason, with relish.

'Which is a remarkable accolade, considering the competition,' Steele observed.

'As slippery as a barrel of eels,' Mason added, apparently feeling the denigration needed more emphasis.

'And this is my father's solicitor? Well, I cannot say I'm surprised.'

'However,' said Steele, 'in present circumstances, Mr Jamieson's dubious record has worked in our favour. By reminding him that we know certain things to his discredit we persuaded him to assist us. We now know a great deal about Meredith Austin's affairs.'

'Well done, gentlemen. Please tell me.'

'Your mother's will was as you surmised. Her money went to your father, and was indeed used to found his business. And it was a condition of the will that he provide you with a home and an income until you marry.'

'Which is why he has always regarded me as a burden.' Clare's voice was bitter.

'His second wife was more cautious. On absconding, she put a large sum in trust for her daughter. Mr Austin must use it for Harriet's benefit only. When she marries, or reaches the age of twenty-one, the money becomes hers.'

'Which is why the wretched man drives away her suitors.'

'A plausible theory, but not one that can be proved, of course.'

'No doubt he would retain the money if Harriet died, or were certified insane?'

'That would be the expected outcome, yes. But neither of those tragedies is likely, I think.'

'You would not think that, if you knew my father as I do.'

'Let us not get carried away, Miss Austin. Thus far, we've uncovered no evidence of illegality. However, Mr Mason and I have both come to distrust the man as much as you do.'

'I'm glad to hear that, Major. Is there anything to be done about the situation?'

'We are still checking papers to see if he's used trust money for his own ends. And our legal adviser is seeing if the trust can be broken, and the money passed straight to Harriet.'

'Alas,' said Clare, 'I fear she would scarcely know what to do with it.'

'That's a bridge we can cross when we come to it. We also have an expert looking at Mr Austin's business dealings. There may be things to uncover there.'

'You are very thorough, Major. We are lucky to have you acting on our behalf.'

'Thank you, Miss Austin. At the risk of sounding pompous, I must say that Mr Mason and I both have a hatred of villainy and a compulsion to try and thwart wickedness whenever we suspect it.'

'Also,' said Mason, slightly embarrassed, 'we are being well paid to catch the Heath Maniac.'

'Indeed,' said Steele. 'And we must now turn our attention to the matter that brought us here in the first place.'

'Of course,' said Clare. 'I have told you I should like to help in any way I can. Is there any progress in that area?'

'The police have recruited an expert from the United States. A ... what does he call himself?' He turned to Mason.

'A criminologist.'

'Ah yes. Our American friends are always surprising us with new ologies. Apparently, this Professor Kane helped to catch the Chicago Axe Murderer. When there's a spate of killings, he claims he can build up a picture of the assassin. A brilliant man, according to Scotland Yard.'

'Has he produced a result?'

'No, he hasn't arrived yet. It seems he missed his boat in New York. In the meantime we get on with our more down-to-earth inquiries. We think we may have a lead to Luke Scully.'

As before, Steele thought he detected a slight nervous reaction in the young woman at the mention of this man. But it was gone in an instant. 'Scully?' said Clare. 'Oh yes, our former gardener. You were asking me about him.'

'We're very interested in Scully.'

'Well, you'll be pleased to hear I've remembered something else about him. I believe at one time he'd been on the stage.'

'Ah!' exclaimed Steele triumphantly. 'Just so! And that is our lead. Tell Miss Austin, Jack.'

'I've been asking round the alehouses. And there's a barman at the Flask who recalls Scully as part of a double act. On the halls. Charlie Challis and Luke Scully.'

'We've discovered that Charlie Challis is still working,' said Steele. 'We're hoping he may have kept in touch with his old partner.'

'Can you find this man Challis?'

'Very easily. He's appearing this week at the Camden Alhambra. We shall go there tonight, to see if he can help us.'

6

I<small>T WAS A</small> lively night at the Camden Alhambra. The place was not quite so full as it would be on Saturday, but the numbers were good for midweek.

Talbot O'Reilly, the Irish tenor, was past the peak of his career, but still had a following, especially in north-west London. His name at the top of the bill ensured steady business.

When Steele and Mason entered, only a few of the red plush seats facing the stage were vacant, and the bar, which ran down one side of the hall, was noisy and crowded with customers. Most of these people would have only one eye on the stage until O'Reilly came on.

The two men took seats in the fifth row, at the end furthest from the drinkers. Steele lit a small cigar; Mason rolled a cheap cigarette.

Nell Waters, billed as the Cockney Princess, was nearing the end of her act, which consisted of four of the songs that had almost made her famous, linked by a well-judged flow of cheeky chat. She was just finishing her third ditty, 'You'd Better Put It Away Now, George', with its telling second line, 'Mother will soon be home.' The song concluded, amid cheers and raucous laughter, with the revelation that the contentious item was the pipe that George was smoking.

Nell had a melodious voice, not quite as good as it had been a thousand gins ago, but still appealing. It served her well in her comedy songs but it was beginning to be a mistake to end her act with a sentimental ballad.

On this occasion, 'He'll Always Be There In My Heart' didn't go well. With no bawdy lines to enjoy, and the sound of a less-than-wonderful voice, the drinkers returned to their glasses and signs of restlessness began in the stalls. There were a few jeers, and the hubbub of conversation began to drown the singer.

As the noise worsened, the need for fair play was aroused in at least one spectator and a powerful voice from the bar bellowed, 'Give the old cow a chance!'

So fierce was this command that the hubbub was hushed. Then the orchestra ground to a halt as Nell Waters advanced, with a sweet smile and a raised hand.

'Thank you,' she said. 'I'm glad there's at least one gentleman in the house.' After that, she murmured to the conductor to cut to the last verse; the orchestra struck up again and the Cockney Princess sang her way through to the end amid cheers and applause. There was almost an ovation as the curtains closed and Nell stepped out through the middle to take a bow. In fact, she took several bows, encouraged by gentlemen in the audience who appreciated the low-cut gown she was wearing.

Over the applause, the orchestra did a brisk reprise of one of her songs as a bridge to the next act. Steele puffed his cigar and reflected, 'It makes you proud to be British, doesn't it? They'll forgive you anything if you make them laugh.'

The Camden Alhambra had taken up the new trend of dispensing with the traditional chairman. Here, acts followed each other without verbal introduction. So once the applause for Nell Waters had stopped, the orchestra abruptly ended the reprise of her song and set off in a totally different musical style, with an onslaught of dramatic Cossack music.

This heralded the appearance of a speciality act, Vladimir and Olga. At first the stage was occupied only by Vladimir, a swarthy man with shiny black hair, a moustache, and a single golden earring. He set up a target at one side of the stage and then, against a low background of urgent Russian tunes, hurled knives at it from the opposite corner. All thudded into the bull's-eye.

It looked easy. So, to make it more difficult for himself, the man retrieved the knives and threw them again, this time propelling them backwards over his shoulder. Next, still facing away from the target, he bent forward and threw the knives between his legs.

Only one failed to hit the bull's-eye, the last knife, and that landed in the next circle. The man muttered a foreign oath, retrieved the miscreant, did a somersault and, as he completed it, threw the knife between his legs again. This time it hit the very centre of the target.

Then, to a crescendo of music, Vladimir took a bow, after which he signalled towards the wings for his partner to join him.

So far, audience reaction had been tolerant rather than enthusiastic. The man could throw knives, so what? This changed with the arrival of Olga, a voluptuous, large-eyed, black-haired beauty, in a white blouse and a long black skirt, slit up to her thigh. The act now had everyone's full attention.

'Bit of all right,' said Mason.

'Some Russian women can be very striking,' Steele pronounced sagely, giving the impression of boundless experience of beautiful women throughout the world. 'Note the fine cheekbones. Cossack blood, I daresay.'

Stagehands had removed the target and replaced it with a white upright board. Olga stood with her back tightly pressed against this, clutching the sides with outstretched hands to keep herself still and steady.

Now most of the orchestra were silent; the only sound was a series of drum rolls, each building up to a climax, as Vladimir's knives embedded themselves in the board around Olga's rigid body. They landed symmetrically, the first within inches of her left shoulder, the next on the opposite side, then one by her left knee and one by her right. The final two knives landed either side of her waist, the last one obviously nicking something vital, as her skirt fell to the floor, revealing long shapely legs clad in black fishnet tights. This brought a roar of approval from the bar area.

Over the applause, Vladimir murmured a few words to Olga, apparently checking that she was ready for the act's perilous climax. Bravely, she seemed to concur and Vladimir returned to his throwing position.

Now there were more drum rolls, accompanied by gasps from the audience as Vladimir threw his knives to make a circle round the girl's head. The first thudded home to the right of her throat, the next by her right ear.

And then, as he worked his way down the left side, something went wrong. The fifth knife landed close to her left ear, but too close, it seemed. Olga let out a little cry and put a hand to the side of her head. Blood began to trickle down her neck.

There was an uproar of alarm from the audience. Drinkers put down their glasses and peered at the stage, eager to get their money's worth. If the man could get it wrong once, next time he might do something worse. This was exciting stuff. They didn't know, of course, that Olga's hand had squeezed open the small sachet of pig's blood hidden in her hair.

Vladimir rushed to his partner to check that she wasn't seriously hurt. A few quiet words were exchanged. He seemed to be asking if he should go ahead with the last knife. With a nervous nod of the head, she appeared to say yes, and Vladimir went back to his mark.

The tension was electric as he prepared to throw the final blade. This time he was slower and more cautious than before. But after ten seconds of suspense, during which the drum roll built up to a crescendo, Vladimir threw the knife and it landed safely, an inch away from Olga's neck.

The audience's relief was audible and their applause generous as the orchestra struck up more of their exciting Cossack music, the curtains swirled together, and Vladimir and Olga trotted out to take their bows, Olga holding a discreet handkerchief to her throat.

'A dangerous business,' Steele observed.

'Very dangerous,' said Mason. 'Pity they're too lazy to learn a comic song.'

'Still, it gives us a clue to your Angel of Death.'

'How so, guv'nor?'

'You were wondering how the Heath Maniac's victims had no chance to defend themselves. These people remind us that the knife could have been thrown.'

Mason stubbed out his cigarette in the little brass ashtray attached to the seat in front of him. 'I suppose it could. But the Maniac would have to be as good as this Russian chap. And I don't suppose this bloke is the Heath Maniac, or he wouldn't be on stage showing everyone what he can do.'

By now, the Cossack music had been replaced by a rumbustious English music-hall tune, obviously associated with the next artiste, the man they'd come to see, Cheerful Charlie Challis.

Swiftly the curtains parted and there he was, ambling on to the stage and affecting a comic trip as he approached the centre. Behind him, the backcloth was painted to look like a brick wall, embellished with advertisements for local businesses.

Charlie was dressed in a bookmaker's loud check suit, and he wore a brown bowler hat with a curly brim. He greeted the audience as old friends.

'How do?' he said. 'How are yer? All right? You're in luck tonight, I'm going to sing for you.'

This brought the expected groans and ironic cheers from the bar, none of them unfriendly.

'Thank you,' said Charlie, 'I knew you'd be pleased. I've got a nice little song I'm going to render for you ... render meaning to tear apart. Ladies and gentlemen, a little song, a little song entitled "If You've Nothing On Tonight, Mabel, I Think I'll Come Round for a Bit".'

There were more jocular moans from the bar but now they were mingled with genuine laughter.

Charlie pretended to hear objections from the front rows. 'All right, lady, I won't do that one. I won't do that one, in case the vicar's in. Instead, I'll do one you all know. It's published by Sanderson Music, and it's called "She Taught Me Lots Of Things I Never Knew". He nodded to the conductor. Thank you, Maestro.'

Then off he went into half a dozen verses, describing things girls had taught him, which all sounded as if they were going to be rude, but never quite were. He finished to good applause but as he went into his patter it seemed he still had critics among the drinkers.

'Thank you,' said Charlie. 'Now I've got to tell you about my neighbour. My neighbour, he's a funny bloke—'

A voice from the bar interrupted. 'Why don't you get off and get him on?'

Charlie's response was quick. 'You wouldn't want him near you, mate. He does pest control for the council.'

Having earned a good laugh and a points victory, Charlie launched into his routine. 'Yes, he's a funny bloke, my neighbour. I saw him with his dog the other day, outside his front door. And he was holding his dog's tail! He was! He was holding the dog's tail!

'I said, "Why are you holding the dog's tail?" He said, "My mother-in-law's coming, and I don't want her seeing any sign of welcome."'

Once launched on the subject, Charlie did five minutes on mothers-in-law, before switching to wives, doctors and varicose veins. Then it was back to life in general. He finished on his current favourite joke.

'This bloke at the pub, he drives me mad. He does, he drives me mad. Anything bad, he says, "Oh well, it could be worse." "Terrible weather!" "Yeah. Still, it could be worse." "But it's been raining all day." "Yeah, well, it could have been raining all week."

'I saw him last night, he said, "Have you heard about her at number eighteen?" I said, "What, Fast Annie?" He said, "Yeah. The one whose husband's a commercial, away all week."

'I said, "What about her?" He said, "Big tragedy. Last week he came home Thursday instead of Friday, caught her with another man. He shot them both."

'I said, "That's terrible!" He said, "Yeah. Still, it could have been worse." I said, "He shot two people, how could that have been worse?" He said, "If he'd come home Wednesday, he'd have shot me."'

Charlie liked to end his act with a straight, heart-warming song to demonstrate that as well as being a funny man he was also a lovable human being. 'There'll Never Be Another Like My Mum' was always well received, and so it was tonight. He concluded to a good round of applause, which lasted while the curtains closed, the band went into his play-off music, and Charlie came out front to acknowledge his reception.

Mason looked at the next item on his list of acts. 'The Parisian Sisters,' he announced. 'A Visit to the Ballet. I wouldn't mind seeing that.'

'Another time,' said Steele, rising to his feet. 'We need to catch Challis before he goes to the pub.'

In his dingy dressing room, Charlie Challis sat down heavily on his chair and exhaled lengthily. It was a moment before he remembered to breathe in again.

Once he'd done so, he found the energy to remove his coat, tie and collar, and finally, with a deep sigh of relief, his boots. Then he undid his shirt buttons, revealing a sweat-stained vest. On his dressing table stood two bottles of Guinness. Charlie opened one, put it to his lips, and took a long drink.

He reckoned he'd gone quite well tonight. Slipping his mate Jim ten bob to heckle from the bar had been money well spent.

There was a knock at the door.

Hastily, Charlie used his make-up towel to hide the second bottle of Guinness. Then he called out, 'Who is it?'

The door opened and in came Gerald Timlin, manager of the Camden Alhambra, and a figure of authority to the likes of Charlie Challis. 'It's your manager,' he said.

'Evening, guv'nor,' said Charlie, sitting up straight. 'Went all right tonight, eh?'

'Yes. All right,' said Timlin. 'They've heard that first song a bit too often. You need to give it a rest.'

'But they love it,' protested the comic.

'Yes, Charlie, and you love the tip from your publishers. But never mind that now. There's two gentlemen to see you.'

'Gentlemen? To see me? There's a novelty!' Charlie gave a derisive laugh. 'Listen, guv'nor, I'm tired. I don't want to talk to no one just now. Unless it's a rich widow, with a good figure and a nice little pub.'

'You have to see these gentlemen. They've brought me a letter of introduction from J.G. Hurst.'

J.G. Hurst owned the chain of music halls that included

the Camden Alhambra, and was not a man to disoblige. He was a member of Henry Steele's London club.

'Oh well,' said Charlie. 'Bring 'em in.' He swallowed the rest of his Guinness and did up his shirt buttons.

The manager ushered in Steele and Mason and, having studied Hurst's letter again, performed the introductions. The room seemed too small for four large men.

'Would you prefer to move to my office?' Timlin offered.

'No, thank you,' said Steele. 'I'm sure Mr Challis is a busy man. We shan't take up much of his time. May we sit down?'

Apart from the chair and dressing table, the only furniture was a shabby red sofa and, as Timlin withdrew, the visitors lowered themselves awkwardly on to this.

'We are private investigators,' said Steele. 'We hope you may be able to tell us about a man called Luke Scully.'

'Luke Scully?' The comedian sucked in air through his teeth. 'Yeah. I can tell you a lot about Luke Scully. We used to work together.'

'So I'm told,' said Steele. 'How long ago was that?'

'Well ... we'd been a double act for three or four years. And we split up about two years ago. Bit more, perhaps. I got sick of carrying him.'

'Carrying him?'

'Yeah. He weren't no good no more. The demon drink.' Charlie picked up the empty Guinness bottle for dramatic effect. 'Drink's a good whore, but a bad mistress.' As his guests pondered these words of wisdom, he put down the bottle and continued. 'Course, it weren't the beer with Luke. Gin was his downfall. Mother's ruin. Pickled himself in gin, silly bugger.'

'And that affected his work, obviously.'

'Not half. Forgot his words. Lost his timing. Picked fights with people. I had to give him the boot.'

'How did he take that?'

'Badly. Got very angry. And he could be violent, Luke Scully. Tried to fight me, poor sod. I gave him one little push and he fell over. Too sozzled to get up again.'

Steele was silent for a moment, thinking of Scully's tendency to violence. Mason took up the questioning.

'After the split, did you keep in touch?'

'Couldn't avoid it at first. He kept turning up, saying he was sorry and looking for a handout. I usually gave him a quid and told him to cut out the gin.'

'Did he do any work?'

'Not on stage, no one would have him. He was in the boxing booth at Hampstead fairground for a bit. He was quite handy with his fists, before the gin got him. He'd been a soldier once.'

Steele was alerted. 'He'd been a soldier?'

'Yeah. Weapons was always his hobby. 'Course, they don't allow weapons in a boxing booth, so he didn't last long. Got what was left of his brains knocked out.'

'What sort of weapons was he interested in?'

'All sorts. He'd kept his pistol from the army, which you're not supposed to do.'

Steele nodded. 'Serious offence. We could hold him for that, if we need to.' And then he added, 'Once we find him. Anything else?'

'Yeah. He used to mess around with some sort of bow and arrow. If he was somewhere like Clapham Common, he'd try to bring down a few birds. Oh yeah, and he had a knobkerrie. One of them things the fuzzy-wuzzies bash people with in South Africa.' Charlie sniffed. 'All a bloody waste of time.'

'D'you know what he did after the boxing booth?'

'He was working for some toffs up on the Highgate Road, gardening and odd jobs and such. I think he gave up drink for a bit; there was a girl up there he fancied.'

'A girl?'

'Yeah. Well, where Luke was concerned there was always

a girl. Or two. Or three. But I heard this one was special. Then it all went wrong. The toffs give him the sack, accused him of stealing. Course, that was well out of order. Luke's done a lot of silly things but he was never a tea leaf. They say he was very bitter about that.'

Steele picked his words. 'They say? You haven't seen him yourself?'

'Not for a year or more, eighteen months maybe. This is all gossip from the pub. The Black Swan, he still has a few mates there. They say he took it very hard, ended up hating all the toffs in Highgate. Started drinking again. Last I heard, he was living rough on the Heath.'

'Can you tell us how to get hold of him?'

'Very carefully,' said Charlie. 'Like I said, he can be violent.' He laughed heartily at his little joke, then became respectful again. 'Sorry. Yeah, I know what you're asking but I don't know the answer. You could try the public bar at the Black Swan. Or there's an agent we both used to use, maybe Luke kept in touch with him. Ernie Treadwell, 63 Charing Cross Road.'

As Mason made a note, the door was flung open and a woman burst in, a shabby dressing gown flapping loosely over her underwear. Minus her splendid black wig, her mousey-coloured hair was in a mess and without her stage make-up her face was grey and starting to show a few wrinkles. In crumpled slippers, instead of high-heeled shoes, she seemed considerably shorter but, with mounting dismay, Steele and Mason began to recognize her.

'For God's sake, Charlie, give us a fag!' implored the woman they knew as Olga. 'Alfie's gone and smoked the whole bleedin' packet! I'm gasping!'

'Mind your manners, Gladys!' said Charlie. 'I got two gentlemen here.'

'Beg pardon,' said the woman, drawing her dressing gown

closer around her. 'Got the bailiffs after you again?'

'No,' said Charlie, reaching into a drawer for his ciga-
rettes. 'They're trying to find Luke Scully.'

'Cor!' said the woman. 'That toerag? Well, I can soon tell
them where to find Luke Scully.' She turned to the detectives.
'Worth a quid, is it?'

In his austere little office at Dunblane, Charles Stone heard
the thump of the front door knocker downstairs but he knew
the manservant would answer it and, after a swift glance at
his watch, he continued working on the accounts. They had
got slightly disordered due to recent dramatic events and
this would displease Dr Frankel, which was not a wise thing
to do.

A minute later, bony knuckles rapped on his own door.
'Come in,' he called, and the door opened to admit Prosser
and a youth, about eighteen years old, in working clothes.

'This young man is from Slaughter's,' said Prosser.

'Right,' said Stone. 'I'll deal with this. Dr Frankel is not to
be disturbed before eight o'clock.' A thought occurred to him.
'What is for dinner tonight?'

'Sirloin steak,' said Prosser. He was a man of few words.

'Make sure it's rare. And have a bottle of the Burgundy
decanted.'

Prosser left the room without response, closing the door
behind him. The youth seemed nervous. He advanced to the
desk, took a large envelope from inside his rough jacket, and
handed it to the secretary. Stone slit it open with a large
metal paper-knife, which was rather sharper than it needed
to be, and checked the contents.

Satisfied after a minute's perusal, he put the envelope in
a drawer on the left-hand side of his desk. Then he opened a
drawer on the right-hand side, took out a package wrapped
in brown paper, and gave it to the youth. 'Instructions are

inside,' he said.

The youth turned to go but Stone stopped him. 'One moment, young man,' he commanded.

The youth, somewhat alarmed, turned back to face Charles Stone, who was looking stern.

'Dr Frankel tells me our arrangement will have to be renegotiated,' said the secretary. 'His costs have increased, and the business is dangerous.'

The youth had trouble with the word 'renegotiated' but he grasped the essence of what Stone had said. 'I don't know nothing about that,' he protested. 'You'll have to talk to Mr Slaughter.'

'Exactly,' said Stone. 'Tell Slaughter to come in person next time.'

Winter had come early to Lambeth: the two tired-looking trees that graced Gravelly Road had long since shed their leaves, and their bare branches glistened with moisture. Some sparrows hopped around the railings that fronted the basement steps, chirruping bravely to keep their spirits up, but it was a bleak scene. Both sides of the street were lined with long rows of grey terraced houses that had seen better days.

When Steele and Mason reached number 53, they were heartened by the first show of human spirit in that long thoroughfare: an aspidistra in the front window offered some defiance to the general gloom.

Mason raised the knocker and rapped three times on the black front door. After half a minute he rapped again. There was a further short delay, then the door was opened halfway and a female face peered round it. It was a grey, weary-looking face, and it registered suspicion.

'Yes?' said the woman.

'Madge Scully?' asked Steele.

'Yes,' said the woman again. 'Who are you?'

'I'm Henry Steele and this is John Mason. We're inquiry agents.'

Now the woman's face expressed alarm. 'You're police!'

'No, we're not. We're private citizens. One thing we do is try to bring people together, or put them in touch. We have a message for Mr Scully from his friend Charlie Challis.'

'Charlie Challis? Cuh!' The woman's voice was bitter. 'Fine friend he turned out to be!'

'We also bring greetings to you from your sister Gladys. It was she who told us your husband was here.'

'Oh. Gladys.' The voice was now a little more amenable. 'Is she all right?'

'Gladys is fine,' said Steele. 'We saw her last night at the Camden Alhambra. She and Alfred are a big success.'

'That's a nice change,' said the woman.

'People were remarking on her fine Cossack cheekbones.' Mason couldn't resist the jibe.

'What?' Madge Scully was bemused.

Steele smiled tolerantly. The men's relationship had always thrived on a little gentle ribbing.

'Your sister is in good health and hopes to see you next time they play south London,' he said.

'Well ... give her my love. And thanks for bringing Charlie's message.'

She seemed about to shut the door but Mason's foot had somehow edged on to the threshold. And then her eye was caught by Steele feeling in his waistcoat pocket, and producing what looked like gold coins.

'We haven't delivered the message yet,' Steele pointed out. 'Also, the Camden manager has discovered that Mr Scully is still owed some money from last time he worked there. He's asked us to bring it to him.'

'Oh. That's good.' The woman opened the door wider and reached out for the cash. 'I'll give it to him.'

'I'm afraid we must hand it over to him in person. We have to get him to sign a receipt.'

'Oh,' said the woman again. 'Well, I suppose you'd better come in.' At last the door was fully opened and the men entered. The woman led them through what might have been called the hall, but was actually a dark passage.

'I'll have to find out if Luke can see you,' she cautioned. 'He's not well, you know.'

'No,' said Steele. 'We didn't know that.'

'You could have guessed. If he was well, he wouldn't be home here, would he? He'd be up north of the river, chasing girls and toadying to the toffs.'

They reached a door at the end of the passage. Mrs Scully knocked, opened it an inch, and called out, 'Luke! There's two visitors to see you!'

The voice from within was weak and unwelcoming. 'I can't see no one. I'm ill.'

'They've got some money for you!'

The pause was short, and the voice became less hostile. 'All right. Tell 'em they can have five minutes.'

Mrs Scully opened the door wide and the men went into a small, depressing room, which contained little more than a narrow bed and a wooden cabinet beside it. On the cabinet stood a large china bowl, with a water jug standing in it. Beneath the cabinet was a chamber pot, mercifully empty.

One look at the wreck of a man in front of them was enough to answer the question that had brought them here. Through gaps in a torn nightshirt, an emaciated body could be seen, shiny with sweat. The face was deathly white, with watery eyes sunk deep in dark sockets, and cheekbones strained against papery skin. Thin arms moved slowly and painfully, as the man tried to prop himself upright against the pillows. The effort exhausted him and he fought for breath, which came in short gasps.

Having no warning of their visit, Scully could not be dissembling. Anyway, no actor could simulate quite that degree of human devastation. So it was certain that Scully had not been stabbing and murdering people on Hampstead Heath in the last month.

Still, he might have some useful background information. Steele and Mason advanced to the bedside. 'Good morning, Mr Scully,' said Steele, with what he hoped was an encouraging smile. 'Charlie Challis sent a message.'

'Yeah?'

'He said, "Cut out the gin."'

This affront raised a small spark of animation in the invalid. He seemed about to spit but then, remembering his wife's presence, confined himself to a contemptuous snort and moved on to the important matter. 'You got some money for me?' He held out a shaky hand.

Steele put three sovereigns in the palm. 'You're owed this from your last job at the Camden Alhambra.' He didn't bother to pursue the fiction about the receipt.

'Blimey!' wheezed Scully. 'That'll be three years ago! Mean sods! Three years they've hung on to this!'

He took a grubby handkerchief from under his pillow, wrapped it round two of the coins, and put the small bundle back under his pillow. He held out the third coin for his wife.

'Get me half a dozen bottles of gin, Madge. And you can keep the change.'

Madge took the coin firmly. 'One bottle will do for you, my lad. And the change will pay off some of the back rent.' She nodded at the pillow. 'I'll have the rest of it later.' She moved towards the door.

'D'you mind if we stay and have a word with your husband, Mrs Scully?' asked Steele, looking round for a chair. There was a rickety upright one in the corner. Mason fetched it for him, and then perched himself uneasily on the end of the bed.

'Please yourself,' said Madge. 'You'll not get much out of him. I never do. At least, not much that makes sense.' And with that she left the room.

The conversation with Scully mainly confirmed what they'd already heard from Clare Austin and Charles Challis. Scully's voice was feeble, and his words sparse as he reluctantly answered questions about his time working for Meredith Austin; indeed, only the sight of another sovereign glinting in Steele's hand induced him to do so at all.

He admitted that he hated Austin, and said the theft charge was a bloody lie, trumped up as an excuse to get rid of him. The real reason he had to go, said Scully, was that he wouldn't kow-tow to Austin all the time, as the tyrant expected. But Scully showed no passion for revenge. Again, when asked about Clare Austin, his response was muted. She was 'all right', he said, 'the best of the bunch'. Briefly, he seemed about to say more, but either from weariness or inhibition his voice trailed off.

Nor did he have much to say about his ten months living rough on the Heath. He'd existed by shooting birds and rabbits with his bow, and catching ducks by the ponds; he'd learned survival techniques in the army.

But it had obviously been a time of great privation, which had finally destroyed a body already ravaged by drink, and it had eventually sent him slinking home to his wife. He acknowledged that he was lucky to be married to a saint. 'She's a real Christian,' he said. Clearly she'd still felt bound by her marriage vows.

It was only when, unasked, he went back further, to his years on the stage, that Scully's voice mustered a little strength and his mind some enthusiasm. His story differed from that which they'd heard from Charlie Challis. He averred that he had been the star, and it was jealousy that had caused Challis to push him out. He described great audience reactions and, having checked that his wife had not yet returned, recalled colourful adventures with theatrical ladies.

These excitements tired him; his voice began to peter out and his eyes to close. He was silently enjoying happy memories as he fell asleep.

On this occasion Scully's timing was perfect. It was as he began to produce little snuffles and snores that Madge came back with the bottle of gin.

'Nodded off, has he?' she said. 'It's best if he's sleeping.' She opened the bottle, replaced the stopper, put an upturned glass on top, and placed the gin on the far side of the cabinet. 'Don't want him reaching it too easy.'

The men rose to leave. 'Thank you, Mrs Scully,' said Steele. 'Your husband's done his best to be helpful.'

'Well, there's a miracle! Perhaps he's seen the light at last,' said Madge, as she led them out through the door and back along the passage. 'I've been trying to get the parson to come in, that's if Luke'll see him. It's time he made his peace.'

'We heard you talk about rent arrears,' Steele ventured. 'Perhaps you'd allow us to help a little further.' He handed Madge Scully two more sovereigns.

'God bless you, sir, and thank you,' said Madge, putting the coins in her apron pocket.

'You must find things difficult. How do you manage?'

'I'm out cleaning five days a week,' replied Madge. 'Nice lady I'm working for. She even give me money to have a doctor look at Luke.'

'What did he say?'

'Consumption. His lungs is almost gone.'

'I'm sorry,' said Steele. He meant it. What had happened to Scully was hideous.

Mason remained practical. 'Should we leave a card, guv'nor?'

'Oh yes. Thank you, Jack.' Steele gave Mrs Scully one of their business cards. 'We're engaged in the hunt for the Hampstead Heath Maniac,' he said. 'We hoped Mr Scully might remember something useful from his days in Hampstead, but he wasn't able to do so today. If he recalls anything later, would you please let us know. And if at any time you need help, Mrs Scully, you can call on us.'

'Thank you, sir.' Madge Scully put the card in her apron pocket alongside the sovereigns, a handkerchief and a comb, which she would use from time to time to straighten her husband's remaining strands of straggly hair.

Steele could not resist a final cautionary word. 'Excuse my asking, but did the doctor say it was all right for your husband to go on drinking gin?'

'He said it won't make no difference now. He's only got a few weeks to live. It's best to keep him happy.'

Frankel descended the stairs, crossed the hall, and went down the three stone steps into the kitchen area. He was enjoying some pleasant anticipation, though no one would have known that from his face.

He was recalling that there had been a lot of good meat left on the lunchtime roast chicken. In particular, he was savouring an enticing mental picture of a plump chicken leg, still in place on the bird.

Three hours had elapsed since lunch, and there were three more to get through before dinner. His gastric juices, seldom idle, were starting to make their presence felt. It was time for a snack. He remembered that there were a few cold sausages as well.

He walked through the kitchen, opened the door of the spacious larder, and marched in. And then he let out a howl of rage.

A figure was already there, standing in front of the marble

shelf, cutting off a slice of chicken breast with a sharp knife: a small piece, whose absence he hoped would not be noticed.

Hearing the door opening behind him, the boy swung round, his face a mixture of terror and disbelief. This was a time when the kitchen area should normally be deserted.

Frankel grasped him by the front of his shirt, hoisted him off the ground and began shaking him violently, berating him as he did so.

'You scoundrel!' he thundered. 'Wicked little thief! Vile wretch! How dare you!'

'I'm sorry! It was only a little bit ... I'm sorry!' was all the frightened lad could say, as he was jerked about in the big man's grasp. There was no excuse he could think of.

His words only inflamed his master further.

'I'm sorry, *sir*!' he shouted into the boy's ear. 'You'll be a lot sorrier before this day is over! And don't you ever speak to me again without saying "sir"!'

Then Frankel released his grip and, as his victim tottered on his feet, dealt him a fierce blow to the side of his head with a swing of his huge hand. The boy crashed to the floor. For a moment he showed a brief surge of defiance and reached out for his knife, which he'd dropped when his assailant first seized him.

Frankel saw the movement immediately, having already glimpsed the gleam in the boy's eyes. He brought a heavy boot smashing down on the outstretched hand, and the boy let out an animal cry of pain. Frankel kicked the knife away, and the boy lay there trembling. The doctor shook his fist at him.

'Go for your knife, would you, you cur!' he roared. 'So! You'd be a murderer as well as a thief!'

'I'm not a thief,' mumbled the boy.

'Not a thief? Not a thief? Then why are you meddling with this chicken? Why are you in here? You know full well you are allowed in the kitchen only when you're working. And you should never come in this larder at all! Never! You know that! And now I catch you in here, putting your filthy hands on the meat! How dare you?'

The boy said nothing. He was fighting back tears.

'Answer me, you blackguard!' Frankel bent forward to fix his prey with a savage glare. 'Why do you disobey me?'

A few words came out painfully. 'I was hungry ... sir.'

'Hungry? You're not hungry, you're greedy! You cannot be hungry, when you are given two meals every day! Good meals, better than you ever had before I brought you here!'

The boy didn't argue. It would have been unwise to protest that the black bread, bought in bulk, could scarcely be called a good meal. It was usually stale, often mouldy, and could only be consumed after immersion in the thin grey soup which was the other component in his diet. Occasionally, there would also be some poor-quality fruit, sold cheap because it was bruised or squashed. The doctor didn't want scurvy in his household.

Frankel went back to the door and bellowed orders in a voice that would have brought down the walls of Jericho.

'Stone! Prosser! Come here at once! In the larder! Now!'

He came back, picked up the knife, and put it in his pocket. Then he glowered down at the quivering youngster.

'You evil, ungrateful little tyke! I rescued you from the streets of Kentish Town! Living rough with a pack of urchins! No doubt the unwanted child of some whore! I've fed you, given you a roof over your head and a dry bed to sleep in! And this is how you repay me!'

Again, the boy sensibly refrained from contradicting his furious master. He did not assert that the dirty old mattress on the floor of the attic, with its stuffing spilling out, was not the best sort of bed to sleep in. Nor did he point out that the roof over his head leaked when it rained and let in a draught when the wind blew. The experience of being taken to the bedroom of one of the men was never pleasant but, on stormy nights, it was almost a relief.

Now he was prudent enough to lie still where he was. Had he got up he would have been an easy target for further blows.

The lightly built Stone responded to Frankel's summons more swiftly than the lumbering Prosser. He quickly took in the scene: the boy cowering on the floor and his employer, red-faced and white-knuckled, standing over him. Stone's sympathy was not with the victim.

'Has this young lout been up to mischief, sir?' he enquired.

'Not just mischief, wickedness!' Frankel declared. 'I found him stealing food, on top of which he was insolent! And then he made to attack me with his knife!'

'With respect, sir, I did warn you that this one was a rogue, always likely to create trouble. There's bad blood there. We were better off with the red-haired boy.'

'Never mind your fancy tastes! This boy is with us now, and we must teach him how to behave! He will soon learn.'

Now Prosser had arrived and was silently awaiting instructions. Frankel soon delivered them.

'This young knave has been stealing, abusing our hospitality. He will be fined five shillings. And he's to be locked in the coal house for forty-eight hours, with nothing but bread and water. And only the rats for company! He will be able to reflect on the consequences of disobedience.'

Stone seemed a little disappointed.

'Is that sufficient punishment?' he queried.

'By no means,' said Frankel. 'Each night at ten I shall give him a good thrashing. He will have all day to look forward to it.'

For a few seconds the secretary's features were slightly stirred by the hint of a crooked smile.

7

EVENTS ON THE Highgate Road were old Mrs Burnaby's main source of daily entertainment. Her flat above the Hill Top Cafe faced squarely on to the street and, sitting in her chair by the window, she could spend all day surveying the scene.

At night, Highgate Road could be bleak and lonely, the gas-lit street lamps casting long shadows, but in daylight hours all was hustle and bustle. Hansom cabs taking businessmen to the City passed in the opposite direction to elegant carriages delivering the gentry to stately Kenwood House. Riders trotted their horses on their way to canter on the Heath. Pedestrians ambled to and from the Highgate Village shops, or headed west towards Jack Straw's Castle, one of London's more magnificent public houses. On a fine day some of the strollers would stop to gossip with friends, or to buy hot chestnuts from the man with the brazier.

Mrs Burnaby was used to the sight of adventurous youths risking their necks on ill-controlled bicycles: indeed, last week she had even seen one of the dangerous new horseless carriages spluttering past.

And, of course, the houses on the other side of the road were a modest source of interest too. A little further west she could spy the small forecourt and front gate of Dunblane, from which various men emerged at different times of day. There was a large, lumbering man in a heavy cloak and dark, broad-brimmed homburg hat. He was carrying a black bag. Mrs Burnaby had heard he was a doctor but he didn't seem very caring. Several times she had seen him barge into other people and then walk on without stopping. From the same house there sometimes came a short, busy man in a smart overcoat and bowler hat, who often had a brief-case. Occasionally there was a more shabbily dressed fellow, in cloth cap and muffler, often accompanied by a boy. There were also random male callers, whom she saw once and never again. There seemed to be no women at Dunblane.

By contrast, there appeared to be several women living at Hillside, the house directly opposite. Indeed, Mrs Burnaby had decided that there was only one man there, who must be master of the house. This was a neat, prosperous-looking man, of middle height and middle years. She saw him leave home at 7.30 every morning and march off energetically towards Highgate Station.

Later on, three ladies could be glimpsed individually leaving Hillside and returning at different times of day. Two were young and nimble, the third older and more sedate. She usually carried a shopping basket.

What currently intrigued Mrs Burnaby was the conduct of two workmen in blue overalls, who'd been admitted to Hillside three days ago, in the middle of the afternoon, and had stayed little more than an hour. They hadn't arrived yesterday or the day before, but they'd appeared again this afternoon.

'What sort of workmen worked only two days a week,' Mrs Burnaby asked herself, 'and then stayed only an hour?' Why were they privileged to use the front door, instead of the tradesman's entrance? And why did one of the workmen carry a silver-knobbed walking stick?

All these things were giving Mrs Burnaby food for thought that afternoon.

'You've found Luke Scully?' Clare Austin's voice was firm, betraying no strong feeling, just polite interest. But, as before, Steele felt there was an undercurrent of emotion that the young woman was working hard to conceal.

He and Mason had discussed this before they came back to Hillside. Both sensed that there may have been some sort of friendship between the repressed and disfigured spinster and the womanizing rogue who, two years ago, must still have been virile and raffish.

Scully was now excluded from their inquiries so the two men agreed that there was no point in discussing the matter further. Revealing full details of Scully's current situation would surely distress Clare Austin unnecessarily. They had resolved to dismiss the subject as quickly and lightly as possible.

'Yes,' said Steele. 'We found him living in Lambeth. He was able to prove that he hasn't been north of the Thames for six months. And, alas, he wasn't able to tell us anything useful.'

'A pity,' said Clare. And then there was a moment's silence.

'He spoke very warmly of you, Miss Austin,' said Mason. 'He said you were the only kind member of this household.'

'He was not well treated by my father. I tried to show him some courtesy.' Then the young woman's voice became brisk and businesslike. 'So that avenue has come to a dead end.'

'I'm afraid so,' said Steele. 'However, we have many other areas to explore.'

'Has the American professor got to work yet?' Clare Austin seemed intrigued by this topic.

'Yes. He managed to catch the next boat, and is now installed in an office at Scotland Yard, using up a great deal of paper and ink. He has four clerks on call to supply every conceivable detail of the Heath crimes and carry out errands for him.'

'Four clerks?'

'One for each murder. He likes to be thorough.'

'A thorough nuisance,' Mason interpolated.

'As I told you, he aims to create what he calls "a profile" of the Heath Maniac, so that he can tell the police what sort of person they should be looking for.'

'Has he made any progress?'

'Oh yes.' Steele allowed himself a wry smile. 'He's already reported that the killer is physically strong, but may be mentally unstable.'

'Which the office boy could have told him in two minutes,' Mason observed drily.

'He thinks the Maniac may be a basically pathetic individual, incapable of normal relationships. In fact,' Steele continued, 'he did draw up an initial profile. He told the Scotland Yard boys that the culprit would turn out to be an ugly, inadequate man, with a quick temper and irrational habits.'

'So that's what they'll be looking for?'

Mason came in with a quick reply. 'No. They've already found him.'

'They've found him?'

'He came walking down the corridor. They realized it was an exact description of the assistant commissioner.'

For the first time in their presence, Clare laughed, a small, gentle laugh but genuine laughter nevertheless.

'A slight distortion of the facts,' Steele corrected. 'As you'll have gathered, my colleague has little faith in those theoretical studies.'

'That's true enough,' said Mason. 'In my opinion, Professor Kane is a great waste of time and resources.'

'Hmm.' Clare was thoughtful. 'And what is your opinion, Major?'

'I am rather more open-minded,' said Steele. 'The study of the human mind is still in its earliest stages. Eventually, it may be a useful tool in crime detection. There is a doctor in Vienna who is developing mental research into a science, like medicine.'

Clare's reply surprised him.

'Yes,' she said. 'I've read about Sigmund Freud. His work is very exciting.'

'It certainly has possibilities,' the major agreed. 'Perhaps one day scientists may be able to predict human behaviour, possibly even to change it. In the meantime, Professor Kane's work gives the bigwigs at Scotland Yard something to chatter about.'

'There are more practical possibilities, aren't there, sir?' said Mason with a touch of impatience. 'Are we allowed to talk about Strauss?'

'Certainly,' said Steele. 'We need to get more people looking out for him.'

'Who is Strauss?' asked Clare.

'A criminal lunatic,' said Steele. 'And a very dangerous one. He's able to conceal his darker side most of the time and appear entirely normal. But he can fly into homicidal rages without warning. He was convicted six years ago of killing a business colleague who'd made a joke at his expense.'

'A business colleague? He's a businessman?'

'Oh yes. Intelligent. Good appearance, we're told. He was an executive with a pharmaceutical company. It turned out he'd done two previous murders and got away with them. He was found Guilty But Insane, and sent to Broadmoor. Two years ago he escaped.'

'And he's still at large?'

'At large and undetected. There was a possible sighting

in Dover, shortly after his escape, and it was thought he fled abroad. But eighteen months ago an acquaintance thought he saw Strauss in a Hampstead street. It was just a glimpse through the window of a moving cab but it led to a big search. This failed to find him, so the hunt lapsed. Now it's on again, because of the Heath murders. All policemen are carrying his description, and an artist's sketch of the man.'

'Truly, the world is a dangerous place,' said Clare with a sigh. 'Are there any other lines of inquiry?'

'There are many. As always with these sensational crimes, Scotland Yard gets scores of letters from imbeciles claiming to be the killer and taunting the police. They come from idiots but they all have to be followed up.'

'How tedious. Are you gentlemen involved in that process?'

'Fortunately not. Mr Mason and I continue our own investigation. As you know, we are interviewing all members of the Heath Association.'

'Do you learn anything useful, Major?'

'We never know if anything's useful or not until we've researched it, Miss Austin. For instance, Sir Charles Greenwell told us that his butler left on bad terms last year, after a fight with one of the gardeners. Now we are trying to trace the man.'

'Have you talked to Commander West yet?'

'Yes, I think you can say we talked to him. Actually, we mainly listened.' Steele smiled at the memory. 'He is a man of very strong opinions.'

'Ah yes. Commander West is our local firebrand.'

'He's certainly fiery. We saw him at nine in the morning, and already he was red in the face and thumping the table.'

'I think he puts pepper on his porridge,' said Mason.

Steele continued. 'He proposes that all local residents should be provided with guns, so they can walk freely on the Heath and shoot anyone who looks suspicious.'

'Although I'm sure he'd prefer the Maniac to be taken alive, so he can be hanged on Highgate Hill,' Mason added.

'We had to warn him about taking the law into his own hands,' said Steele.

'Did you?' For the second time, Clare seemed amused. 'How did he take that?'

Steele chuckled. 'How would you put it, Jack?'

'I'd say he took it like an angry bulldog having his bone snatched away. He said he'd do what he damn well liked.' Mason checked himself. 'Oh. Forgive the language, Miss Austin.'

'Of course,' said Clare. 'I'm sure you spared me the worst. Whom have you yet to see?'

Mason was the one with the diary in his hand. 'We have an appointment with Dr Frankel at 4.30 this afternoon.'

The young woman looked dubious. 'Dr Frankel? I don't think you'll find him very co-operative.'

'We shall do our best with him,' said Steele. 'In that connection, we have to ask you a favour.'

'You know I'll do anything I can, Major.'

'It would be unwise, I think, to appear at Dr Frankel's in our plumbers' outfits. We have our normal clothes with us.' Steele indicated the toolbags on the floor. 'May we have the use of a room to change in?'

'Of course.' Clare Austin smiled again. 'We must find you a place where Mrs Butters won't come upon you. She might not survive the shock. Use the conservatory here, and I will stand guard outside the door.'

'Thank you,' said Steele. And then a thought struck him. 'Did you encounter the Greenwells' butler at any time, Miss Austin? His name's McDonald.'

'No,' said Clare. 'We don't tend to hobnob with the local aristocracy. We're regarded as trade, you know. But Luke Scully sometimes mentioned the man. I believe that he too had quarrelled with him. An unpleasant person, apparently. Servile to his masters, and a bully to his peers.'

'Hmm,' said Steele. 'Not so servile at the end, it seems. Sir Charles says he went off swearing and shouting threats. I think we must talk to McDonald sooner rather than later.'

'I've put the word around the local pubs,' said Mason.

'True devotion to duty,' Steele observed. 'We must also mention this to George Willoughby. Get the police on the job.' He sighed. 'I'm afraid this investigation has a long way to go. But we shall get our man in the end.'

And then the hall door was thrown open, and Mrs Butters came rushing in without knocking. She was breathless with excitement and waving a newspaper.

'They've got him!' she cried. 'They've got him!'

'What is it, Mrs Butters?' Clare demanded, a little frostily. 'What are you trying to tell us?'

Mrs Butters checked herself, suddenly abashed at her unseemly behaviour.

'Oh. Sorry. Excuse me protruding, Miss Clare. I couldn't wait to tell you. The evening paper's just come. They've caught the Heath Maniac! It's in the late news bit!'

Apparently at a loss for further words, she thrust the newspaper forward. Mason took it and read out the blotchy words hastily printed in the Stop Press column.

'"A man, believed to be the Heath Maniac, was rescued by police from an angry crowd in Camden Town this morning. He was arrested and taken to Camden Town police station. More details in next edition."'

8

'Is there anything more I can get you?' asked the waitress, and Mason thought he saw a twinkle in her eye.

Thus encouraged, he said, 'Yes, love. I reckon you could get me excited. But I've got a wife waiting at home, so I'd better settle for another toasted teacake. Plenty of butter, please.'

The waitress moved off, not displeased, and Steele said, 'Is that wise? You had three biscuits with your coffee at the Austins'.'

'Got to keep my strength up, guv'nor. I don't suppose this Frankel will offer us anything.'

'I'm sure you're right about that.' Steele drank some tea and looked at his watch.

The detectives were back in the Hill Top Cafe, waiting until it was time for their visit to Dunblane.

Clare Austin had urged them to stay on at Hillside but Steele preferred not to be seen leaving the Austin house and going straight to Dr Frankel's. He was convinced that someone at Dunblane kept a close eye on local activity.

Also, they needed some quiet time to consider the startling news they had just heard. At Hillside all was chatter and excitement. Mrs Butters had found more words and was distributing them generously. Harriet, too, was jubilant with relief.

Only Clare had managed to remain calm, almost as if the Heath Maniac was a side issue. Her main concern seemed to be that the detectives should continue probing her father's affairs. Steele had assured her that they would.

Now, over a pot of tea, and back in their normal clothes, the men were considering their position.

'Are you sure we should go ahead with the Frankel call?' asked Mason. 'I mean, now that things have changed? It looks like the hunt is over, doesn't it?'

Steele was unequivocal. 'We should most certainly stick to our plans,' he said. 'I'm very keen to speak to a doctor who is not on the list of London GPs but who regularly prescribes strong sedatives to a young girl, especially one who appears to have nothing basically wrong with her.'

'But we're going there to discuss the Heath Maniac. Will he answer questions about himself?'

Steele smiled. 'Come, Jack, we're experts at learning about certain things while apparently talking about something else. And we've always managed to extract information from people who thought they weren't co-operating. It's part of the challenge.'

Mason grinned. 'You're thinking of the man at the Foreign Office.'

'Amongst others, yes. He certainly gave us a good account of Middle East policy while thinking he was being questioned about his foreign travels. Anyway, we must definitely call on Dr Frankel. Apart from anything else, I don't think things have changed.'

Mason peered into the other man's eyes. 'You don't believe the Maniac's been caught, do you?'

'I think it's very unlikely. I didn't want to spoil the rejoicing at the Austins' just now but I've a feeling in my bones that this is too sudden. When we spoke to George Willoughby yesterday, he didn't say they were following any new leads.

If there'd been a serious suspect, he'd have known. And, if there'd been an arrest today, he'd have got a message to us by now.'

'You think the local police have made a mistake?'

'Or the paper got it wrong. Both things have happened before. Until someone's been charged, we continue our investigation.'

The waitress brought Mason's second teacake. 'It's got extra butter,' she announced.

'Ta,' said Mason. 'That looks almost as tasty as you do.'

'You're very cheeky,' said the waitress, but as she moved off she was smiling.

'I wish you'd refrain from vulgar badinage when we're working together,' Steele observed mildly. 'I think we should maintain a little dignity.'

'Sorry, guv'nor,' said his assistant. 'I thought she might be a useful contact; she must know everything that goes on around here. I was just softening her up.'

'Ah. Was that it?' said Steele, without much conviction.

Mason returned to the main topic. 'The thing is, will Frankel see us, now everyone thinks the Maniac's been caught?'

'He may not know yet. Not everyone has an evening paper delivered. If he does know, we shall say we still need background information, to help the police bring their charges.'

The cost of the extra teacake had turned Mason's mind to fiscal matters. 'There's another point. If the Heath Association reckon the job's done, they won't want to pay us any more.'

'It seems you didn't read the contract, Jack. They pay our fees until the culprit is convicted.'

'Let's hope for a long trial, then.'

'Don't be mercenary. The government bonus for the Portsmouth job will keep you in beer and baccy for a good while yet. Personally, I'm not letting go of this case till the real Heath Maniac is on his way to the gallows.'

'All right, guv'nor. Point taken.'

'Furthermore, I shan't rest till Meredith Austin's schemes have been scotched.' Steele swallowed the last of his tea. 'That's another thing. Frankel may let slip something about his crony. Oh yes,' he concluded, 'I think an interview with the bad doctor is essential.'

Dunblane was separated from the Highgate Road by a space that may once have been a front garden. But now there was no trace of greenery: the entire surface was paved with slabs of tombstone grey.

Between heavy brown drapes, net curtains shrouded the front windows, and both men had the feeling that there was a presence behind the net: a person watching their approach. Somewhere at the back of the house a dog began barking in a sharp, aggressive way.

A thick iron ring hung in the middle of the front door. Mason rapped it twice on the dark plate beneath, with only moderate force. But with such a heavy knocker it was hard not to sound aggressive.

The dog's barking became fiercer. Then it seemed the hound was being restrained, its noise reduced to a low grumbling, and then to silence. Mason could not help wondering if it had been thrown a human limb to munch.

After a short delay the door was opened by a tall man with close-cropped hair and a hostile expression. He looked at the detectives but said nothing.

Steele's manner was affable. 'Good afternoon. Major Steele and Mr Mason to see Dr Frankel by appointment.' He handed over their card.

Still without speaking, the man opened the door wide for them to enter and, as they did so, Charles Stone came walking briskly down the hall.

'All right, Prosser,' he said. 'The Heath Association requires Dr Frankel to see these men. I'll take them to the laboratory. Come there in fifteen minutes to escort them out.'

The silent servant handed back Steele's card, and then melted away into one of the downstairs rooms. Both detectives felt an inward glow of relief. Clearly, news of the alleged Maniac's arrest had not yet reached Dunblane.

'Come this way,' said Stone, a command rather than an invitation. He led the detectives up four flights of stairs to the second-floor landing, where he knocked on a door.

'Come,' said a voice.

Stone opened the door and the three went in.

'The Heath Association's inquiry agents,' the secretary announced. 'Have you time to see them now?'

On the far side of the room, by the window, the large, heavy man in a white overall was mixing things in an earthenware dish. He spoke over his shoulder, in a deep peremptory voice, with a hint of some European accent.

'As well now as later,' he said. 'Better to get it over and done with. Come back for them in ten minutes.'

The secretary left, and Dr Frankel turned to face the visitors. He said nothing.

The business card was still in Steele's hand. He gave it to Frankel, who put it down on a workbench without looking at it. He remained silent.

'As you know,' said Steele, 'we have been asked to look into the atrocious crimes recently committed on the Heath. As part of our investigations—'

Frankel cut him short. 'If you have legitimate questions for me, you must put them quickly. I am in the middle of an experiment.'

Still striving to be genial, Steele smiled. 'Ah yes, of course. We realize you're a busy man. I believe you are engaged on research.'

'Yes.'

'Very interesting. May I ask in what area?'

'No.'

There was complete silence for a moment. The man in the white coat stood motionless and impassive, his arms folded across his chest.

Steele ignored the affront. 'I see. No doubt it's confidential. Work for the government, perhaps?'

There was no response, so he tried a new tack. 'We think the murderer may be seeking revenge on one or all of the Heath dwellers, by disrupting their lives and creating a climate of fear. So we are learning all we can about local residents. I believe you have lived here for only eighteen months?'

'Nineteen.'

'And prior to that, you were conducting your research elsewhere?'

'My life before I came here has no relevance to your inquiries.'

Steele bit his lip. His failure to dent this brick wall was making his boasts in the cafe sound hollow, and he suspected that Mason was chuckling inwardly. But he pressed on. 'It might be relevant, Doctor, if you acquired an enemy in previous years.'

'I am a man of science. I cannot waste my time on trivial speculation.'

'Very well. If we must confine ourselves to the basic issue, have you any theory about the Heath murders?'

'A lunatic. It is time the police caught him. Then he must be hanged.'

Frankel's words were familiar, and Steele recalled that Meredith Austin had said almost exactly the same thing. He continued doggedly.

'Dr Frankel, I believe you cross the Heath frequently on the way to your club with Mr Austin. Have you ever noticed any suspicious or unusual behaviour?'

'No. At this time of year it is dark when I go to my club.'

'Have you ever felt threatened?'

'Only by people seeking to distract me from my work with stupid questions.'

Steele swallowed hard, then took a deep breath and tried again. 'Have you ever had occasion to—'

He was interrupted by a sharp knock on the door, which brought an instant shout of 'Come!' from Dr Frankel. Charles Stone hurried in.

'Dr Frankel, the Heath Maniac has been arrested. Prosser heard the news at the butcher's, and he got hold of an evening paper which confirms it.'

Frankel showed no emotion. 'Good,' he said. 'Then the matter is closed. I am not obliged to give these men any more of my time. You can show them out now.'

Steele was not giving up easily. 'Even if the Maniac has been caught, a case will have to be built up. It would help if—'

'I have helped you enough. You must go.'

'Dr Frankel, we need to know if—'

'You need to know nothing. Stone, if these men do not leave immediately, tell Prosser to bring the dog.'

Prosser was still wordless, as he closed the front door behind them.

Mason, on the other hand, could not resist a comment. 'My word, guv'nor! It's remarkable how you manage to extract information from people who think they're not co-operating.'

Steele was unperturbed. 'The interview wasn't wasted. Did you notice that Frankel is left handed?'

'I did, guv'nor. Also he has a scar on his right wrist.'

'Well done. Two things that might be useful if we have to trace his past life, which I rather think we might.'

As the detectives walked down the path, a man who had been approaching along the Highgate Road opened the front gate and turned in. His eyes met Steele's, and there was surprise and recognition on both sides.

'Well, well,' said Steele. 'Tommy Slaughter.'

The newcomer was middle-aged, well built, in a check suit, grey overcoat and felt hat. 'Yeah,' he said, and his craggy features registered unease. 'Have we met?'

'Indeed we have,' said Steele. 'At the National Sporting Club. And at various racetracks around the country. And in another place, as well.' He paused a moment to study the effect of his last phrase: more unease. Then he continued. 'I'm Henry Steele.' He fixed Slaughter with a steady gaze, which brooked no denial.

'Oh yeah,' said Slaughter. 'Inquiry agent, aren't you? What brings you here?'

'We have some business with Dr Frankel. As no doubt you have.'

'Yeah.' Slaughter looked at his watch. 'Better not keep him waiting, eh?' He knocked at the front door, which this time was opened quickly. Prosser had been observing events through the front window. As before, he said nothing. Slaughter evidently didn't need to introduce himself: he walked straight in and Prosser closed the door behind him.

'Not very chatty, is he?' Mason observed. 'He and Frankel should get on well. Like a monks' night out.'

'I don't think Slaughter was pleased to see us. He's allergic to people connected with the law.'

'I think I remember him now. Some sort of dealer, isn't he?'

'Sometimes. Also racehorse trainer. Unlicensed bookmaker. And occasional boxing promoter. Allegedly involved with one of the Brighton race gangs.'

'Oh yes,' said Mason. 'I've got him now. Wasn't he a witness at the Boscombe fraud trial?'

'He was. By a strange quirk of the legal system. By rights, he should have been in the dock.' Steele was pondering as they walked off down the road. 'Now, I wonder what connection the unscrupulous Mr Slaughter has with the unspeakable Dr Frankel?'

The curiosity was mutual but, in Slaughter's case, it was mixed with anxiety.

'What were them two narks doing here?' he demanded. 'Did you know they're the law?'

Frankel was a little more communicative when talking to clients, but no less cold. Obviously, Slaughter was not someone he regarded as a friend.

'They are private detectives, hired by local busybodies to help our bungling police catch the Heath Maniac. I was required to see them.'

'Your flunkey says they're often in this neighbourhood.'

'They've been spending time at the house next door. It seems they're interested in my neighbour. Don't worry, they're as incompetent as the police.'

'Don't kid yourself – those two aren't incompetent! That bleeding Steele is as sharp as a ferret down a rat-hole! And just as dangerous! He spotted me straight off just now.'

'You're known to him, are you?'

'Yeah. And his mate. They wrecked a nice little jig of mine a few years back. Earning me good money, that was, till those two got on to it. The rozzers would never have sussed. Those two bastards got my pal sent down for two years.'

'Perhaps he was careless.'

'Well, I'm not. I got to think what to do about that pair.'

'Now the Maniac's been caught, they shouldn't be coming this way any more.'

'Don't you believe it! I could see that bastard's mind working when he saw me, wondering what I was doing here.

You shouldn't have made me show up.'

'I cannot talk business with underlings. And, speaking of business, we have financial matters to discuss. I take it you want our arrangement to continue?'

'Of course I do. And so do you. We're both doing well out of it. But not if those two vultures are going to be on my back.' Slaughter thought for a moment. 'Where's his business, that Steele? I might have a few friends call on him. Where's he live?'

'I have no idea. They are of no interest to me.'

'Well, they should be. If they make trouble for me, they'll make trouble for you.'

Then Frankel remembered. 'Ah. The man gave me his card.' The big man picked up the card and gave it to Slaughter. 'This should tell you what you want to know. And now perhaps we can talk business.'

They did, and ten minutes later reached an agreement that was beneficial to each of them, though not to various unsuspecting citizens.

When the business was concluded and Frankel was slightly more amenable, Slaughter asked him for more details about Steele and the Heath Association.

Harriet Austin stood by the window, contemplating a fine early-winter night. She was in a melancholy mood, thoughts of Robert Kemp constantly intruding on her reverie: he had loved the prospect that now spread out before her. Yet it was here that he had met a brutal death. And then there was Ella. Was she lost somewhere out there, facing cold and starvation?

Behind her, Clare was busy at the bookshelves, peering at titles, trying to find what she needed. Some of the volumes were in poor condition, their covers torn or missing, and she had to remove these and study them closely.

Harriet pulled herself together, determined to be positive. 'It's a beautiful night, Clare,' she said. 'One can see the lights of Holborn twinkling in the distance.'

Clare continued her search. 'I would expect that, Harriet. It's what lights are supposed to do.'

'And the moonlight stretches right across the Heath. It's almost as bright as day.'

'Not good for wildlife. There'll be no hiding from predators.'

Harriet sighed, her effort at cheerfulness deflated. 'How sad it is that beauty is so often mixed with cruelty.'

'I fear that is part of life, dear sister. Have you seen Hawthorne's *Nature Walks of London* anywhere?'

'No. I'm afraid I didn't know we had such a book.'

'Of course we have. Unless someone's taken it. Hawthorne gives a good account of Hampstead Heath in the last century.'

'Oh. I should like to read that.'

'I shall pass it on to you when I've finished with it. If I find it.'

'Thank you.' Harriet was admiring the evening star, which Robert had taught her to identify.

'I can't think where it's got to. I need some facts for a piece I'm writing. The Heath was a wilder place a hundred years ago.'

'I suppose it would be. Wilder, no doubt, but at least there was no murdering maniac at large. What a shame the police were wrong about that man yesterday. I really thought the danger was over.'

'Did you? I can't say I did. And I could see Major Steele was not convinced. It's pathetic that the police should make such a mistake! A drunken braggart telling lies in an alehouse!'

'I suppose they had to arrest him to find out the truth.'

'Perhaps. But why release the news to the press? They should have known the papers would blazon the story as if it were fact.'

'Is it certain the man was lying?'

'Apparently. When questioned, he got the details wrong. And it was proved he was in Birmingham when the man Tate was killed. So they let him go.'

'And left us all as frightened as ever.'

'There's no sense in being frightened, Harriet. We have to get on with our lives. "The coward dies a thousand deaths, the brave man dies but one."'

9

SINCE HIS WIFE'S death, Steele had lived in a serviced flat in St John's Wood. This suited his lifestyle. He wasn't troubled by domestic tasks – cleaning and maintenance were all taken care of – and meals were always available in the restaurant. In fact, in good military fashion, the major brewed tea and coffee for himself in his tiny kitchen. He even grilled his own breakfast toast. (Though he was sometimes grateful for one of life's more benign coincidences: that, when the milk boils over, it often extinguishes the burning toast.) Apart from that, Steele usually dined, and occasionally lunched, at his club.

The main assets of the apartment were a pleasant bedroom overlooking Regent's Park, and a neat but spacious sitting room, which he used as his office. Not officially, for this was a residential building, with no business or trading allowed, so there was no plate outside his door. But it was here that Mason joined him each morning and it was here that their files and records were housed, and where they sat down to plan their work. The manager of the block, an old army friend, turned a blind eye.

Steele's arrangements would seem satisfactory to most people, but one individual disapproved. John Mason's wife, a motherly soul, felt that no man should be allowed to live on his own, since the male sex were incapable of looking after themselves.

Steele kept himself fit with an active life and regular exercise, notably a weekly session of real tennis at Lord's. He carried no surplus flesh but his lean face and slim body were interpreted by Emily Mason as signs of under-nourishment.

So, apart from urging her husband to persuade his colleague to find a second wife, she loaded him with wholesome supplements to augment the major's diet. These would vary from scones to rice puddings to rock cakes with, as a special treat, an occasional steak and kidney pie.

Most of these were well received, since the two men shared the spoils and both were hearty eaters. Some were less welcome: indeed, the rice puddings tended to finish up with the cat from the next apartment.

Today's offering was a big success. Mason arrived bearing a cardboard box containing a cream sponge cake that both men fancied. But they agreed to resist temptation until the mid-morning coffee break. There was work to be done.

They began by noting a piece in *The Times*, which confirmed that the Heath Maniac was still at large and stated that the arrest report in an evening paper had been an irresponsible error. (The evening paper was owned by a rival proprietor.) Mason again congratulated Steele on his perspicacity and Steele graciously refrained from saying 'I told you so'.

Then they turned to studying a letter from their contact at Scotland Yard, which had arrived in the seven o'clock post. George Willoughby said that Surrey police had found Dan Croucher and were questioning him at length about what he'd seen on the Thames all those years ago. He'd been told he wouldn't be charged with poaching and he was talking freely, obviously keen to ingratiate himself with the law. He'd said that he'd seen a man push a woman off a boat and then punt away from her.

This seemed damning enough, but Willoughby cautioned that a court would be unlikely to accept Croucher as a reliable witness. However, the police were taking the matter very seriously, and would interview Austin once they'd assessed the evidence.

Steele smiled. 'I think Meredith Austin's villainies will soon be brought to an end. Even if he's not charged over his wife's death, the illegal activities we've learned of from Jamieson should be enough to get him locked up. We'll send the file to Willoughby once we have Randall's report.'

'Let's pray he's put away before he succeeds in driving his poor daughter out of her mind.' Mason spoke with unusual fervour. 'And before the evil Dr Frankel can poison her for him.'

'Indeed. And that's another evil man who'll soon be brought to book. I'm not sure if irresponsibly prescribing excessive drugs is a criminal offence, but I plan to have a word with Archie Lennox at the club tonight.'

'Archie Lennox?'

'He's on the General Medical Council. He'll know how to proceed. And we must also mention Frankel's activities to George Willoughby.'

'Poor George. He was hoping we'd help solve the Heath Murders. Instead, we just keep dumping fresh problems on his desk.'

'Well, I don't think he's best pleased but he's a good copper, he'll always do his duty. Besides, we're not idle on the main job. We talk to more Heath residents tomorrow, I think.'

'Yes. The Aspinalls in Highgate Close.'

There was a little click from the hall, as the eleven o'clock post came through the letter box and landed on the mat. Mason fetched it and brought it to the sitting-room table.

There was a bill, which Steele moved to the bottom of the

pile. There was a thick foolscap envelope, which he hoped would be a report from their accountant, Giles Randall. And, intriguingly, there was a small, cheap brown envelope addressed to Major Steele in clumsy capital letters, written in pencil by a childish hand. Both men peered at it. Mason was the first to speak.

'What d'you make of this, guv'nor? A child or a crank? Or an idiot?'

Steele considered for a moment longer before giving his opinion. 'None of those, I think. This is a person bright enough to find this address, which is not widely known. Cranks usually write to us care of Scotland Yard, don't they?' He picked up his thin ivory paper-knife. 'Well, let's see, shall we?'

He slit the envelope open, and drew out a sheet of inferior paper, lined, as if torn from a school exercise book. He held this flat on the table so that both men could read the words, which were written in the same scrawl as the envelope.

THEY SAY YOU BEEN PAYD TO CACH THE HEATH MAINAIC. I CAN HELP YOU. I SAW HIM KILL TATE. COME TO THE VALE OF HEALTH THURSDAY 5 O'CLOCK. WARE A FLOWER ON YOUR COAT SO I NOW YOU. WAIT BY THE ROYAL OAK. BRING TWENTY POUNDS. NO COPPERS.

'That makes sense,' Mason observed. 'Twenty pounds in coppers would be far too bulky.' He enjoyed his little joke.

'Interesting,' said Steele. 'He can't spell "paid" or "wear", but he can spell "wait" and "coat". Full stops in the right places. This is a person with a little education pretending to be illiterate.'

'D'you think it's a hoax?'

'Well, it's not what it purports to be, I'm sure. But I believe someone knows something and wants to tell us, without giving himself away. It's the sort of ruse Austin or Greenwell, or even Frankel, might use if they wanted us to know something, but couldn't speak openly for some reason.'

'But we'd recognize them when they came to the rendez-vous.'

'If it is someone we know, he probably won't come in person. He'll send a hired hand, or a deputy, with a message.'

'I suppose you're right. That's why you have to wear the flower.'

'Anyway, we can't ignore this, it's our only positive lead at present.' Steele pondered. 'Thursday, that's tomorrow, isn't it? What time are we due at the Aspinalls?'

'Three o'clock.'

'That fits. We can walk to the Vale of Health when we leave Highgate Close. There's nothing to lose.'

'Except our lives, of course. It could be a trap.'

Steele snorted. 'Jack, you and I have coped with more traps than a plumber's mate. Still, I'll ask George Willoughby to have some plain-clothed officers close by the Royal Oak just in case.' He looked at his watch. 'Eleven-fifteen. I'll make the coffee. You put the cake on a plate and fetch a knife.'

'Right, guv'nor.' Mason rose with alacrity. Then a thought struck him. 'Perhaps you should take a slice to Mr Willoughby when you go to the Yard this afternoon. Cheer him up a bit.'

Clare came briskly into the room and made straight for the bookshelves as usual. She seemed less on edge this evening, immediately finding the volume she wanted and taking it out.

Harriet put down her embroidery and looked up at her sister. 'Ah, Clare. Did you ever find that book you were looking for?'

'The Hawthorne?' said Clare. 'Yes, I found it last night.'

'Where was it?'

'In the bottom drawer of Father's desk.'

Harriet gasped. 'You looked in Father's desk? You know we're forbidden to do that!'

'I had to. I'd searched everywhere else. Then it occurred to me that he might have taken the book to spite me. He knows I need it for my research. And it seems I was right.'

'Surely not. If he'd wanted to spite you, he could have destroyed it. Or thrown it out.'

'Oh well,' Clare conceded, 'perhaps he actually needed it himself, for some strange reason. Come to think of it, he had made some pencil marks on the map of Hampstead Heath.' She had taken tonight's book to a table, and was making a brief note on her pocket notepad.

'For heaven's sake, Clare! If you think Father's using that book, you must put it back at once before he misses it!'

'I shall put it back when I have extracted all the information I need. And not before.' Clare completed her note, put away the notepad, and turned to face her sister. 'And if I need more information later, I shall take it out again.'

'Clare! Please don't make him angry again! He's been calmer this week. And I'm trying to pluck up the confidence to ask him something.'

'It shouldn't be difficult for a girl to seek her father's advice. He might even feel flattered.'

'But this is such an odd question. Something Major Steele wants me to put to him.'

'I'm glad to hear you're co-operating with Major Steele. Only don't mention his name to Father.'

'Of course not. But I need to find Father in a good mood.'

'That's like hoping for a heatwave at Christmas,' Clare observed.

'No, Clare, it can happen. As long as nothing occurs to provoke him.'

'And that's like hoping for rain in the Sahara. What is it the major needs to know?'

'Believe it or not, he wants me to ask Father if he can swim! I can't imagine why.'

'Ah, I can,' said Clare, in a knowing way. 'I shan't tell you, though. It might make it harder for you to sound natural. But rest assured, there is a good reason.' Clare returned her book to the shelf and began running her fingers along the neighbouring titles.

'I fear there's little chance of my sounding natural,' Harriet lamented.

'Nonsense! You must! Just lead into it casually. Talk about bathing in the ponds. Many people do that. You could even suggest that Father might take you.'

'I hope I can find the courage.'

'Courage is always there, if you take the trouble to look for it.'

'I try, Clare. I do try. But whenever I think I've found a little, something happens to drive it away.' Harriet sighed. 'I saw that awful tramp again yesterday, staring over the wall into our garden.'

'Ah yes. Your tramp.'

'I'm sure he's up to no good.'

'It's strange, Harriet, that no one but you has ever seen this man.'

'I suppose I'm the only one with time to look out of the window. You're always working in your room, Father's out, and Mrs Butters is busy in the kitchen.'

Clare glanced at the clock on the mantelpiece. 'Not so busy this evening, I see. Dinner is already five minutes late.'

'It's hardly surprising. Mrs Butters has so much work to do.'

'That's true. The more so since Father saw fit to sack the maid. And is too mean to hire a replacement.'

Harriet paused in her work. 'Poor Daisy. I wonder what's become of her.'

'I think she went off with that young man who was always hanging around.'

'Do you? I don't think he'll be very good for her. Very surly, wasn't he?'

'Extremely. On one occasion I thought he was going to come in and set about Father. But, alas, luck was against us.'

'Oh, Clare, how can you talk like that?'

Clare felt this was a rhetorical question that needed no answer. She took a new volume from the shelf and leafed through the first few pages.

'Anyway, she's gone,' Harriet resumed. 'And now Mrs Butters has to do everything. So we shouldn't complain if meals are five minutes late.'

'It's a wonder she stays,' said Clare. 'There must be kinder employers to be found.' She decided to take the book she was holding. She closed it and began walking towards the door.

'She looked so weary at teatime,' Harriet continued. 'And, of course, she has this problem on her mind.'

Clare stopped. 'Mrs Butters has a problem?'

'We were talking the other day, while you were upstairs. Now we know the Maniac's still at large, she's back to wondering if she should confide in Major Steele. About her find.'

'What find is this?'

'Didn't I tell you at the time? Mrs Butters found a strange object in the garden shed. Behind the logs. She thinks it may be some sort of weapon. I persuaded her to tell the major, but she missed her chance. Will the detectives be coming here again?'

'I'm sure they will.'

'Also, Mrs Butters thinks Father has been prying in her room.'

'That doesn't surprise me,' said Clare.

As she turned to go, the door opened and Meredith Austin came in. He didn't smile.

'Dinner is already nine minutes late,' he declared. 'Does anyone know why?'

Clare's reply was cool. 'Harriet believes Mrs Butters is not feeling well.'

'She'll be feeling a lot worse if I have to wait much longer for my food,' said Austin.

'Excuse me,' said Clare. 'I have to take this to my room.'

She sidled neatly past her father, without making contact, and left the room, closing the door behind her.

Austin scowled. 'If that young woman spent less time scribbling and deigned to help with the housework, we might get our dinner on time.'

'Perhaps we should all do more to help,' Harriet ventured.

'Good heavens, child, I can't have you doing physical work, you're far too delicate. Your duty is to rest and improve your health. But as for that one and her foolish jottings ...' Austin exhaled contemptuously.

'Writing is important to Clare, Father.'

'And what does it earn her? Pennies! She should have sought a position as a governess, as I told her.' Austin went to the mantelpiece. 'She will come to regret defying me.' He took up the little pot that stood there, looked inside, and reacted with alarm. 'What the devil! My desk keys are missing!'

Harriet looked up and peered around. 'It's all right!' she cried. 'They're in place in your desk. In the bottom lock.'

'What? Let me see.' He stormed across to the desk and took out the keys. 'What the deuce are they doing here? I never leave keys in the lock! Damnation! Someone has been meddling at my desk!'

'I swear I have not touched anything!'

'I would never suspect you of such a thing, Harriet. But there are people who wish me harm, and are eager to spy on our affairs.' A thought struck him. 'Those infernal detectives who invaded this house last week. Were they ever alone in here?'

'I think not. I believe either Clare or Mrs Butters was always with them.'

'Hah. Not that that is much reassurance. One of them may be in league with those interfering knaves. Or, more likely, both of them.' Austin was looking in all the drawers, checking the contents. 'I shall be questioning the pair of them. And, by thunder, I'll get some answers! And from now on, these keys will stay in my pocket. It is outrageous! I am beset by rogues and traitors!' Austin's face had gone an alarming shade of red. Harriet watched him anxiously.

'Please do not upset yourself, Father. You have had so much on your mind lately. Perhaps you forgot for once and left the keys there yourself.'

'I do not forget things! Not even for once!' Austin had concluded his search, and he slammed the last drawer shut. 'Someone has removed a book I had taken from the bookshelf.' He reflected for a moment. 'And that was just two days ago. So it cannot have been the detectives.' He frowned. 'Unless they have been back here without my knowledge.'

Harriet quickly shifted the focus. 'Is anything else missing?'

'I think not. However, some things seem to have been disturbed. It is intolerable that ill-wishers should have been prying into my papers. Well, I shall get to the bottom of this in due course.'

'I'm sure there'll be an innocent explanation.' Harriet continued her attempts at conciliation. 'Is there anything I could do to help?'

Austin mopped his brow with the handkerchief from his breast pocket. Then his manner softened a little. He had seen an opportunity.

'Well … as it happens, I am reminded of a more pleasant matter that needs to be dealt with. I had thought we should do this tomorrow but there's no time like the present.'

He opened the top drawer again and took out a foolscap envelope, from which he withdrew some documents. 'Some business on your behalf.'

Harriet was surprised. 'Is it not a little late for business? I'm rather tired, and dinner must soon be ready.'

'This will take only a moment, Harriet. Simply two papers that require your signature.'

Austin could produce a certain amount of charm when required. It was this, plus his energy and strength, that had persuaded two women to marry him. Now he turned it on his daughter. He smiled and patted her hand.

'Something attempted, something done will earn a night's repose,' he reminded her. 'Let us get this job out of the way.'

'Very well, Father. What are these papers?'

'Just formalities. But they will enhance the value of your trust fund.'

'You know I do not understand these things.'

'Of course not. Why should you, when I am here to organize your affairs? Come to the desk here. You can sit in my chair.'

Harriet put down her needlework and did as she'd been told. Her father put a pen in her hand and laid the pages in front of her.

'Now, just sign here, my dear … good. And here, on the next page … well done. There, that is all the business completed.'

Austin sprinkled sand on the wet signatures from the small glass bowl on his desk. 'Your work is done, Harriet. You have earned your dinner.'

While Harriet returned to her armchair, Austin tipped the sand off the papers and into the wastepaper bin. Then he returned the documents to the envelope and put it back in the drawer. He glanced at his daughter.

'How is your embroidery progressing, my dear?'

'Oh, quite well, thank you.'

Austin sat at his desk chair and regarded Harriet with what might almost be taken for approval. She had evidently pleased him. 'You have been working at it very diligently lately,' he observed.

'It is one of the few ways in which I can pass the time.'

'That is only for a while, my dear. Once your strength is restored, you may be able to take up music again.'

With a mixture of excitement and fear, Harriet realized that this was a heaven-sent opportunity to do her duty: a chance that might not come again. Her father seemed almost friendly; at least, he was not actually scowling. And it was he who had brought up the subject of her health.

With her gaze firmly locked on to her needlework, trying to speak lightly in spite of her racing heart, Harriet took the plunge.

'I sometimes wonder if I shouldn't have a healthier activity. Something in the fresh air.'

'A sensible thought, Harriet. I might get a croquet set for the garden.'

'That would be enjoyable. But I was thinking of something a little more strenuous.'

'Strenuous?'

Harriet's mouth was going dry, but she pressed on. 'Sometimes on a summer's day the ponds on the Heath look inviting. It crossed my mind that I might take up bathing.'

'Bathing? In Highgate Ponds? Highly dangerous! You know the water is deep?'

'Yes, I have been warned of that. But I'm told they have lifeguards.'

'Common fellows! I would not want them laying hands on

my daughter. And that is what they would do, if you got into difficulties! It is unthinkable!'

'Actually, Father, I was hoping you might escort me. I expect you're a good swimmer.'

All trace of geniality left Austin in a flash.

'Then you expect wrong! I cannot swim! And, furthermore, I have no wish to. If God had intended man to swim, he'd have given us fins. Put this foolish idea out of your mind, my girl! It is out of the question.'

Harriet felt crushed, and astonished by the violence of his reaction. But she was also a little proud: she had an answer for Major Steele. She hoped he would realize what it had cost her.

As Harriet bent over her embroidery again, Austin rose from his chair and began pacing up and down, complaining to the world in general. 'Why is my dinner not served on time? And why is there no order in this house?'

Then the door opened, and an anxious Clare came in.

'I can't find Mrs Butters,' she announced. 'I went to the kitchen to ask about dinner but she's not there. And the back door is wide open!'

'Wretched woman!' said Austin bitterly. 'She is always leaving that door open. To let the steam out, she says. Not caring that she may be letting thieves in!'

'But where can she be?' asked Clare.

'No doubt she's in the cellar, sampling the wine.'

'That's not fair, she doesn't do that. I'm worried about her.'

'You'd do better to worry about yourself, my girl!' Austin grasped Clare's arm in an iron grip and glared into her face. 'I believe you have been meddling at my desk and, if you have, you will be sorry!' He let go of his daughter and pointed towards the door. 'But first things first. Go and close the back door at once, and lock it. Then find Mrs Butters and tell her that if dinner is not served at once she will lose a month's wages!'

Rubbing her arm, Clare left the room and closed the door behind her.

Austin began pacing back and forth again, and resumed his grumbling. 'It is not good for the digestion to have to wait for dinner! Why is the woman suddenly failing in her duties?'

'As Clare told you, I don't think Mrs Butters is well. She seemed very tired this afternoon.'

'She should go to sleep earlier, instead of sitting up reading trashy novellas! There is no need for her to be awake after 9.30, once the washing-up is done. The woman has no common sense.'

'Please do not be too hard on her, Father. She is very kind. Yesterday she offered to find me a new kitten if Ella does not return.'

Austin stopped walking and looked sternly at his daughter. 'Indeed? Well, do not assume I shall give my permission. You know I am averse to animals in the house.'

'But surely you would not have me live without a pet?'

'We shall see. We shall see. But let us have no more talk of swimming.'

Austin sat down wearily at his desk and began writing on a piece of paper. As he did so, the door was thrown open and Clare rushed in, ashen-faced and trembling and struggling for words.

Harriet was shocked. 'What is it, Clare? Are you all right?'

'What's the matter, girl?' Austin barked. 'Where is Mrs Butters?'

'Mrs Butters is lying at the bottom of the cellar steps!' cried Clare. 'With her head in a pool of blood!'

The Dunblane coal store was brick built and stood ten yards from the house. Fortunately for the boy, it was to the south-west of the building and was thus somewhat sheltered from the north wind. Nevertheless, it was bitterly cold, and the boy had no outer coat to combat the freezing winter night. Every few minutes he would exercise his arms and run on the spot to keep his circulation going but it brought scant comfort.

The jagged lumps of coal, which would soon be warming Frankel's rooms, were at present dead and cold, stacked in a sullen heap that covered most of the floor. The boy had arranged some of the top pieces to form a crude seat for himself. There was nothing else to sit on.

A chipped enamel water jug was on the ground, and the paper bag with the black bread was on the coal beside him. He'd put it there in the hope of protecting it from the rats, which scuttled about the floor from time to time.

The only ventilation came from a small grille at the top of one of the walls. This had been installed many years ago, when a previous owner kept dogs in there. (These days Frankel's dog slept indoors at night, for extra security.) Luckily, the wall with the grille faced the Highgate Road, so a tiny amount of light filtered in from a street lamp. There was no other illumination.

For a long time at the start of his incarceration the boy had been absorbed in self-pity, an emotion to which he was well entitled. Life had been cruel from the start.

Bad memories of a hostile and drunken woman, who must have been his mother, mingled with visions of various men who came and went in the back rooms of the slum house. Most of the time the men ignored him but sometimes he was kicked or cuffed if he was in the wrong place at the wrong time.

Only the sailor called Joe had shown him any kindness. Joe stayed longer than the others, and took an interest in the boy. He seemed to enjoy telling the lad stories of his adventures at sea and in foreign lands. Joe it was who taught the boy the rudiments of reading.

But one night there'd been a terrible quarrel, and the woman hit Joe with a hammer. The sailor had left the house with his head bleeding, never to be seen again. And then came the day when the woman turned her hammer on the boy, and he too had fled for his life.

After that came jumbled recollections of the turbulent period that followed, when he was living with the street boys, sleeping in doorways, huddled together for warmth, scavenging food from the rubbish outside taverns and eating-houses, begging for money, or stealing the odd coin if the opportunity arose.

There'd been some comradeship in those days but there'd also been fear and violence, with bigger boys always eager to impose their supremacy with fist and boot.

It had seemed like an escape when the prosperous-looking stranger had approached him in the park. The man had been sitting on a bench watching the urchins play football with an old cabbage, found in the gutter after the market closed.

The boy had fallen and cut his knee, so he was still there, trying to wipe off the blood with a handful of grass, when the cabbage disintegrated and the other boys moved off in search of new diversions.

The man had tended the injured knee and asked questions in a friendly voice. Then, when he'd established that the boy had no home and no family, he'd invited him to come and live in his house, and be a servant for sixpence a week.

The boy had jumped at the chance. The idea of living in a house and receiving wages seemed a dream come true. Alas, the reality had proved a bitter disappointment. He'd simply exchanged one grim existence for another. For him, life at Dunblane was a wearisome round of drudgery, accompanied by harsh words, and punctuated by beatings and other humiliations. Furthermore, always under the watchful eyes of three men, he had lost his freedom.

These sad thoughts had filled the boy's mind for several hours, creating a mood of resignation. The optimism he'd shown Harriet last week was now extinct. He'd begun to accept that misery was his lot in life. He was doomed to suffer. He would sit there shivering in the dark, taking just enough of the cheerless bread and water to stay alive. He'd endure the loneliness and the beatings, and then resume his dreary routine of slavery. It was the line of least resistance.

But then came the stirring of something different. There was within the boy a spark of resilience, a streak of determination, even of pride. On the Heath he'd seen a better side of life. Before the fear caused by the Maniac there'd been happy well-fed people with smiling faces, walking for pleasure, flying kites, playing games. Why shouldn't he be part of that world?

And then there'd been the girl. She'd smiled at him, let him touch her, treated him as a human being. There might be other girls out there who'd give him smiles and let him touch them.

He'd boasted to this one that he'd escape when the time came. Suddenly, he decided that the time had come. He must get away now.

For a while, when the boy first came to Dunblane, Frankel had paid him the promised sixpence a week. Before long, of course, the doctor had started forgetting, or withholding the wage as a fine. But there'd been occasional tips, including the cat-money. He now had five shillings and fourpence wrapped in a rag and hidden beneath a loose floorboard in the attic.

That might be enough to survive on for a few days, while he found the London docks the sailor had told him about. He could get a job on a ship and sail the seas, like Joe.

Next time he was allowed out on the Heath, or sent on an errand, he must be sure to have his savings in his pocket. And then he'd run! He knew where the river was. He'd go in that direction. The docks must be somewhere on the river.

And then he recalled Frankel's malevolent words, which had been almost lost in a haze of fear and pain. He was to be fined five shillings! The tyrant must have guessed the boy had savings and had resolved to grab them, to prevent him escaping.

Once the rest of the punishment had been served, his master would get his hands on the money, there was no doubt of that. Even if Frankel didn't find it in its crude hiding place, he'd beat it out of him.

And then the boy would have no means of subsistence for his first days in the outside world, if he managed to get there.

But now the boy's mind was racing.

He realized he'd have to make his bid for freedom this very evening. Apart from rescuing the cash, this might be the best chance he'd have, while he was out of sight, and disregarded by the rest of the household. If he could somehow get out of this prison, he could sneak upstairs, collect his money, and steal away before his absence was discovered.

Frankel was coming to thrash him at ten: it would be good to avoid that. The Highgate church clock had just struck seven. So there'd be three more hours during which the men would give him no thought.

Frankel worked in his laboratory till eight, and then he and Stone sat down to dinner, which was cooked and served by Prosser. Until dinner, Stone would be in the office, working on papers and sipping gin.

The window of the laundry room was usually left ajar. The boy could reach it by climbing up the drainpipe; he'd done it before. Then he would make his way to the attic and back, using the dark places and short cuts he knew well.

But how was he to get out of the coal house?

A memory had been lurking at the back of his mind during his hours of dejection. And now, as his energy began to flow, it came to the fore. He remembered the trick Titch had bragged about last year.

Titch, of course, had been the smallest of the street gang, but what he lacked in inches he made up for in cunning and dubious skills. He claimed that he could always escape from a locked room and, for a ha'penny each, he'd told the rest of them how it was done.

The boy felt in his pocket and was reassured to find the matches he always carried, to light the fires at six o'clock every morning. The other essential for that task was old newspapers, and a pile of these was kept alongside the coal. He groped around in the gloom and found a broadsheet. He took a double page from the centre, thought for a moment, and then added another to make a double layer.

He knelt down and slipped most of his paper mat through the gap beneath the coal-house door, retaining only a few inches on his own side.

The key of this door normally stayed in the outside keyhole, and he fervently hoped that today would be no exception. He would soon find out.

He took one of the long lucifers from the matchbox, inserted it into the lock, and pushed. To his joy, it met something hard. The key was there.

He pressed the matchstick hard against the tip of the key, attempting to dislodge it. The match snapped. He tried three more matches and they all broke.

Desperately, he racked his brains to try and think of something stronger to use, and it occurred to him that there was an item on his belt that might do the trick. The buckle had the usual small metal spike to go into the holes at the opposite end. He removed his belt and eased the spike into the keyhole. Would it be long enough?

After a moment he let out a sigh of relief. Metal had met metal. The spike was touching the key.

He pushed hard with his new tool and felt the key move slightly but not enough to fall out. For five minutes the boy prodded and probed with the spike, attacking the key from every possible angle. In spite of the cold, sweat began to form on his brow.

And then, just as he was about to despair, he felt the key move decisively and heard it fall to the ground outside. It was not yet time to rejoice. Had the key landed safely on the newspaper? Or had it bounced off and ended up out of reach? And was the space below the door big enough for the key to pass through?

The boy's hands trembled as he pulled the paper gently towards him. The light was too faint for him to see if the key was there. He ran his fingers cautiously over the paper to feel for it. And suddenly, amazingly, there it was! Titch had got it right! His key to the outside world was sitting there on the middle crease of the newspaper.

Carefully, he picked it up and put it briefly in his pocket, while he stood up and restored the belt to his trousers. When he was ready, he put the key in the lock, turned it, and heard the tongue withdraw to its housing with a pleasing click.

Then he turned the handle and began to push the door open, gently, so as to reduce any creaking. When the door was halfway open he slid out sideways, with the minimum of movement.

He was surprised to find bright moonlight outside. He blinked, and exhaled heavily after his exertions. He allowed himself a moment of exhilaration. He was free. He peered around him eagerly.

And now came the shock. A man was leaning against the wall opposite, only a few yards away! It was Prosser, and he was staring at the coal-house door, as if waiting for the fugitive to appear.

For an instant the boy froze with fright.

Then he turned to run but already Prosser had taken four swift strides and had an iron grip on the boy's arm, and a large hand over his mouth.

The boy was too shaken to struggle as Prosser pulled the door wide open, steered them both inside, and closed the door behind them.

'If you know what's good for you, don't make a sound!' he ordered, removing his palm from the boy's face. Now deflated, the boy stood helplessly awaiting his fate, which he assumed would be another savage beating to add to the one he was expecting later.

Prosser spoke quietly and, to the boy's surprise, without hostility or anger. 'Good trick that with the key. I ain't seen that done for years.' Was the man playing cat-and-mouse with him? 'I was on my way to let you out when I seen the key moving. I thought I'd let you get on with it. See if it still works.'

'Let me out?' gasped the boy. This must be some new refinement of torment. 'You was going to let me out?'

'Yeah. And you'd better get a long way away from here bloody quick. Only don't go without your dosh.' He took from his pocket a small cloth bag, in which was the rag containing the boy's savings. 'I put it in a bag, see. Be safer. That weren't a clever place you was hiding it.'

The boy's surprise had turned to astonishment. He could scarcely find his words.

'You mean ... you're letting me go?'

'Yeah,' said Prosser. 'Better that way. Frankel's in an evil mood. Crazy with rage, you might say. And he'll be worse when he's had his wine. I don't want murder done in this house. One of us could swing for it.'

Obviously, he wasn't going to tell the boy about his moment of weakness an hour ago. After three pints of beer he'd lapsed into melancholy.

In truth, although an enthusiastic bar-room brawler, Prosser had never cared for wanton cruelty. And the thought of what Frankel would do to the boy later had begun to disturb him.

And then had come that extraordinary thought. Recalling drunken nights in Kentish Town, it had occurred to him that he could actually be the father of this boy! Or of another just like him. His conscience, which he had regarded as dead and buried years ago, had revived enough to nag him. Perhaps there'd been something wrong with the beer.

This stupid softness still had a hold on him.

'If you've nowhere better to go,' he found himself saying, 'go to the Horse and Groom down Archway. My brother works in the taproom. Tell him I sent you. He might give you a hand, if his feet aren't plaguing him.'

In a daze, the boy remembered that if someone did you a kindness you were supposed to say 'Thank you'. It had happened so rarely in his life that he had scarcely ever used the phrase. But he used it now.

'Thank you, Mr Prosser,' he said. And he liked the sound if it, so he said it again.

By now Prosser was surfeited with all this kindness and affability and was beginning to feel ashamed of himself. He managed to regain a proper gruffness as he said, 'Now listen, boy. Don't you never tell no one what goes on here. You bring Frankel down, you bring me down.'

'I'll never say a word, I swear it!' the boy assured him.

'You better not,' said Prosser sternly, 'cos if you do, I got mates who'll find you wherever you are and cut out your liver. Now go, quick!'

Stuffing the moneybag in his shirt and some bread in his pocket, the boy went: swiftly on to the Heath, and then swiftly off it, getting on to the Highgate Road as soon as he was clear of the houses. Then he headed towards Archway.

In ten years' time, he would own a sheep farm in Australia. And five years after that he would be Mayor of Kilby, New South Wales.

But he had many more of life's slings and arrows to experience before that.

Thoughtfully, Prosser left the coal house, closing and locking the door behind him. After a few paces and a moment's thought, he went back and unlocked the door, leaving the key on the inside.

10

THE LITTLE CLUSTER of homes and gardens, greens and pathways that nestles in Hampstead's Vale of Health is a remarkable phenomenon: a country village in the middle of a wild heath, in the heart of a great metropolis.

It began and grew, and acquired its name, between the years 1400 and 1700, when the City of London was often ravaged by disease: first, the Black Death, and then the recurrent Plague. At the first sign of an outbreak, prosperous city-dwellers would flee to the Hampstead uplands and especially to the hollow in the middle. Here there was fresh air, and a wide barrier of grassland between them and the dreaded bacilli.

The Vale of Health had rural lanes and a country pub beside a placid lake, where herons and smaller waterfowl prosper under the overhanging trees.

This hamlet lies on the west side of Hampstead Heath, and Highgate is to the east, so, on leaving the Aspinalls', Steele and Mason had more than a mile to walk across damp turf and country paths. It was a pleasant prospect, the ground firm underfoot and the air still mild at the end of a sunny, early-December afternoon. The two men had much to talk about.

The Aspinalls had proved hospitable: Mason had

especially enjoyed the fruit cake. But their hosts had been very anxious. The wealthy businessman and his wife no longer walked on the Heath, a deprivation they bitterly resented. But their main concern was their youngest son who, at twenty-three, seemed a likely target for the Maniac. Yet the young man insisted on crossing the Heath each day to go to work in Hampstead, often returning quite late in the evening. And on Sunday nights, he was liable to stroll across for a drink at Jack Straw's Castle. He adamantly refused to be accompanied by a bodyguard. Nevertheless, the Aspinalls were employing a burly ex-soldier to follow him, at a distance and without his knowledge.

The trouble was that the ex-soldier had twice been detained by police patrols, who thought he was the killer stalking his next victim. An unpleasant atmosphere of fear and suspicion pervaded the area.

Herbert Aspinall maintained that this was the whole purpose of the Maniac and, probably, his accomplices. He believed it was all a revolutionary plot to undermine London's reputation as a safe and pleasant place to live, or to come and do business. Beyond that, he'd had no practical ideas or useful information to offer.

As they walked amid the little hills and trees and hedgerows, the detectives reviewed the case. Neither had heard of Mrs Butters' death, which had occurred too late for the morning papers. In fact, the two men had not met today until they both arrived at the Aspinalls'. Steele had spent the morning in the chambers of their accountant, Giles Randall, discussing the implications of his report. They'd then lunched at his club. Mason had manned the office, catching up on paperwork, after which he'd eaten a mound of brawn sandwiches, lovingly prepared by his wife.

Steele told Mason about his meeting with Randall earlier and went on to report on the previous day's visit to Scotland

Yard. He had informed Willoughby they were building a file on the activities of Austin and his shady lawyer, and had been surprised to learn that the police were already investigating Jamieson on another matter.

'It doesn't surprise me,' said Mason. 'The man's as crooked as a barrel of snakes. What's the latest on the Heath Maniac?'

'They've traced McDonald, the Greenwells' man: the chap who fell out with everyone. He's eliminated from the inquiry.'

'Oh yes,' Mason recalled. 'The bullying butler. Don't say he's gone home to die too.'

'Not quite. He's gone home, but he seems in robust health. He's back in Scotland, living with his parents and working as a labourer. It's established that he hasn't been south of the border this year. So there's no need for you to go on asking around the alehouses.'

Mason bore the news cheerfully. 'Oh well. There'll soon be something else we need to know. What more did the big chief say?'

'He's looking into the anti-homosexual theory.'

This was a possibility that had been mooted early in the investigation. Certain parts of the Heath had long been regarded as a meeting place for homosexuals. Was the Maniac out to destroy those he regarded as deviants? None of the four victims so far were thought to be homosexual but, as lone men walking on the Heath at night, they might have appeared so to a deranged mind.

Willoughby had considered the idea at the outset but it was not an easy avenue to pursue. There was a homosexual community in London but they had to maintain strict secrecy, since their activities were illegal. Obviously, they could not confide in the police. So there had been no way Scotland Yard could learn if they faced a special threat. Until now. Steele brought the story up to date.

'The police raided the home of a Turkish man this week, in connection with an assault. They found scores of letters and leaflets calling for the extermination of homosexuals. The man had already fled but he'll be caught; there's a warrant out for his arrest on the original assault charge. We'll know more when they bring him in.'

'That shouldn't take long,' said Mason. 'There aren't that many Turks walking the streets of London. Did you tell Mr Willoughby about this meeting at the Royal Oak?'

'I did, and he's put several plain-clothes men on duty. They should be lurking in the Vale of Health already. So if there is any danger, help will be at hand.'

But the danger wasn't in the Vale of Health. It was much closer.

One of the scenic delights of Hampstead Heath is the number of ponds, some large, some small, some tidied and tended for swimming, others still wild and natural. In most cases, the footpaths simply skirt around the water. But, in the middle of the Heath, one lake is spanned by a brickwork bridge, twenty yards long. It was when Steele and Mason were halfway across this bridge that the attackers struck.

The detectives were suddenly aware that three men, carrying cudgels, had emerged from the trees beyond the end they were approaching and were walking towards them. There was no doubt of their intentions.

Steele and Mason were used to physical combat but they were also prudent. Since they were outnumbered and the advancing men were armed, discretion was the better part of valour.

'I think we should turn round,' said Steele calmly.

But as they did so, three men, also bearing heavy sticks, appeared at the end from which they'd entered the bridge. Their retreat was cut off.

Steele cursed his own stupidity. He'd been prepared for a

trap at their destination but not on the way there. Someone must have guessed the route they'd be taking.

'Sorry, Jack,' he said. 'I got this one wrong.'

'Never mind, guv,' said Mason cheerfully. 'There's only six of them. Backs to the wall, eh?'

The brick parapets at each side of the bridge were generally waist-high but in the middle they arched up a little higher. So anyone standing close to the brickwork could not be attacked from that direction. The two men backed against a centre section, standing a well-judged five feet apart so that, if one of them ducked a blow, it would not go on to hit the other. And each man could hit out without fear of striking his partner. They had been in this situation before.

Each man took off his coat and wrapped it round a forearm as a protective pad. Steele took a police whistle from his pocket and blew the longest loudest blasts he could produce. In the still air they would surely carry to the waiting police half a mile away.

But how long would it take rescuers to reach the bridge? Five minutes? Ten? By that time both men could be dead or crippled.

The attackers shouted oaths and war-whoops as they went into action. Apart from the swearing, there were no words. They seemed very professional.

The first blow was aimed at Steele's head, but he took it on his cushioned arm, and then rammed the silver knob of his walking stick very hard into his assailant's face. The man staggered back, blood pouring from a broken nose, but then he came on again.

As a club swung towards his skull, Mason grabbed it and used its impetus to hurl its owner to the ground; then he kicked the man ferociously under the chin.

The detectives' shrewd positioning meant that, in trying to hit them, the roughnecks were getting in each other's way.

One thug heaved himself up on to the parapet to attempt an assault from behind. But Steele saw the action instantly and, as the man tried to straighten up, dealt him a sharp blow which sent him toppling into the muddy water twenty feet below.

For more than a minute Steele and Mason fought off the attack, ducking the blows or fending them off with their padded forearms while inflicting damage on their own account, Steele with his stick, Mason with a pair of doughty fists.

But, eventually, numbers told.

As Mason ducked a blow from one flailing cudgel and warded off another with his arm, a more cunning opponent delivered a sweeping strike at his legs, knocking them from under him. Then, while Mason was falling, a fierce blow landed on his head. He crumpled to the ground and lay inert.

Steele moved quickly to stand over his friend and shelter him, swinging his stick, kicking out and shouting defiance.

But now the situation was hopeless. Amid his desperate efforts, Steele's mind was racing. The thugs were clearly under orders. Had they been told to kill their victims, or just to disable them permanently?

And then, as Steele's stick was wrenched from his grasp, there came the gunshots: two, in quick succession. One of the gang fell, as his leg gave way under him. The others turned and saw a man hurrying towards the bridge with a pistol in his hand. He fired a third shot, which took another of the thugs in the shoulder.

The gang didn't wait for a fourth. Three of them began running full tilt towards Highgate; the man with the wounded shoulder staggered more slowly behind them. And, finally, the thug who had struggled out of the pond went stumbling blindly in the same general direction.

The man who'd been shot in the leg still lay clutching his knee and groaning.

The newcomer ignored him as he strode confidently up to Steele. 'Good afternoon, Major,' said Commander West. 'Not safe to walk on the Heath these days without a gun. I thought I told you that.'

The Reverend Ernest Littlejohn closed the door silently behind him and began walking quietly down the dark passage. He felt he should talk to the lady of the house before leaving, but she was nowhere to be seen. He paused and coughed, in a discreet clerical way.

This traditional English signal worked, as usual, and Madge Scully came bustling out of the kitchen, drying rough red hands on a rough grey towel. She greeted the parson respectfully.

'Oh. Excuse my wet hands, sir. I was doing some washing. Are you off now?'

'Yes, I have to be, I'm afraid. And your husband is asleep. I don't want to trouble him further.'

'Was he all right? I mean, he wasn't rude or anything?'

'Not at all, Mrs Scully. He wanted to talk. He's ... er ... had a colourful life, has he not?'

'If you like to call it that. I think he'd have been better off getting a proper job.'

'Oh well, the Lord has made us all differently. We serve him in varying ways. Your husband has given people the priceless gift of laughter.'

Madge Scully was concerned. 'He didn't spend all the time bragging about his success on the stage, did he? He was supposed to be confessing his sins.'

'Well, the two were often intertwined.' The Reverend Littlejohn smiled indulgently. 'But, yes, he did confess his sins extremely fully. I have to say, a little more penitence and a little less detail might have been fitting. But confess he did.'

'I'm surprised it didn't take all day.'

'His trespasses were all of the kind the Lord is very ready to forgive. Mr Scully has made his peace with his creator.'

'Well, thank you for coming, sir. Will you have a cup of tea before you go?'

'No, thank you. I have other calls to make before evening prayers. I must be on my way.'

'Do I owe you anything?'

'Good gracious, no. The love of God and the services of his clergy are given freely.'

'Well, that is nice, I must say.'

'Of course, the Church has many expenses, as you know. Any donations to parish funds, however small, are always much appreciated.'

'Oh. Yes. Right,' said Mrs Scully. She thought of Major Steele's gold sovereigns, which she had retrieved from under her husband's pillow. Then she reflected that these were somewhat tarnished and grubby from use. And then she recalled the shiny, bright new shilling, minted only this year, which had turned up in her wages. That looked better, and also it was handier. She opened a drawer in the hall-stand, took out the shilling, and gave it to the parson.

'Please take this, sir,' she said. 'With my thanks.'

'The Church is most grateful,' said the clergyman, pocketing the coin, with a little bow. 'God bless you.'

He moved to the front door, and Madge opened it for him.

'Thank you again, sir,' she said.

'And thank you, Mrs Scully,' said the parson, as he made his exit. 'Let me know when I can help with the funeral arrangements.'

Madge closed the door behind him and walked thoughtfully down the passage. She stopped outside her husband's door and listened.

The call was so feeble that Madge would have missed it, had she not been concentrating intently. But there was no doubt about it. Her husband was calling her name. She opened the door and went in.

'What is it, Luke?' she asked. 'The parson said you was asleep.'

'I was.' Scully's speech was weary, but lucid. 'Then I had a bad dream, and it woke me up. I got something on my mind.'

'You'd better tell me, then.'

'That parson said I had to get everything off my chest. So I did. Then he asked if my conscience was clear, and I said it was. But it ain't.'

'He said you'd owned up to all your past sins and been forgiven. All up to date. You haven't managed to do new sins today, have you?'

'No, Madge, it's something I forgot. When them detectives was here, asking about the Heath murders. I might have helped them, but I didn't. Something I could have told them. Only I decided not to. I never got on with coppers. Now it's on my conscience. I ought to tell them.'

'They're very nice gentlemen. I got their address. I'll get them back, shall I?'

'No, no, I can't go through all that again. You write them a letter, Madge.'

'Me?'

'I couldn't hold a pen no more. And you was always better at writing. If you get a pen and paper I can tell you what to say.'

Madge sighed wearily. 'All right, Luke. If it'll make you easier in your mind.'

She moved towards the door, but then her husband called her back.

'Just one more thing, Madge. Urgent.'

'What is it now?'

'Fetch the gin bottle out from under the bed, will you?'

'What's it doing under the bed?'

'I hid it. I didn't want that parson getting at it, did I? Fetch it quick, Madge, I'm gasping.'

Cedric Jamieson was in buoyant mood this morning.

The post had brought several pieces of good news. Harrison's Wholesale had not queried the exorbitant bill for his services, and had sent a cheque for the full amount. He had caught them at a busy time, as he'd hoped. And he had pitched his fee very nicely: far too much for the work but just short of the sort of figure that any self-respecting client, however busy, would feel bound to challenge.

The houses he owned in Jupiter Street were already attracting offers around £750, now the news of the railway extension was generally released. He had bought them for £200 each, using a shell company to withhold his name, while advising clients in the area that it was about to be blighted by a new sewer development. The advice had been given in strictest confidence so, of course, it had spread like wildfire. Potential buyers were now being reassured that the sewage plan had been abandoned. In fact, of course, it had never existed.

All this had come on top of yesterday's splendid news that Edwin Slattery had been murdered by a fellow inmate at Pentonville prison. This meant that further dust had settled on the Slattery case, and a vital witness had been removed from the scene.

Now Jamieson was sitting back with his feet on the desk, drinking his first whisky of the day, and studying the morning paper. The latter carried the news that Jamieson relished most. The headline read 'Detectives Battered on Hampstead Heath' and the column beneath told a tale which was bringing the lawyer huge pleasure.

*Two of London's leading inquiry agents, Major Henry Steele
and Mr John Mason, have been injured in a violent attack on
Hampstead Heath. This occurred yesterday afternoon when a
dozen thugs surrounded them as they walked near the Vale of
Health and beat them with clubs.*

*The two men have been helping police with the search for
the Heath Maniac: but the assault is not believed to be connected with this investigation, since it was a gang attack and
no knife was used.*

*It is thought more likely to have been a revenge attack on
two detectives who have been responsible for sending many
violent criminals to prison.*

*Both men were taken to hospital, where Mr Mason was
detained and is still being treated for his wounds. Major
Steele was discharged after his injuries had been dealt with.*

Cedric Jamieson had chuckled with glee when his eyes
first fell on the story, savouring the thought of those interfering nuisances suffering injury and pain. He was now reading
the piece for the third time, and wishing there were more
details.

All in all, Jamieson considered that things were going
remarkably well, and he might be entitled to a holiday. There
was a lady in Paris who was always pleased to see him, when
he had money to spend. And there could be more. With his
luck going so well, he might even have a flutter in the casinos
over there.

There was a knock at his door, and Jamieson shouted
'Come in' in a cheerful voice. Could this be more good news?
Gertie upstairs offering discounts on a slack day, perhaps?

In fact, it was Arthur, with some papers he'd laboriously
prepared. He put them on Jamieson's desk and, seeing that
his employer seemed in a genial mood, embarked on a little
conversation.

'Excuse me, Mr J. But them two blokes that was duffed up on Hampstead Heath, wasn't they the ones that was here last week, pushing us around?'

'Yes, the very same,' chortled the lawyer. 'And now they've got their comeuppance.' He'd seen the chance of a little unearned credit. 'No one takes liberties with Cedric Jamieson without paying the price.'

Arthur was duly impressed.

'Strewth!' he said, admiringly. 'You mean you set it up?'

'Now, now, I didn't say that, did I? No names, no pack drill.' Jamieson tapped the side of his nose with a tobacco-stained finger. 'Just work it out for yourself.'

Arthur looked at his employer with new respect.

'Well done, Mr J. I didn't like them two, I don't mind telling you.'

'Well, I don't think they'll be troubling us again.' Jamieson made a decision. 'Now then, my lad, big opportunity for you. I have to go to the Continent on business. I'll go Sunday and stay for the week. You'll be in charge of the office.'

Arthur was taken aback. This had never happened before.

'What, me? On my tod?'

'You know enough to hold the fort for a week. Any new customers, tell them to come back in ten days. Any queries on current business, tell them it's all in hand. You can spend your time chasing the unpaid bills. Anyone gets difficult, get on to Slasher.'

His assistant still looked uncertain.

'I'll give you an extra quid,' said Jamieson. 'And you'll have Gertie upstairs to yourself for a week.'

'Make it two quid, Mr J.,' said the clerk.

'All right, two quid,' said his employer expansively. 'Why not? Money coming in, Slattery out of the way, Steele and his crony scared off. We're in clover, lad.'

There was a loud knocking on the outside door.

'Go and see who that is, Arthur. Might be Father Christmas coming early.'

As Arthur went to the outer office, Jamieson knocked back his whisky and started thinking about seven days in Paris.

Then men's voices were heard in the outer office and, a moment later, Arthur returned to Jamieson's inner sanctum, followed by a large man in a dark-blue raincoat.

'This man says he's from the police,' Arthur announced glumly.

The large man stepped forward. 'Inspector Boyle, Fraud Department,' he said. 'Are you Cedric Robert Jamieson?'

John Mason was woken from a fitful doze by the noise of his door opening and the sound of the nurse's voice. The latter was harsher than the former.

'You mustn't be longer than twenty minutes,' she was saying. 'Be careful not to tire the patient.'

She showed in a familiar figure and then left, closing the door behind her.

'Hello there, Jack,' said Steele. He took in his colleague's hospital room at a glance: bedside chair and table, armchair, wash-stand and, best of all, a large window with a good view of sky: the army benevolent fund was getting value for money. 'Nice little home from home you've got here,' he said.

'It's all right,' said Mason, raising himself further up on his pillow. 'But I'll be glad to see the back of it. The ruddy place is unlicensed. I can't get a drink.'

Steele sat on the bedside chair and looked at the jug on the table.

'Plenty of good refreshing water,' he observed.

'Don't be sarcastic, guv'nor,' Mason pleaded. 'I'm not strong enough to take it.'

'Oh well,' said Steele, delving into his briefcase. He produced a bottle full of light-brown fluid and handed it to the patient. 'If you're really thirsty, this might help.'

Mason took the bottle and read the label with mounting dismay. 'Benevita. Nature's way to a speedy recovery. A unique blend of health-giving herbs and wholesome raw vegetables, designed to comfort the patient, improve bowel function and restore health and vigour.'

At first no words would come. Then he managed to say, 'Thanks, guv'nor. I'll try some later.'

'Have some now,' said Steele. 'And I'll join you.'

'No ... really. Actually, I'm not thirsty any more.'

'Smell it.'

Mason unscrewed the cap and advanced the bottle cautiously towards his nose. Then a grin spread over his face. 'You crafty old devil!' he said. 'This is the real stuff!'

'Of course,' said his friend. 'Only I didn't think the hospital management would approve of bedside whisky bottles. And the Benevita's doing wonders for my window-box.'

Two tumblers stood by the jug. Steele poured some amber fluid into each and added a little water.

'Good health!' said Steele. 'And here's to Commander West!'

Mason joined the toast, took a drink, and exhaled gratefully. Then he reacted to the major's words.

'Commander West?'

It was the first time the two men had talked since the battle on the bridge. Mason had been unconscious when Steele had to leave him at the hospital. Now the major told him everything that had happened since the final blow knocked him out.

'Strewth!' said Mason. 'So the old rascal's carrying a gun after all! I bet it's unlicensed!'

'It is,' said Steele. 'I checked.'

'So how do the police feel about that?'

'George Willoughby came straight over to take charge of

the case. I told him West had snatched the gun from one of the thugs.'

'Cor!' Mason gave a little chuckle. 'Did he believe that?'

'He must have done,' said Steele innocently. 'It's in the official report.' He smiled. 'Willoughby wasn't going to make trouble. He's rather happy about the whole thing.'

'Is he? Including my cracked ribs and battered head?'

'I think he feels that goes with the job. He's pleased because they've nabbed Ned Barker, a villain they've been after for a long time.'

'Oh yes,' said Mason, recalling Steele's narrative. 'I suppose that'll be one of the blokes that Commander shot. They didn't run away with the others, I take it.'

'One did. But not Barker. He won't be running anywhere for a long time. He's under arrest in hospital with a shattered knee.'

'Serves him right,' said Mason.

'Quite. The police believe Barker's behind enough crimes to lock him up for life. They've started questioning him already.'

'About the attack?'

'That and many other things.'

'There'll be the usual trading, I suppose.'

'Of course. They'll offer to reduce some of the charges if he gives them the facts and the names they want.'

'So we should find out who's hired that scum to rough us up.'

'I'm sure of it. Willoughby doesn't let villains off lightly.'

'Who do you think was behind it?'

'There are quite a few people who don't much like us, aren't there?' Steele produced another wry smile. 'Strange, that. Two friendly chaps like us. But we seem to have made some enemies. It could have been any of them.'

Mason sighed and drank some more whisky, while

considering man's inhumanity to man. 'Yes, I suppose so. Austin, perhaps? He may have realized we're after him. Or Frankel?' Then another thought struck him. 'What about Jamieson?'

'Not Jamieson, he's too mean. He wouldn't have paid that many thugs. He'd have hired two men and a big dog. Anyway, we'll soon know. Now then, what about you, Jack? What do the doctors say?'

'Oh, there's hairline cracks to two ribs. They'll soon mend. Apart from that, it's mainly cuts and bruises, plus a bit of concussion. That's wearing off already.'

'Why's there a bandage round your neck?'

'There's a gash at the back. That's got a couple of stitches. So has the wound on my side. The cracked ribs are strapped up. It'll all mend quickly.'

'I hope so. There's work to be done.'

'I can't wait to get out of here, guv'nor. But the quacks say I have to stay a few more days, in case of delayed reaction.'

There was a peremptory knock at the door and the nurse bustled in, looking stern.

'Have you taken your medicine, Mr Mason?' she demanded.

'Yes, Nurse,' replied her patient dutifully.

'Then why is it still on your table?' The nurse was looking at a small glass, three-quarters full of green liquid, hidden behind the bedside Bible, on top of which socks had been folded to add height.

Mason showed huge surprise. 'Oh, is it? Good heavens! I must have mistaken the thought for the deed. Sorry.'

'Well, drink it up now, please.'

'Could I leave it for a moment? I'm just finishing this other stuff. It's not good to mix drinks, is it?'

'Drink your medicine at once, Mr Mason!' For a moment it seemed she might be about to smack him.

'Oh … yes … of course, Nurse. Sorry.' With a grimace,

Mason knocked back the green fluid, and then coughed ostentatiously.

'That's better,' said the nurse. 'Your next dose is at six o'clock.' Her eye lit on the amber liquid in Mason's tumbler. 'What's this you're drinking?' she asked sharply.

'Ah ... er ... it's a sort of patent remedy,' Mason mumbled.

'Indeed?' The nurse looked at the bottle and turned to Steele. 'Did you bring this?'

The major shifted uneasily in his chair, and became somewhat vague. 'Er ... yes,' he conceded. 'I think I must have done. I brought Mr Mason several things.'

'Well done!' said the nurse. 'Benevita is an excellent restorative.'

'Oh yes,' said Steele, recovering swiftly. He screwed the cap back on the bottle. 'I believe it's very wholesome and health-giving. My grandmother swore by it. I thought it might do him good.'

'Certainly it will, it's a first-class tonic.' She picked up the bottle and held it in front of Mason's face. 'Make sure you drink plenty of this, Mr Mason!' she said.

'Oh, I will, Nurse, I will!' said Mason fervently. And then the nurse was gone and the two men were alone again.

Steele had noticed the name on the lapel of the crisp white uniform. 'Nurse Bullimore, I see.'

'Yes. And bloody well named, I must say. Dreadful woman! I'd swear she chews iron filings for breakfast. Washed down with caustic soda!'

Steele rebuked him mildly. 'That's not fair, Jack. She's only doing what she has to do.'

'So did Genghis Khan!' said Mason, and then he gratefully changed the subject. 'Any news from Scotland Yard? Has Professor Kane produced any more bright ideas?'

'Several. Last week he decided the Maniac may have had a deprived childhood. He wanted our friends at the Yard to trace all men who grew up in British orphanages and children's homes in the last forty years.'

'Good God! How did they react to that?'

'With very little enthusiasm. Willoughby's worked out that a hundred policemen working seven days a week would take a year to do the job. He feels they could be better employed elsewhere.'

'Like escorting Professor Kane on to a boat back to America.'

'There is a growing body of opinion in favour of that idea. In the meantime, the professor's announced that he's been working too hard, and his brain needs rest and refreshment. He's going to be walking the Yorkshire moors for a week.'

'Oh well, that'll keep him out of the way for a while. Is he up there yet?'

'He went yesterday. He should have been there the day before, but he got on the wrong train.'

Mason let out a guffaw, which quickly changed to a cry of agony. He clutched his ribs.

'Don't make me laugh, guv'nor,' he pleaded. 'I've got more places that hurt than places that don't.'

Steele's tone became serious. 'Well, there's nothing funny about the next story. I'm afraid there's tragic news from the Austin house.'

'Oh dear. Not that poor frightened girl, I hope.'

'No, the housekeeper, Mrs Butters. She's dead.'

'Good God! The housekeeper? What happened?'

'They found her at the foot of the cellar steps with a fractured skull. Austin called in his friend Dr Frankel, as you might expect, and he said it was an accident, as you might also expect. George Willoughby has his doubts. He's ordered a post mortem, and his men are investigating. There'll be an inquest, obviously.'

'I should certainly hope so. Frankel's verdict will be about as reliable as a cart with three wheels.'

'Mind you, it could have been an accident. You'll have noticed that the lady was somewhat overweight.'

'And overworked as well. Any other details?'

'The back door was open, so there could have been an intruder. Anyway, it wasn't the Heath Maniac. Not his modus operandi.'

Mason peered into his whisky glass and pondered on life's injustice.

'Poor old duck! I liked her. I shouldn't think Austin treated her very well.'

'I'm damn certain he didn't. It's a sure bet he's never treated anyone very well in his life. But he'll soon get his comeuppance.'

'It can't come soon enough.'

'Another thing to tell you is they've arrested Cedric Jamieson on a string of charges. Nothing to do with Austin.'

'Oh well, I suppose we can still carry on building up our own case against him.'

'Certainly. And any more papers we need from Jamieson's office, Willoughby can get them for us.'

There was a pause. Mason drank another mouthful and began to feel more comfortable. But his professional curiosity was still working. 'So what do we do next?' he enquired.

'You lie in bed and get yourself better quick. I may need you back on your feet by Sunday. While you're lolling around here, I'll be doing fieldwork.'

'Fieldwork? What does that mean?'

'It means the office can take care of itself for a day or two. I'm going back on the Heath, with my binoculars. Incognito.'

'More of your scouting missions?'

'Exactly. I want to pry about and see what's happening in and around those big houses. I'm going to observe what goes on at Dunblane and Hillside and the Greenwells' when no one's watching. Or when they think no one's watching.'

'Sooner you than me. It's getting a bit chilly out there. And damp.'

'I'll wrap up warm.'

'What's brought this on?'

'A new line of inquiry, Jack. Perhaps the conclusive one. I've left the biggest news till last.'

'There's more?'

'Considerably more. I've had a very interesting letter from Luke Scully.'

Mason was instantly alert. 'Scully? I wouldn't have thought he could write a letter, even when he was fit and well, and now he's on his deathbed!'

'That's the point. He knows he's about to kick the bucket and something's been troubling him, something he needed to tell us. I expect his wife did the writing; it's a woman's hand. But the words are Scully's.'

'Are they important?'

'If they imply what I think they might, they could solve the mystery. The case could be over on Sunday.'

'What?!' Mason sat up in astonishment and then winced with pain. 'What is this? What have you got up your sleeve?'

'I'm not absolutely sure yet. But I want you fit and ready for action by the end of the week.'

'I will be. Of course. Whatever the doctors say. But will you please tell me what this is all about? What did Scully say in this letter?' Mason grabbed his colleague's arm.

'Don't get carried away!' said Steele. 'It may not mean what I think it means. I have to do some research. And then Willoughby will want proof, and I'm not sure how we get it. I may have to set a trap. And I'll need you for that.'

'For God's sake, guv'nor, stop playing games! Suspense is bad for invalids! What does Scully say in his letter?'

'Calm down, Jack, and I'll tell you. What Scully says is ...'

At that moment there was another cursory knock on the door and again it was opened without delay. The nurse ushered in a pleasant middle-aged woman of medium height – a slightly plump figure built more for comfort than speed. She had a motherly face and a kindly smile.

'Not more than ten minutes today, Mrs Mason,' the nurse was saying. 'Your husband's had a long talk with Major Steele already, and he mustn't get overtired.' She shot a glance at Steele. 'I expect you'll be leaving soon, Major.'

'Oh yes,' said Steele meekly. 'Just a few more points I need to tell my colleague about.'

'Oh dear,' said the nurse. 'Mr Mason needs to relax. You shouldn't be talking business to him.'

'Don't worry, Nurse,' said Steele. 'He never listens.'

The nurse went to the door. 'When I return in ten minutes, I want to find Mr Mason lying down and ready for relaxation,' she declared. And then she left.

'That sounded like an invitation,' Steele observed. 'You may be in luck, Jack.'

Mason shuddered. 'No, thank you! That would be like cuddling a hedgehog! I think I'll stick with my Emily here.'

'I'm glad to hear that,' said Mrs Mason. 'I've just bought a new double blanket.' She bent over the bed and kissed her husband warmly. 'How are you feeling today, dear?'

'A bit like I've been run over by a coach and horses. But it's all right, they've confirmed there's nothing serious.'

'And how are you, Major?' asked Mrs Mason, with a faint note of disapproval. 'You two certainly get into some scrapes.'

Steele rose to his feet. 'I'm fine, thank you, Emily. I let Jack take most of the blows. His skull is thicker than mine.' He looked at the basket the lady was carrying. 'You seem to have brought most of Covent Garden market with you.'

On view in Emily Mason's basket were grapes, apples and oranges, as well as some other objects, unidentifiable in paper bags. She was also carrying a bunch of chrysanthemums.

'Just a few things to cheer him up and make him better,' said Emily, unloading fruit on to the bedside table until it began to look like a harvest festival display. Then she produced a solid item, wrapped in greaseproof paper, and handed it to Steele.

'And I've brought something for you, Major,' she announced. 'I thought I'd see you here today.'

'For me?' Steele eyed the object cautiously.

'It's my special eel and onion pie. I know you don't look after yourself properly. You tuck into that when you get home.'

'Ah. Er ... well, thank you, Emily. Er ... do I heat it up?'

'Doesn't matter. Hot or cold, it's full of goodness. Now what about my Jack? He's been through the mill, hasn't he? He's going to need a lot of rest.'

'I'm sure the nurse will see he gets that,' Steele reassured her.

'Yes, but when he gets out of here. He ought to have a holiday. I hope you're not planning to get him back to work in a hurry.'

'No, no, of course not,' Steele lied.

'He should have time to convalesce. He could do with some sea air. I'll see if I can get us a few days at Mrs Hankey's in Brighton.'

Mason pulled a disapproving face. 'Brighton will be cold at this time of year.'

'Well, we'll see about that in a minute,' said Emily ominously. 'These flowers should be in water. Where can I get a vase?'

'The nurse has a little room at the end of the passage,' said Mason. 'The dragon's lair, I call it. I expect she'll help you if you ask her several times. Turn left as you go out of here.'

'All right,' said Emily, opening the door. 'And when I come

back I'd like my Jack to myself, please, Major. No more business talk for him today.' And with that she set off down the
corridor.

'Oh dear,' said Steele with mock gravity. 'Just when I need
you, you'll be in Brighton.'

'Not bloody likely!' said Mason vehemently. 'Brighton
brings on my rheumatism.'

'But Emily says you need sea air.'

'I'll let her fan me with a kipper. I'll be back on the job
Sunday, if not sooner. Put money on it!'

'I never bet on a certainty, you know that. It's dishonest.'

'Now for God's sake, guv'nor, tell me what's in Scully's
letter, and what you and I have to do!'

Steele told him, and Mason let out a whistle of
astonishment.

Frankel's oaths and cries of wrath could be heard while
he was still outside, first in the coal store and then as he
stomped back to the house. And when he flung open the back
door and stormed in, his rage was incandescent.

'The young vermin's gone!' he roared. 'He's got out! He's
gone!'

Stone and Prosser had been alerted by approaching sounds
of fury from their employer, and by his bellowed demands for
their immediate attendance, so they were waiting for him in
the kitchen. Stone had been wondering what had brought on
this outburst; Prosser, of course, knew the answer only too
well, and had been quietly preparing himself to deal with the
onslaught.

'Gone?' said Stone, with genuine astonishment. And then
he added injudiciously, 'He can't have gone! I saw you lock
him in this afternoon!'

The ferocity in Frankel's voice went up several decibels.

'If I say he's gone, he's bloody well gone, you brainless

dolt! Or do you think he's hiding under the coal? Perhaps you should go and search through it!'

Stone showed no inclination to accept this invitation.

'Sorry, sir,' he said in his weaselly way. 'I wasn't arguing with you. It's just that I can't understand it. The boy must be in league with the devil!'

'The devil himself couldn't have helped him, if you two had kept watch properly!' Frankel glared at his underlings. 'How did he get out? How did it happen, eh? Tell me that!'

Prosser broke the tense silence.

'When you locked him in, guv'nor, did you leave the key in the lock?'

'Dammit, I don't know!' barked Frankel. 'What the hell has that got to do with it?'

'These young villains got a trick where they push the key out and drag it in under the door. When you lock someone in, you oughta take the key.'

At this suggestion of negligence on his own part, Frankel's temper mounted further. 'Never mind that! He should have been watched! All the time! You should have been watching the coal house!'

'You never said that,' Prosser protested. 'You told me to clean upstairs. That's what I been doing.'

'Don't bandy words with me, you oaf! You're idle, that's what you are! Idle and stupid!'

'Can't be in two places at once, can I?'

The veins stood out on Frankel's forehead. 'You're idle, I say! And now you're insolent as well!' The doctor now had a target for his anger. 'I know you, Prosser. Loafing around drinking beer when you should be on duty! You let that young blackguard escape!'

'I told you, guv'nor, I was upst—'

The raging Frankel cut him short. 'Lies! Lies! Don't you argue with me, you cur! I'll have to teach you a lesson!'

He was still carrying the stick with which he'd been looking forward to thrashing the boy. Now he swung a vicious blow at the servant's head.

Prosser ducked and grabbed the stick as it whirled through the empty air. As so often in the past, he would have liked to break it over his employer's skull. But, as before, he reminded himself that it was Frankel who brought in good money for all of them. It was too soon to kill him. So he restrained himself and just broke the stick over his own knee. Then he tossed the broken pieces to the ground and stood looking calmly at his master.

Frankel stared back at him with hatred in his eyes. He was a big man, but Prosser was bigger. And the fellow was useful. There was a moment of suspense, during which Stone moved a little further away from the two large men. Finally, Frankel contented himself with saying, 'You'll pay for that.'

From a safe distance the secretary strove to ease the situation.

'There may still be traces of the boy's blood on the larder floor,' he suggested. 'If we gave the dog a sniff of that, he might be able to track the wretch down. He's probably got no further than the Heath.'

'You mean, you'll take the dog out and search for him?' rasped Frankel.

The secretary's face would have paled had it not been already devoid of colour. As it was, there was just a tightening of the skin.

'I'd rather not, sir,' he said. 'Surely Prosser's the man for that job. I have to finish last week's accounts.'

Prosser was dismissive. 'There'd be no sense in it,' he said. 'The boy could have got out hours ago. Likely he's miles away by now.'

The fire had gone out of Frankel since the failed confrontation. And the wine that had helped to influence his wrath was now becoming debilitating. He sat down on a kitchen chair and scowled at Stone.

'Anyway,' he said, 'I want Prosser in the house for the next few days, in case we get a visit from Slaughter's men. It seems he's not happy with our new arrangement.'

'Then what do we do about the boy?' Stone asked.

Frankel shrugged. 'Nothing. Forget about him. If he doesn't starve on the Heath he'll probably drown in one of the ponds. When I've finished this commission from Lensky I'll go down to the slums and find another urchin.'

11

'I FEAR SOME of the plants are looking poorly,' said Harriet. She closed the conservatory door behind her.

Clare was sitting at her father's desk, writing studiously. She paused and looked up. 'That's because no one's thought of tending them since we lost Mrs Butters. Plants need a little love, like the rest of us.'

'How very remiss we've been,' admitted her sister. 'We should be looking after them in her memory. Well, I've given them all some water now.'

'Not too much, I trust. Plants shouldn't be too wet at this time of year.'

'I don't think I've overdone it,' said Harriet. 'I do hope the hyacinths survive. Their scent is so cheering in the middle of winter.'

'Let us hope we all survive,' Clare responded. 'With the atmosphere we have in this house, I fear it's by no means certain.'

She returned to her work, which was research, as usual. This time she was scanning an enormous volume, open on the desk in front of her, and extracting more facts for her notebook.

Harriet sat down on her customary seat by the window, but now with no view to admire, for the curtains were drawn.

Outside, it was a dark and dismal evening, with spots of rain falling from low clouds, and the wind soughing mournfully in the trees.

Inside, it should have been cosy, but it wasn't. The lamps were lit but the fire in the grate was dull and smoking. Clare had lit it this morning, at her father's bidding. But, in the absence of a housekeeper, too much of the old ash and cinders had been left behind, and the fire had not been properly managed throughout the day.

'How lonely Hillside seems without Mrs Butters bustling about,' lamented Harriet. 'Thank heavens I have your company this evening. It's good that you can sometimes do your work in here.'

'Not for long, I'm afraid. I'm here because I need some information from Hosker's *Flora and Fauna of Southern England,* and it's too heavy to carry to my room. When I have all the facts I need I must return to my manuscript upstairs. You know I work better there.'

'Oh dear.' Harriet shook her head sadly. 'Then I shall be desolate indeed. I would never have believed Father would go out and leave us tonight of all nights. I can't think how he can be so heartless.'

'You refuse to see him as he really is, sister. He is a monster. He cares nothing for either of us.'

'And yet he gives us a home.'

'Because it brings him money. From my mother's will, and your mother's trust. Funds which I'm sure he intends eventually to steal.'

'Oh, Clare, I can't believe that.'

'Also, of course, he now has the services of an unpaid housekeeper. That reminds me. I have orders to lay out a meal for him to eat when he comes home. I must search the larder for something that will give him indigestion.'

'Oh!' Harriet cried out in anguish. 'I cannot bear all this

hostility!' She picked up her embroidery and began to work at it listlessly.

For a while all was quiet, as the sisters got on with their different tasks. The patter of rain on the windows had abated. Harriet found the silence oppressive, and her nervous fingers dropped the needle. She put down her work in frustration and found a new topic of conversation.

'I wonder when Father will find a replacement for Mrs Butters.'

'Not for a long time, I fear.' Clare continued writing, clearly able to work and talk at the same time. 'Probably not until he thinks he's losing face with his friends because he has no paid servants. Till then, he'll be happy to go on using me as a slave.'

'Perhaps I could help, if you would show me what to do.'

'Thank you, but it's usually quicker to do things oneself, rather than try and explain them to someone else. Besides, you are too delicate for heavy work.'

'I would do my best.'

'You would not like it. My back ached terribly yesterday, after I spent two hours cleaning the downstairs floors. And then Father came in and walked all over the kitchen in muddy shoes.'

'That was just thoughtlessness. You should have told him.'

'And give him an excuse to hit me again?' Clare was now warming to her subject. She put down her notebook. 'I was wrong just now when I said that Father didn't care about you and me. The truth is, he hates us!'

'Oh, surely not. That cannot be true.'

'It is true. Did you know that after Mrs Butters was murdered, the inspector offered to have a policeman on duty here for the next few weeks and Father refused?'

'What?' Harriet was shocked. 'He refused to let us have police protection?'

'I heard the conversation. Father was rude and truculent. He told the inspector to his face that he didn't trust the police and wouldn't have them in the house any more than necessary.'

'And now he deserts us to go and play whist! On a Sunday night! With the Maniac still at large! Doesn't he realize that I'm almost frightened to death?'

'I'm sure he does. Your death would suit Meredith Austin very well.'

'You cannot mean that!'

'Of course I mean it. Major Steele has confirmed that if you die unmarried, your father keeps your mother's money.'

'Please, Clare! I cannot bear to think of these things!'

Harriet's voice was becoming shrill with emotion. Clare sought to placate her.

'Well, that situation may not last much longer. Major Steele is working on your behalf. There may soon be big changes in your life.'

'I do not want big changes!' cried Harriet. 'I just want my books and my garden and my cat, if only she would come back to me! And I want to be free of all this fear and anxiety!'

Clare resumed her note-taking, and made no reply.

Harriet strove to regain control of herself. She picked up her embroidery and tried again. But once more she found the silence too stressful, and broke it with another question. She forced herself to speak more calmly.

'Is it certain that Mrs Butters was murdered?'

'Oh yes. Quite certain.' Clare's answer was terse and casual, as she pressed on with her scribbling.

'Dr Frankel said it was an accident, didn't he?' Harriet protested. 'And those cellar steps are very steep.'

'The devious Frankel said it was an accident to please Father, who obviously didn't want a police investigation. But, as you must have heard, the police doctor said no. Mrs

Butters had head injuries she could not have got in the fall.'

'But who could have wanted to kill her?'

'Some footpad, perhaps. Taking advantage of the open door. As you know, some housekeeping money seems to have gone from the kitchen drawer.'

'What does Major Steele think?'

'I don't know. I've had no contact for several days. That assault on the Heath may have diverted his attention.'

'Pray God he has not deserted us!'

'I thought you were against accepting his help.'

'I was, but now … oh heavens, I don't know what to think. These are such desperate times!'

Again both young women were mute for a while, Clare busy with her research and Harriet sinking into nervous thoughts and wild imaginings.

And then suddenly, loud and clear, came the stark sound of a dog howling, somewhere out in the darkness: an awful sound, half threatening, half anguished.

Harriet gasped with fright. 'Dear God!' she cried. 'What was that?'

Clare retained her composure. 'I daresay it's that big black hound that Dr Frankel keeps. The animal is almost as unpleasant as its master.'

'It's never howled like that before! I've heard it barking occasionally, but not that terrible noise.'

'As you say, sister, these are desperate times. No doubt the dog shares your apprehension.'

As the fearful sound went on, Harriet put down the tray-cloth she was working on. 'I cannot continue with this,' she declared. 'My hands are shaking.'

Clare did not look up from her work, and her advice was simple. 'Well, read a book. There are plenty here.'

And then the noise ended abruptly. The beast's last howl changed halfway into a sort of strangulated whimper. After that all was quiet again.

'Ah. Someone has silenced him,' said Clare. 'And rather brutally, from the sound of it.'

'It can't be Dr Frankel – he's playing whist with Father, isn't he?'

'So we're told. All we know is, they went out together. So no doubt the deed was done by that evil secretary of his.'

'Mr Stone? Is he evil?'

'I would say so. I have seen him from my window, whipping that dog unmercifully while the creature was chained to a post. Mr Stone seemed to be enjoying himself.'

Harriet winced. 'How horrible!'

'I have also seen him prowling on the Heath at dusk. He carries field glasses, and I believe he peers into lighted windows. What I think is called a Peeping Tom.'

'Then you're right, he is indeed a wicked man,' said Harriet. And then, more urgently, 'Clare, I meant to tell you. I have seen that hideous tramp again, staring at our house. He terrifies me!'

'Oh dear,' said Clare insincerely. 'Well, I suppose we should feel flattered to be attracting so much attention.'

Harriet recognized that she had been rebuffed. She was suddenly aware that the noise of the wind had ceased abruptly, as if turned off by an unseen hand. And somehow the absence of any sound was more baleful than the baying of the hound had been.

She rose and began pacing up and down. This annoyance soon drove Clare to a more positive reaction. She stopped what she was doing, sighed, and looked around.

'Do sit down, Harriet!' she commanded. 'Look! There are the poems of Alfred Tennyson. Read some of those. You will find them diverting.'

Her sister stopped walking, briefly comforted by a familiar thought. 'Tennyson, yes, perhaps I should. That was the last book Robert gave me. We used to read it aloud together. I shall be able to think of him.'

She picked up the small leather-bound volume, returned to her window seat, and began to turn the pages, looking for something soothing. It was a modest anthology of some of the poet's better-known works, and eventually she found a poem that seemed suitable. She settled down and made a valiant attempt at concentration. Then, after reading a dozen lines to herself, she realized that she had taken in nothing. So she went back and started again, and at last the words began to mean something.

Clare took advantage of the five-minute interlude to round off her efforts and bring tonight's research to a satisfactory conclusion. Then she put down her pen and stood up.

'There!' she announced. 'I think that's all I need on this subject.' She turned to her sister. 'Harriet, I have stayed with you as long as I can.'

Harriet was aghast. 'Oh, Clare! You are not going to abandon me so soon?'

But Clare had already closed Hosker's mighty tome and managed to tuck it under one arm. She was now heading for the bookshelves.

'You know I cannot do creative work down here. And the rough draft of my article is strewn around my room. Now that I have these facts I must go up and begin the final version.'

'Could I not come and sit with you?'

Clare spoke firmly. 'No, sister. Your presence is too distracting.'

'I promise I wouldn't say a word.'

'It is foolish to make promises one cannot possibly keep.' Clare heaved the massive volume up onto the lowest shelf and began levering it into the space it had previously occupied.

Her words had injected a small spark of anger into her

sister's gloom, and there was a hint of sharpness in Harriet's reply.

'Are you saying I talk too much?'

'Heaven forbid,' said Clare. 'However, if this work is ever published, it will carry a dedication. "To my dear sister, without whom this piece would have been written in half the time."'

'You are very unkind!' Harriet protested. 'How can you joke at a time like this?'

'I find humour a great relief from life's horrors. I recommend it.'

'There's little humour in our present situation, I must say.'

'Perhaps you'll find some in Lord Tennyson's poems,' said Clare. 'Though, on the whole, I doubt it.' She gave Hosker's book a final push into place and moved off towards the door.

Harriet's small defiance had evaporated. She rushed to intercept Clare and put a restraining hand on her arm. 'Sister, please don't leave me here alone! Not tonight! I have not even my cat for company!'

'Harriet, I have to go! There is no need to fret. I shall be back within the hour. And Father may be home even sooner. In the meantime, the doors are locked and the windows are fastened. You cannot possibly come to any harm.'

Harriet looked round desperately for some delaying tactic. 'Clare!' she cried. 'I think the fire has gone out!'

Clare gave it a casual glance. 'Quite possibly,' she said. 'However, I think it is still hot enough to deter any enemy from coming down the chimney.'

'But surely ...'

'That's enough, Harriet! Show some spirit! Before very long you are likely to need it!'

Clare detached herself decisively from her sister's grasp and was gone, closing the door behind her.

Now there was just Harriet and the dim gas lamps, the big

chilly room with its dark corners, and the brooding silence: that overpowering, deafening silence.

After a moment's bewilderment, Harriet went to the fireplace, knelt down, and began to stir the smoking embers with a poker. She noticed a wad of papers mixed in with the coals, presumably dumped there earlier in the day for instant destruction. But some of the papers had stuck together and, instead of being consumed, had merely smouldered and choked the fire.

The papers were almost entirely brown and burned, but the young woman noticed a small piece where some writing was still legible. She stared at it and made out the words 'mental institution' but the rest was too charred to be read.

Her efforts with the poker produced some extra smoke, but no flame. She got up, went disconsolately back to her perch by the window, and sat down edgily. She picked up the Tennyson book and found that she couldn't recall which poem she had been reading. So she started leafing through the pages again.

Then, once more, the dog howled: a brief lament this time, three distinct howls, none of them cut short. The sequence simply came to an end, as if the animal had completed its message.

Harriet shuddered, but kept control. Clare had explained that this was their neighbour's dog. And dogs do howl from time to time, even if she had never heard the Dunblane dog do so before. Holding the book in trembling hands, she chose a page at random and compelled her eyes to focus on the words.

The wind had begun to moan again, the unseen hand having brought it back into action: not such a steady force now, a gusty wind that rattled the windows and caused some small object to roll about on the paved area outside.

Without warning, there was a crash from across the room.

Fearfully, Harriet raised her head and looked for the source of the noise, which had sounded like a door being slammed. But Clare did not slam doors, and, anyway, Clare's room was in the opposite direction. There was nothing untoward to be seen. Harriet told herself that the catch must have failed to engage when she closed the conservatory door. No doubt the wind had blown it open and then swung it shut. Yes, that must be it. And yet, deep inside, she was sure she had closed the door properly: it was something she always did.

With her thoughts scrambled and her heart racing, Harriet forced herself to remember those happy times reading aloud with Robert Kemp. Reading aloud was what she must do now. The discipline would compel her to lock on to the words. And it would remind her of Robert.

She rose and, as if giving a public performance, declaimed the lines from the book held in front of her.

The woods decay, the woods decay and fall,
The vapours weep their burthen to the ground.
Man comes and tills the field, then lies beneath,
And after many a summer dies the swan.
Me only cruel mortality consumes,
I wither slowly ... Oh!

It was not the right poem for the occasion. She hurled the book to the ground, subsided on to the sofa, and buried her head in her hands.

For the third time the dog started howling, now continuously, neither tiring nor being restrained. And, curiously, the sound seemed to be closer. Was it her imagination or was the dog approaching the house? And what was it that was moving out there, sliding around on the paving stones?

Suddenly, Harriet felt she must find out what was going on outside. She was drawn irresistibly to the window, though she dreaded to think what she might see beyond.

She abandoned the security of the sofa and advanced nervously towards the window. Looking at the view through this pane of glass had so often brought her solace and joy. Tonight the prospect was frightening.

Would she see some monstrous hound, slinking towards her with bared fangs? Or the Heath Maniac stalking another victim?

As she reached the window and touched the curtains, a wave of fear swept over her. She lowered her hand and moved back, to stand frozen with terror and indecision.

But Clare's words about spirit had lodged in her mind and triggered a small stirring of self-respect. She attempted to swallow, but her throat was too dry. Then she stepped forward, seized a curtain with each hand, and pulled them firmly apart. And, as she did so, she began screaming.

From no more than a foot away, an awful face was staring in at her: a great grey face, lined and pock-marked, with piercing eyes and an expression that was scarcely human. It was the face of the tramp, the tramp she had seen before, but previously only at a distance. Now the ghastly creature was here to confront her close up, with a look of icy malevolence.

Harriet retained enough sense to pull the curtains together and then, for a few seconds, she stood there, rooted to the spot, unable to flee, as in a nightmare. But eventually movement returned and she ran across the room and out through the hall door, shrieking and crying and calling for Clare.

For a few seconds the room was empty and silent, save for the receding cries of Harriet as she fled upstairs. Then the handle of the garden door turned, the door was opened quietly, and the tramp came in, looking warily around him.

Satisfied that he was alone, he went to Meredith Austin's desk and began rummaging in the drawers, obviously looking for something. His search was interrupted by approaching voices, Harriet's shrill and desperate, Clare's cool and censorious.

The tramp hastily closed the drawers and scanned the room for a bolthole. The conservatory was the obvious place and that was where he went, shutting the door behind him.

'Harriet,' Clare was saying, as the young women entered the room, 'this is madness! You must stop such nonsense, you're imagining things!'

'I'm not, Clare! I'm not! Please believe me! He's there! Outside that window!'

Clare strode briskly to the window in question and pulled the curtains aside. There was nothing to be seen but spots of rain on the glass and pitch darkness beyond.

'You see!' she proclaimed. 'There's no one there! Nothing to see!' With a look of contempt she pulled the curtains together again.

'There was, I swear it! The tramp! He was there, staring in!'

'Well, he's not there now! For heaven's sake, girl, sit down and calm yourself.' Clare guided her sister on to an upright chair. 'I've brought your sedative tablets.'

'But I've already had today's dose,' protested Harriet. 'I'm not supposed to take more.'

'You may in an emergency.' Clare went to the sideboard, where stood a fluted jug of water. She poured some into a glass. 'And this is certainly an emergency. You've worked yourself into a state of hysteria.'

She handed the glass to Harriet and took a pill-box from her pocket. Harriet looked at the cold stale water with distaste.

'Eugh!' she shivered. 'This water is horrid! I think I need something stronger.'

Clare pondered. 'Perhaps you do,' she conceded. 'There's a

flask of Mrs Butters' blackcurrant wine in the conservatory.'

Harriet rose and walked across to the conservatory door. 'A good idea,' she said. 'The cordial. That might make me feel better. It's in the cool cupboard, isn't it?'

'It is. But you mustn't mix the sedative with wine. Take the pills with water now. And then after five minutes you can have a little wine as a reward.'

Harriet hesitated outside the conservatory, again beset by indecision. Then she turned back. 'Yes,' she said. 'Perhaps that would be best.'

Clare handed her two pills from the box. Harriet put them quickly into her mouth and swallowed them both with one gulp of water. Then she shivered again, returned to her chair, and sank down, inert with nervous exhaustion.

'Well done, sister.' Clare was becoming conciliatory. 'Now you must rest and relax before you make yourself ill. Read your book, or do your embroidery. Do not go to the window. I tell you again, here indoors you are perfectly safe.' She moved off towards the hall door.

Alarm banished Harriet's exhaustion. 'Clare!' she pleaded. 'You're not going to leave me again?'

'I have to. As I said, I must complete this piece in time to offer it for the Christmas editions. And before I settle down I have to prepare Father's cold supper.' Clare paused in the open doorway. 'If you are in dire distress, I can be here in a matter of moments. But please don't trouble me again with trivia and mad ideas!' And, with that, Clare was gone and the door was closed behind her.

The dog had ceased its long howling session. Now the only sound was the swirling of the wind, occasionally rising to a sharp crescendo.

Harriet sat rigid, with hands tightly clasped, again determined to regain control of herself. She watched the clock on the mantelpiece and muttered some feverish disjointed prayers. As soon as she saw that five minutes had passed, she got up and hurried to the conservatory. She opened the door and went in. And then she began to scream again.

This time, her screaming was cut off by a large rough hand, placed across her mouth. And an arm went round her waist, holding her still. A harsh voice spoke close to her ear.

'Be quiet! Stop struggling! Answer my questions by nodding your head. Understood?'

The terrified girl responded by moving her head up and down twice.

'Right. Is Mr Austin at home?'

Harriet shook her head in the traditional sign of denial.

'Is there a policeman in the house?'

Again she gave a negative nod.

Reassured, Major Steele moved his hand, released his grip on the girl's waist, and reverted to his normal voice.

'Ah. Then there's no further need for subterfuge.'

He removed the rubber mask from his face.

'I'm sorry to have alarmed you, my dear. I have had to take certain precautions.'

A mixture of relief and astonishment engulfed Harriet. 'Major Steele! Dear God! It's you!'

'Forgive the masquerade, Miss Austin. I assure you, it was entirely necessary.'

'So it's you I've seen watching our house.'

'It was essential for me to observe the activities in this area without being recognized, and without attracting the eagle eye of Dr Frankel. There were places I had to search.'

Harriet's mind was churning as she strove to make sense of things. 'So why have you come in now and revealed yourself?'

'Because my search is done. And, more importantly, because you are in deadly danger. It was time for me to make a move.'

'How did you get in?'

'Through that door. Your sister gave me a copy of the key. I unlocked it earlier, in case I had to come in quickly.'

Harriet gasped. 'You mean … the door has been unlocked all evening? Thank God I didn't know that.'

'You were safe enough all this time. I was standing guard outside. But now this dreadful business is moving to its climax. You must stay close to me.'

'I shall be very glad to do that, Major.'

'And you must do as I say. And please keep your voice down.'

Amid the sighing of the wind there came a sound which could have been that of a door closing.

Harriet clutched the major's arm. 'What was that?' She spoke quietly as instructed.

'That was almost certainly the sound of the front door being shut.'

'The front door? Then Father must be home.'

'Not quite yet, I think. Stay still.'

Steele walked noiselessly to the hall door and opened it a few inches, enough to see down the hall. Then he pushed it shut and returned to Harriet's side.

'As I thought,' he murmured. 'The hall is empty. The noise was not made by someone coming in. It was someone going out.'

'Going out? Who could have gone out? Clare is busy upstairs. And you know that Mrs Butters is dead?'

'Sadly, yes. And I am deeply sorry that I failed to act in time to prevent that.'

'So, when Father is out, Clare and I are the only ones in the house …'

'Perhaps.'

'What do you mean, perhaps? It is a certainty.'

'Few things are certain in this world, Miss Austin.'

Harriet was not inclined to debate the question. There were more urgent matters. 'Major, if Clare's gone out, she may come to harm! It's Sunday night. And the Maniac is loose! I must go to her!'

Steele took hold of her arm again. 'Stay where you are!' he commanded. 'Whatever happens, you must remain in this room.'

Harriet's voice rose. 'Will you please tell me what is happening! I need to know!'

'I asked you to speak quietly, Miss Austin.'

'I'm sorry. But surely I'm entitled to an explanation.'

'Very well,' said Steele. 'I believe an ambush is being prepared. We have to await the outcome and be ready to help.'

'An ambush? What sort of ambush?'

'A potentially lethal one. But a plan is in hand to ambush the ambusher and avert the fatality. Furthermore, if I am right, we shall shortly know the identity of the Heath Maniac.'

White-faced, Harriet trembled. 'You mean … I am actually to see the Maniac?'

'I am confident that we both will. But have no fear, you will not be hurt if you stay at my side.' He glanced at the clock. 'Ten-fifteen,' he observed. 'I think it would be wise to turn the lights down a little.'

Steele left the girl briefly and adjusted the gas lamps to a moderate glow. Then he returned, put a hand on Harriet's shoulder, and guided her to the sofa.

'We might as well sit down, my dear. We can do nothing at present but await events. They will not be long in coming.'

So the two of them sat side by side, watching the garden door. Steele had taken a small automatic pistol from an inside pocket. Harriet regarded it with mixed feelings. Of course, it made her feel more secure. But she had never heard a gun fired before: she wondered if the noise would be unbearable, and she prayed that it would not happen. Questions teemed in her mind.

'Do you know who the Maniac is?' she asked.

'Yes,' said Steele. 'I'm sure I do.'

'Then could you not have told the police and had him arrested?'

'Unfortunately not. The police require proof and there is none. I have only a theory: it is necessary for the Maniac to be caught in the act.'

'You can't mean ... someone else has to be killed?!'

'No. As I said, I have taken steps to prevent that.'

The dog began to howl again, now distant, as at first.

'Oh, that dog!' Harriet complained. 'It has been making that horrid noise all evening. Yet I never heard it do that before.'

Steele's response echoed Clare's. 'Animals sense the presence of evil.'

After this exchange, the pair fell silent. Again, the wind seemed to be abating, its sound decreasing as the tension in the house mounted. The fire in the grate seemed finally to be dead.

And then a hideous, anguished cry rent the night air. It came from oufside on the Heath, but not far away: one brief shriek, high-pitched with pain, but surely a male voice.

Harriet shrank closer to Steele. 'Dear God, what was that?' she cried. 'It sounded like a man! A man in agony!'

Steele was equally shaken, and his reply was grim. 'Yes. Yes, I fear so. I pray it doesn't mean that ...' He checked himself, as a hubbub erupted outside.

Suddenly, the bleak night was full of violent noise: angry voices, running feet and police whistles. Harriet's horrified reaction was compounded by a fearful blend of recollection and premonition.

'Oh, God!' she cried. 'I fear that something awful is

happening! Like the night poor Robert died. But then there was no uproar outside. We heard only banging on the door.'

'Things are different tonight,' rasped Steele. 'I hope that the outcome will be different also.'

And now came the banging on the door. First a short burst of hard blows, then a few more, slower and feebler, as if delivered with diminishing strength. The thuds were accompanied by a dismal moaning. Harriet's recall was now appallingly complete, and her response was the same as before.

'Dear God! Someone is in terrible distress! We must open the door!'

This time there was no argument.

'Yes,' said Steele. 'You stand back. I will open the door.'

With his pistol raised, he advanced to the garden door and opened it wide.

On the doorstep stood a man, unsteady and glassy-eyed. For a moment he swayed on the threshold, then one fist beat weakly at the empty space where the door had been. The momentum carried the man forward and he fell full length, face down, on the floor. A spike protruded from between his shoulder blades and blood bubbled up through a gash in his overcoat.

As Steele bent over the body, feeling for a pulse, Harriet leaped forward with a wail of despair. She put a hand under one of the man's shoulders and seemed to be trying to turn him over. Steele restrained her.

'Do not attempt to move him, Miss Austin. He's dead, I'm afraid.'

'But he's my father! What's happening? He's my father!'

'Yes. He was also your tormentor. And, I have to say, your mortal enemy. You must come away now or you'll be covered in blood.'

Harriet began to sob hysterically. Steele put an arm round her and led her to a chair.

'This is not the way things were meant to happen,' he lamented. 'But perhaps it is for the best. You would not have enjoyed seeing him on trial at the Old Bailey. Anyway, what's done is done. Help will soon be here.'

Now the raised voices were coming closer and, as Harriet watched in amazement, three figures came in through the garden door. The one in the middle was Clare Austin. Her right arm was held by John Mason, her left was supported by a constable. More policemen could be seen outside.

Harriet's sobs were interrupted by a relief that was almost joyful. 'Clare!' she cried. 'Thank God you're safe!' She jumped to her feet and was about to run to her sister, but Steele held her back, gently but firmly.

'Not now, Miss Austin,' he said.

John Mason looked down at the corpse of Meredith Austin and said, 'I'm sorry, sir. We were just too late to prevent this.'

'Evidently,' said Major Steele.

'But you were right,' Mason added. 'It was a crossbow.' He held up the weapon he was grasping in his free hand.

'It had to be,' Steele pronounced. 'The silent Angel of Death you once spoke of. Coming from nowhere to strike the victim down. Once the man had fallen, the bolt was withdrawn, and a knife thrust in and out, to make it look like a stab wound.' He glanced at the spike in the dead man's back. 'Tonight, of course, the assassin hasn't had time to do that.'

Harriet's relief turned to renewed horror.

'You mean the Maniac is still out there? For God's sake, shut the door!'

'No, Miss Austin. The Maniac is in here.'

'What?!'

Steele indicated Clare Austin, standing sullen and hostile between her two guards. 'Your stepsister.'

'Clare?!' Harriet was astounded and could only blurt out, 'What are you talking about?'

'I'm talking about an embittered and jealous woman. A woman unhinged by frustration and ill-treatment.'

'No!' Clare came to life with a defiant shout.

'There's no point in denying it, miss,' said Mason. 'You were holding the crossbow when we caught you.'

Clare spoke passionately. 'I'm not denying that I've rid the world of some evil men. I'm denying that I'm unhinged. My brain is sound and my mind is clear.'

'Well, that will be a matter for the experts to decide,' said Steele. He turned to the policeman. 'Inspector Willoughby is watching the front of the house. Tell him to come and arrest the Heath Maniac, will you? And bring the police doctor.'

The policeman said, 'Very good, sir,' and left to carry out his mission.

Harriet was trying to come to grips with the astonishing events and revelations of the last five minutes. She stared wildly at her sister and found herself saying, 'Clare! Clare, what have you done?'

'I've eliminated another male rodent. Not a handsome young seducer this time, but a wicked brute who's ruined more than enough women's lives.'

John Mason was crestfallen. 'We should have saved him, sir, as you planned. We saw the woman come out of the house, like you predicted, but then we lost sight of her in the dark. We didn't see her again till Austin arrived and she let fly.'

'No need for sackcloth and ashes, Jack,' said Steele. 'He's no great loss to society. He was a bully and a cheat, and he certainly murdered his first wife. You've saved the hangman a job.'

'But he was my father,' sobbed Harriet.

Steele put a comforting hand on her arm. 'That is not certain, Miss Austin. It is known that your poor mother sought relief from his brutality in the company of a better man.'

Clare turned bitterly on her sister.

'And don't you realize, you ninny, that Meredith Austin was bent on driving you out of your mind? Your guinea pig stolen, the whistling in the night, the dead rabbit, and God knows what he's done with your wretched cat! I have despatched a monster from your life!'

'But Clare! You killed all those young men! You murdered my dear Robert!'

'Your dear Robert!' Clare spat out the words. Her resentful resignation was now burgeoning into anger. 'He was my dear Robert until he saw your silly good looks! And then, like other male nincompoops, he decided he preferred a china doll to a real woman!'

Harriet gasped. 'I can scarcely believe this!'

'You wouldn't believe it, you useless milksop!' Clare's anger had now fermented into an insane rage. 'You never believe in anything real, anything practical! You think your pretty face will carry you through life without any problems!'

Clare broke loose from Mason's mild grip and gave him a fierce shove. Caught off balance, he toppled to the floor as Clare, now unrestrained, ran across the room. 'But it won't!' she cried. 'Because it won't be pretty any more!'

The demented young woman snatched one of the daggers from the wall and charged at her bewildered sister.

The blade was no more than a foot from Harriet's face when Steele fired his pistol and Clare's arm dropped to her side.

Harriet's ears were still deafened by the gunshot as she watched her sister sink slowly to the ground.

12

M ASON LOOKED AT his watch. 'What time is Mr Willoughby
coming?' he enquired.

'He said he'd be here at eleven,' said Steele.

'So he's already half an hour late.'

Steele was in a tolerant mood. 'We shouldn't be too hard
on our constabulary, Jack. They always have much to do.
Besides, Richard Cresswell won't be here till noon. And,
while we're waiting, Mrs Butters' blackcurrant wine is very
pleasant, is it not?'

'Yes, it is, guv'nor. But should we really be drinking it?'

'Of course we should. Miss Austin told us to make ourselves at home. Anyway, there's no one else to drink it now,
and it's far too good to waste.'

He poured a little more wine into Mason's glass and a lot
more into his own, which had been almost empty. 'We owe it
to poor Mrs Butters to ensure it's fully appreciated. And it
may help to keep us warm.'

It was a cold, bright December morning and the south-facing sitting room was catching a little watery sunshine. But
after only four days with no resident, Hillside was already
beginning to feel chilly and desolate. It was the detectives'
first visit to the house since that momentous Sunday evening
which had changed two lives and ended a third.

When that night's drama had finally come to an end, Steele and Mason had driven the distraught Harriet Austin to Mason's home, where Emily Mason had gladly taken her under her wing.

The cab had then carried the men to the hospital, so that Mason could receive treatment. Clare Austin's violent and unexpected push had sent him sprawling and he had crashed his head against the cast-iron fender that surrounded the fireplace, causing a large gash close to where the previous one was only just starting to mend. To Mason's dismay, after stitching the cut, the doctor had suspected renewed concussion. He had insisted the patient stay there for three days' observation, in the care of Nurse Bullimore, who, of course, scolded him roundly for being careless.

While Mason languished in hospital again, Steele had been busy. He'd worked with Chief Inspector Willoughby at Scotland Yard, tidying up the outfall from the Heath Maniac's arrest and dealing with matters relating to Meredith Austin. And he'd also been pursuing some inquiries of his own.

On Tuesday afternoon he'd visited his disgruntled partner and cheered him with the news that Ned Barker, the felon arrested after the bridge attack, had finally yielded to a mixture of pressure and promises, and revealed who was behind the assault. It was Tommy Slaughter, obviously anxious to put a stop to the detectives' probing.

Slaughter had been swiftly arrested, on a charge of conspiracy to murder, and was now himself under interrogation. The police were especially keen to find out why he had been visiting Frankel, and what business the two men had which called for such desperate measures.

Since Monday morning the Hillside grounds had been invaded by excited reporters. The capture of the Heath Maniac was the big news of the week, and they wanted some background for their lurid stories. The house itself had been inhabited only by police, checking the scene of Mrs Butters' death, gathering evidence against Clare Austin, and keeping the newshounds outside the building.

This morning, though, other activities were afoot in Hillside. Steele and Mason were there to meet Inspector Willoughby and show him some papers in Austin's desk, which would be used in the prosecution of Cedric Jamieson. They had brought Harriet Austin with them, so that she could choose and pack things that must go to her new home. She was upstairs now, making her selection.

After today, Hillside would be left to the police and, when they'd finished their work, the house would be locked up, and its contents covered with dust-sheets. Steele was determined that Mrs Butters' wine should not suffer this indignity.

He sipped some more, gently savouring its fruity flavour, and mused on good developments.

'Harriet Austin looks a different person,' he reflected. 'Remarkably, she seems to have put on weight already.'

Mason grinned. 'No surprise there, guv'nor. The poor defenceless girl has been stuffed with Emily's eel and onion pie. And her saveloys and mash, with piccalilli.'

'Has she been sleeping well?'

'Like a log, apparently. Apart from that first night, of course. Emily's been sharing the same room, to keep an eye on her. She says Harriet goes out like a light as soon as she lies down. No need for sedatives now.'

'Ah.' Steele smiled and lit a small cigar. 'Just the relief from fear and tension. Of course, Austin was behind all the things that scared her, but Clare was happy to stoke them up. And now they're both out of her life.'

There had been little chance for the two men to talk this week, and Mason had questions to ask. 'So it was Scully's note that put you on the right track,' he ventured.

'Scarcely a note,' said Steele. 'More like a full-length

confession. But, yes, that was what opened my eyes. It's clear that Scully and Clare Austin were lovers, though he doesn't actually say so: no doubt because his wife was writing the letter. They spent a lot of time together and he taught Clare self-defence and the use of some weapons, including the crossbow.'

'Funny thing to be doing with your girlfriend.'

'Weapons were his hobby, remember. And it would have been an amusing pastime on the Heath. Then, when he was booted out in a hurry, he left his crossbow behind.'

'Why didn't he go back for it?'

'Probably because Austin said if he ever showed his face there again he'd shoot him on sight.'

'Well, that makes sense, I suppose.'

'Long afterwards, thinking deeply on his deathbed, Scully was haunted by the thought that the Heath Maniac might be using that crossbow.'

'So he shopped his bird? In this letter he sent you?'

'Not specifically. He just said he'd left the thing at Hillside. Anyway, they'd actually parted on bad terms. Clare turned hostile when she suspected, no doubt correctly, that he had other women on the go. And, when she caught him in fla-grante delicious with the parlourmaid, she told her father at once: adding a few lies about both of them thieving. Austin sacked the pair of them immediately.'

'Not the sort of woman to get the wrong side of,' Mason observed.

'As her father recently discovered.' Steele was warming to his subject. 'So I came up here looking for the crossbow. And when I found it in the garden shed, with dried blood on the bolt, I reckoned that was the murder weapon. It had been carefully hidden behind a pile of logs. I think Mrs Butters saw it there and that's what she was trying to pluck up the courage to tell us, that day when she was interrupted.'

'Ah yes, I remember. Someone came in, didn't they, and she shut up like a frightened oyster. So Clare Austin must have killed her to make sure she didn't try again.'

'That's what Willoughby thinks. And so do I.'

'I suppose she pushed the poor old girl down the cellar steps.'

'More than pushed, I think. The doctor says Mrs Butters had head injuries that suggest a violent blow on the back of the head. I'm afraid the lady was as deadly with a blunt instrument as she was with the crossbow and the knife.'

'Knife? Oh yes, you mean the one she used to enlarge the wounds.' Mason glanced at Austin's ornamental daggers on the wall. 'D'you think she used one of those for the job?'

'I doubt it. She would scarcely risk being seen taking it down. And kitchen knives are easy enough to come by.'

Another thought occurred to Mason. 'Why was the woman so ready to help us, when she was the culprit we were out to catch?'

'We can only guess at that, Jack. I suppose her main purpose was to ruin her father, and we were the best means of doing that. Also, helping us meant she always knew what we were up to.'

There were three sharp knocks on the front door.

'That may be Willoughby,' said Steele.

Ten seconds later came another three knocks, even sharper.

'Definitely Willoughby,' Steele added. 'He's not a man who likes to be kept waiting.'

They heard the front door opened by a duty policeman, who treated the newcomer with great respect, and evidently took his hat and coat.

A moment later Willoughby entered the room, red-faced, puffing slightly, and rubbing his hands together to warm them up; not a tall man, but one who gave the impression of strength and authority. His sandy-coloured hair was beginning to show some grey streaks at the sides.

'Good morning, gentlemen,' he said. 'And a damned cold one, too.'

'It is indeed,' said Steele. 'We have some good strong wine here that is keeping our circulations going. May I pour you a glass?'

Willoughby raised a flat hand, as if holding up the traffic. 'No, thank you,' he said.

Steele smiled. 'Ah. No wine while working, eh?'

'Exactly. That is my rule,' said the inspector. 'In fact, I very rarely take wine. Blurs the judgment. I have my own survival kit.'

He took a silver flask from his pocket, sat down heavily in an armchair, and took a hefty swig of Scotch whisky. Then he exhaled heavily and rubbed his hands again.

Steele looked at him with mock disapproval. 'Drinking spirits on duty, George?'

'I'm entitled to this. I've been up since five this morning, and engaged on Her Majesty's business.'

'Good heavens! What could Her Majesty have wanted you for at that time of day?'

'A matter which I think will interest you. As you know, we have been questioning that rogue Slaughter since Monday night, mainly about his involvement with Otto Frankel, a person we've been interested in for some time.'

'A nasty piece of work,' observed Mason.

'Undoubtedly. He came to our attention in connection with contraband items seized by Customs at Dover. There was insufficient evidence to pursue him at that time. But we were intrigued that Frankel keeps a large house and several servants, but seems to have no legitimate income.' A note of triumph entered Willoughby's voice. 'Well, now we have the explanation.'

'I would imagine,' said Steele, 'that he has been doing quite well from his trading with Tommy Slaughter, supplying him with the wherewithal to drug horses and manipulate the result of races.'

Willoughby's jaw dropped. 'You scoundrel! You knew! Why didn't you tell us?'

Steele corrected him gently. 'Not so, George. I didn't know. It was just a theory. After all, Slaughter's record as a race-horse trainer is not exactly unblemished. We were going to investigate Frankel once the Maniac had been caught.'

'Well, you won't need to now. Slaughter agreed to tell us everything, once we consented to reduce his charge. It's been changed from attempted murder to grievous bodily aarm.'

Mason rubbed his head ruefully. 'It felt like attempted murder to me!'

'Don't worry, he'll still go down for a long time. Anyway, it seems Frankel is well known to London's underworld, as a sort of all-purpose crime doctor. For a lot of cash, he's been treating wounded criminals who daren't go to hospital. And, besides supplying stuff to affect horses, he's provided drugs for all sorts of illegal purposes. We think he may even have sold explosives to anarchists!'

Mason whistled with surprise.

'I'm pleased to hear you talk of his villainy in the past tense,' said Steele.

'You can be sure of that.' Willoughby swallowed a little more whisky, and the triumph returned to his voice. 'I led a raid on Dunblane just before dawn this morning and arrested both Frankel and his secretary, Charles Stone. We had to move fast, there was a chance they might flee the country.'

'Was there a struggle?' Steele enquired.

'Yes. Between the villains. Frankel blamed the secretary for getting the police on to them. Apparently, Stone's little game was stalking women on the Heath till he got them alone, and then exposing himself.'

Mason winced in disgust. Steele drew on his little cigar and said, 'I must say, that doesn't surprise me.'

'In fact, Frankel was quite wrong. We hadn't heard about those goings-on. Women too embarrassed to report it, I suppose. Anyway, that's what Frankel thought, and he laid into Stone with a stick. Then the manservant, Prosser, joined in and knocked them both down. Said he'd been wanting to do that for months.'

Steele smiled. 'I can believe it. We've met Prosser. An extremely robust character, I'd say.'

'As tough as a threepenny chop,' Mason confirmed. 'Not the sort of man to get the wrong side of.'

'Well, the bad doctor seems to have done that all right. We had to hold Prosser back or he'd have killed him. Prosser says Frankel's been abusing and ill-treating boys: young lads who've worked for him. If we get him on that, the swine will go down for an extra fifteen years, on top of twelve for his other villainy.'

'Will you be able to prove it?'

'I'm sure we will. Prosser's eager to testify in court. And he says he can find two recent victims who'll speak up.'

'That should do it,' said Mason.

'It seems Stone was at it, too. I think he'll turn Queen's evidence to make it easier for himself.'

'A very nasty household,' Steele observed.

'More scum than we've got on our water-butt,' said Mason.

'Extremely nasty,' Willoughby agreed. 'I'm very glad to have rounded them up.'

This time the inspector's triumph was not deflated.

'Well done, George!' Steele's admiration was genuine.

'Congratulations, sir!' Mason exclaimed. 'The Highgate Road has got rid of three evil men in one week!'

'A splendid week for the law,' said Steele. 'Two cases

concluded already, and it's only Thursday!'

'Three, in fact,' said Willoughby. 'Surrey police have closed their file on the death of Florence Austin. It's clear her husband killed her, and it's a shame he's escaped the proper penalty. Still, he has come to a suitably unpleasant end.'

'Yes,' agreed Steele. 'At the hands of one of the daughters he tormented.' He paused for a moment, while all three reflected on the poetic justice. Then he asked, 'How is Clare Austin?'

'Physically, she is recovering well. Your shot to the shoulder was well judged. Mentally, I'm afraid she goes from bad to worse. She has become quite wild, and attacked a male nurse who was tending her. She now has an armed guard at her bedside.'

'Do the doctors let you talk to her?'

'She demands to see me, in order to brag about her crimes. She admits killing Grace Butters, who she calls "a silly old woman, too feeble to stand up for herself".'

Steele shook his head thoughtfully. 'Do you think she might escape the gallows on the grounds of insanity?'

'Quite possibly,' said Willoughby. 'Since the M'Naghten ruling, courts are making many more allowances for mental disturbance.'

He was referring to the case of Daniel M'Naghten, a Scottish carpenter who, some years earlier, had shot dead Sir Robert Peel's secretary under the delusion that he was assassinating Peel himself. He claimed he thought the Prime Minister had been out to kill him. He escaped the death penalty, when his counsel convinced the court that M'Naghten suffered from other delusions as well, and was not responsible for his actions at the time of the killing. After that, it was accepted as a possible defence that some people can suffer from monomania, a form of madness that causes occasional bouts of homicidal hysteria, while leaving the individual intellectually sound. It was a defence of which the police, and many of the public, did not approve.

Steele was familiar with the rule.

'The M'Naghten Rule applied to a single homicide, did it not? Miss Austin killed several times.'

The inspector sniffed. He was clearly one of those who didn't care for the current trend.

'I've no doubt a clever lawyer could argue that the condition could be recurrent,' he said. 'Anyway, two medical experts are to examine the woman next week.'

'I hope they may be merciful,' said Steele. 'The poor wretch has been much ill-used.'

'I shall do nothing to send her to the hangman,' Willoughby assured him. 'I am content that no more young men will be murdered on the Heath. At least, not by Clare Austin.' He cleared his throat. 'Now, gentlemen, to a more pleasant topic. The younger sister.' He glanced at Mason. 'I understand you have been looking after her.'

Steele intervened. 'Mrs Mason has. Jack himself has been relaxing in hospital. There's a nurse there he's much attracted to.'

Mason ignored the jibe. 'Yes, Emily has been treating Harriet like a daughter. She'll be sorry to say goodbye to her.'

'Miss Austin is moving today to a more permanent home,' Steele explained. 'We've managed to trace her mother's brother, Richard Cresswell, living in Richmond and unaware of his niece's problems. He's delighted to have her join his family. And he'll be here to collect her shortly.'

Willoughby was a kindly man and he smiled with genuine pleasure. 'Ah! A happy outcome indeed!'

'Which we hope may become even happier. Cresswell is in touch with Harriet's mother in Australia, where she has a gentleman friend. He thinks they may come to England and marry, now Austin's dead. So, in due course, the girl may experience the novelty of having loving parents around her.'

The hall door was knocked and opened, and a uniformed policeman came in. He addressed the inspector.

'Excuse me, sir. The postman just delivered this letter for Miss Clare Austin. Sergeant Atkins thought you would want to deal with it.'

'Quite right, Constable. It may contribute to our investigation.' Willoughby nodded at Steele. 'This may give us some clue as to the girl's state of mind.' He took the proffered letter, produced a penknife from his pocket, slit the envelope, and produced a folded sheet of notepaper. As he pulled it out, a smaller piece of paper fluttered to the floor.

'Hello,' said Willoughby, 'that looks like a cheque.' He picked it up, and it *was* a cheque.

Steele's mind raced. 'Good Lord! I wonder ...' He paused. 'What does the letter say?'

Willoughby read it aloud.

Dear Miss Austin. Thank you for sending us the above story, which we would like to publish in our February issue. I enclose our cheque for ten guineas in full payment. Please let us know if this is acceptable to you. Yours faithfully, J.G. Blythe, Assistant Editor, Strand Magazine. *P.S. We would be interested to see any other stories you write.*

'What's all this about?'

Steele's face wore a sad smile as he answered. 'The girl aspired to be a writer. She told us she had sent her first story to *The Strand*.' His eye fell on the letter-heading. 'Good heavens! Look what her story's called!'

'Tell me.'

'The Hand of Justice.' Steele gave a little mirthless laugh. 'Life has its cruel ironies, has it not?'

Ever practical, Mason asked, 'What happens to the letter and cheque now, sir?'

Willoughby took the letter back from Steele. 'They are not relevant to our inquiries, so I shall hand them to Miss Austin in one of her more lucid moments. She is not yet a convicted felon, so she is entitled to receive mail. And money, of course.'

'Rather too late,' Steele observed. 'Still, perhaps it may be some consolation to the poor creature. Her wretched life has not been without some worthwhile achievement.'

The constable had been standing respectfully silent, but he now gave a discreet little cough, and spoke up.

'I have another message, sir.'

'Yes, Phillips?'

'Miss Harriet Austin asked me to let these gentlemen know that she's done her packing. When she returns from the garden, she'll be ready to leave.'

Willoughby was astonished. 'The garden? In this weather? What the devil is she doing out there?'

'I couldn't quite follow, sir. Something about a rabbit.'

'Hm. Well, women do strange things. Thank you, Phillips.'

Constable Phillips withdrew, and Willoughby turned a puzzled face towards Steele. 'What on earth would induce the girl to go out in the garden on a day like this?'

Steele's reply was somewhat self-satisfied. The blackcurrant wine had made him quite mellow. 'I think she may be reacting to a discussion we had on the way here.'

'Oh, the lost cat!' said Mason. He told the inspector about Austin's cruel hoax.

'Good gracious!' said Willoughby. 'That actually happened, did it? Clare Austin described it in one of her mad ravings. I thought she might be fantasizing.'

'No, it really happened,' Steele confirmed. 'And after that the cat, Ella, disappeared, to Harriet's great distress. Today I realized where the creature might be found.'

'Another of your theories,' said Willoughby, with a hint of mockery.

'My dear chap, I prefer to think of it as deduction,' Steele purred. 'Obviously, Austin will have set out to kill his daughter's pet rather than just pretend to do so. But Ella saw him coming, sensed the man's evil intentions, and fled the house.'

'A sensible thing to do,' Willoughby observed.

'Very sensible,' Steele agreed. 'She will have needed a refuge. She must have felt cold and unloved,' he continued. 'In need of comforting.'

'I know the feeling,' said Willoughby. He took another swig of whisky.

'She will have sought a friend. And today, in the cab, Harriet told us how her cat loved to play with Herbert, her rabbit, and Freddie, her guinea pig.'

'The guinea pig's gone,' said Mason.

'So he has,' said Steele. 'But his abandoned hutch will still be there, with a strong scent of Freddie left behind. I suggested Harriet might look inside.'

At this moment they saw Harriet coming up the garden path cradling a cat in one arm and carrying a straw basket with the other. Above the rim of the basket two furry ears could be seen. Mason jumped up and opened the garden door and she came in, glowing with happiness.

'You were right, Major!' she declared. 'Ella was playing with Herbert in Freddie's old cage. They'd torn back the wire so they could get in and out. Thank you a million times! Now I can take them both to Uncle Richard's!'

'Let's hope Uncle Richard is an animal lover,' said Mason.

'He should be,' said Steele. 'He's a vet.' He turned to Inspector Willoughby. 'Make that four cases concluded this week, George.'